KILLING SARAH

by

Jonas Saul

PUBLISHED BY:
Imagine Press Inc.
Ebook ISBN: 978-1-927404-32-4
Paperback ISBN: 978-1-998047-06-2
Hardcover ISBN: 978-1-998047-31-4

Killing Sarah

The Sarah Roberts Series

Dark Visions (One)
The Warning (Two)
The Crypt (Three)
The Hostage (Four)
The Victim (Five)
The Enigma (Six)
The Vigilante (Seven)
The Rogue (Eight)
Killing Sarah (Nine)
The Antagonist (Ten)
The Redeemed (Eleven)
The Haunted (Twelve)
The Unlucky (Thirteen)
The Abandoned (Fourteen)
The Cartel (Fifteen)
Losing Sarah (Sixteen)
The Pact (Seventeen)
The Terror (Eighteen)
The Chase (Nineteen)
The Betrayal (Twenty)
Sarah's Return (Twenty-One)
The Hunt (Twenty-Two)
The Delivery (Twenty-Three)
The Trap (Twenty-Four)
The Ultimatum (Twenty-Five)
The Depraved (Twenty-Six)
The Condemned (Twenty-Seven)
Payback (Twenty-Eight)
The Unknown (Twenty-Nine)
Wrath (Thirty)
The Damned (Thirty-One)
The Game (Thirty-Two)

Jonas Saul

The Decoy (Thirty-Three)
The Disappearance (Thirty-Four)
The Whole Truth (Thirty-Five)
Alex (Thirty-Six)
Parkman (Thirty-Seven)
Darwin (Thirty-Eight)
Aaron (Thirty-Nine)
Remains To Be Seen (Forty)

The Jake Wood Novels

The Immortal Gene (Book One)
The Immortal Target (Book Two)

Standalone Novels

'Til Death Do Us Part
The Drowning
The Woman in the Woods
The Threat
The Specter
The Mafia Trilogy
A Murder in Time
Frequency of the Dead

Co-Authored Novels

Collision Course (Written with Gary Ponzo)
There Will Be Blood (Written with Rania Stone)
The Soulless (Written with Rania Stone)

Short Story Collections

Twisted Fate (Tales of Horror)

Killing Sarah

Twists of Fate (Tales of Hope)

5

Chapter 1

Overwhelmed, Sarah felt like everyone, and everything was killing her. How much could one person take? How much should someone endure for the safety of others?

The decision was long overdue. It was time to leave it all behind before someone succeeded in killing her. There had been too many close calls and bullets that depended on a fraction of a second in time to determine if they would kill, maim, or miss.

The scars accumulated over the years had become a collage of good and bad memories.

But now it was time to stop and live for herself.

Sarah hadn't left Aaron's apartment in the week since she returned from Europe. He ran the errands, got the groceries, and handled the phone whenever it rang. That life had grown on her, and she liked it. No one talked to her but Aaron. No one called. She had been missing for two months, and the world assumed she was dead.

Only Darwin and Rosina in Italy knew she was alive. They had nursed her back to health after her near-death experience there.

But no one else knew she was finished. It was over. No more chasing notes from Vivian and dealing with the police, who had a severe case of never trusting her even though she had proven herself countless times. It was over. She was committing to this new life with Aaron.

The alternative was death.

One day, somehow, no matter how much Vivian led the path and protected her, Sarah figured someone would get lucky. Someone would kill her.

The door to the apartment opened, and Aaron stepped inside.

"Crazy night at the dojo," he said as he shut the door. He looked at her on the couch and stopped. "You okay?"

Sarah nodded. "Just doing some thinking."

"About what?" he asked. He kicked off his shoes and moved into the kitchen. A moment later, he entered the living room, a beer in hand, and sat in the leather chair opposite her. "What were you thinking?"

"What if I told you I wanted to continue being a vigilante for as long as possible? Even in my fifties? How would you feel about that?"

He looked at his beer a moment, then raised his gaze to meet hers.

"Sarah, I love you. If that's what you want, I will support it."

"What if I got seriously hurt or was killed?"

"Then I would have to live with that." He smiled at her.

"After I hunted down who hurt you, of course." He drank from his beer. "I'd live with it because doing what you do is your decision. What we're doing together," he waved a hand between them, "wouldn't work if I didn't validate you and your decisions. I stand behind you. We've talked about this before. I felt it was too dangerous for you to do it alone. But I was wrong."

He took another long pull on the bottle.

"Now flip the debate the other way," Sarah said. "What if I told you I was going to quit? No more notes from Vivian, no more chasing the bad guys. I would stay home, make dinner, and go to the movies with you."

"Same answer. That's what love is, Sarah. Support. You have to do what is right for you. The people in your life either understand, care for, and support you, or eventually, they're not in your life. What is all this about? You leaving me or something? Moving out?"

She studied his face, his eyes. He always hung on her every word as any good listener would.

"I've decided what I want to do going forward."

"Which is?" Aaron moved closer, sitting on the edge of his chair.

"I'm getting out."

"Getting out? You haven't left the apartment in a week. Okay, come with me to the dojo one night. Or we can go for a walk. That'll get you out."

She stared at him for a moment, then laid her head back on the couch and looked up at the ceiling.

"Something tells me I'm not getting it," Aaron said. "Are you saying you're quitting? As in, not taking notes anymore?"

"I'm done with being a vigilante."

"What?" Aaron sounded genuinely surprised. "Since when?" he whispered.

This was what he wanted. They had discussed this earlier in the year. He tried to get her to stop, but she had argued she was duty-bound to do what was right. That's why she went to Italy. He wanted to go to protect her if she wasn't going to quit. She could use the backup, he had said.

But she refused. A part of her longed to continue with Vivian, but with all she had been through, and now in her mid-twenties, she wondered if there would ever be a life for her. Would she ever get married? Could she have kids? How much would her stab wounds and bullet holes ache in old age? She had contemplated what day would be a good day to stop and decided that now was the time while she was still young.

If something minor came up and Vivian assured her it was important, she would be interested, but there had to be a point where it stopped completely. Going after mafia hitmen and hunting rogue politicians in foreign countries was over the top, even for her.

She explained her reasoning to Aaron. "I hope you understand."

"Understand?" He wiped a tear from his cheek. "I'm being selfish when I say this, but I'm so happy you made that decision. Oh, Sarah." He got up and sat beside her on the couch, wrapped his arms around her, and held her tight.

They sat there for a few minutes until the phone rang. Aaron didn't move to answer it.

"Aren't you going to get that?" she asked.

"No. Leave it. They can call back."

"It might be Parkman."

"So?" Aaron leaned away to look at her.

"I'm supposed to meet him tonight," she said. "He's in town to talk to me about something."

Aaron leaned over and grabbed the handset on the fourth ring. He nodded when he looked at call display.

Sarah took the phone. "Parkman?"

"Oh, good, you're home. We need to meet."

"I know. Do you want to come up here?"

"No. I can't. Too dangerous. You have to come to meet me. Alone."

She looked at Aaron. "Okay, but why all the cloak and dagger stuff? You in trouble?"

"Not me."

Sarah's stomach dropped a notch as it filled with acid.

"Where do you want to meet?"

Aaron shook his head and mouthed the words, *no way.*

"Do you remember that burned-out warehouse on Keele Street? The one the Leap Year Killer blew up?"

"How could I forget? I was inside at the time."

"Meet me in the front parking lot at midnight. Trust me, Sarah, you'll want to hear what I have to say."

"And I've got something to tell you, too, Parkman. Be prepared. You might be in for a shock."

"Nothing shocks me with you, Sarah. Nothing."

"See you then," she said.

As she pulled the phone from her ear, Parkman shouted something else. She brought the phone back up. "What was that? I missed what you said."

"I just said to come alone. Don't bring anyone else with you, or you risk their safety."

"Risk their safety? Great. What about mine?"

"You're with me. Don't worry about that. And, if anyone can take care of themselves, it's you. Just be there. It's important."

Sarah hung up and handed the phone to Aaron.

"What's going on?" he asked.

"I'm meeting Parkman at midnight."

"Why?"

"He wouldn't say, but I'm assuming I will know when we meet."

"Are you being a smart ass or just sarcastic?"

"Maybe a little of both."

She made a funny face, stuck her tongue out at him, got off the couch, and walked to the balcony doors. The lights on the streets below split the darkness. Straight lines cut through the inky blackness, leading people through the night.

"I heard from Vivian," Sarah said.

"What did she say? Does she have an opinion on you quitting the family business?"

Sarah glanced over her shoulder at him and fixed him with a cold stare.

"Sorry, didn't mean it to sound like a joke."

She turned back to the window. "Vivian agrees it's time to lay low, take a break, or even quit altogether." She took a couple of deep breaths. "That's what scares me."

"What does?"

Sarah walked back to the couch and plopped down. She pulled a piece of paper out of her back pocket and unfolded it.

"The fact that Vivian agreed so easily scares me." She read a few lines of the note to herself, then looked up at

Aaron. "This recent note tells me she sees something dangerous coming my way that I will avoid by quitting. Otherwise, she would've argued against it. Vivian was the one who started this message-giving business. I just got swept up and enjoyed it." She shook her head. "This last trip to Italy proved how easily I could be killed. I almost didn't make it this time, and all that kept going through my head were you, my parents, and Parkman, how I didn't spend enough time with the people I love. Aaron, we need to talk about marriage, how many kids you want and buying a house one day. I've still got money from when my mom and dad moved to Santa Rosa—"

"Okay, okay, slow down. We'll have plenty of time to do all that. Who else knows you're alive, and who knows you're quitting?"

"Only you, Vivian, and the people who brought me back to health and saved my life in Italy. I planned on telling Parkman tonight."

Aaron nodded. "Okay, are you still going to meet him?"

Sarah ruffled the pages in her hands. "Let me paraphrase some of what Vivian said."

Aaron grabbed his beer, took a swig, and sat back on the couch. "Go ahead."

"She said it's important for me to have closure with all the people who have helped me along the way, including Parkman, as he's been there for me for many years. More than anyone else. But if I'm really going to quit, I can't meet him tonight."

"What? Did you read that wrong? *Can't* meet him tonight? Didn't you mean *can*? Could you have misinterpreted her message?"

"I don't think so. That never happens. Sometimes the message comes through in a riddle, or there are words I have to look up like street names, but if Vivian says it's black, it usually is."

"So then you're not going tonight?"

"I am going," Sarah said. "Parkman deserves to hear this in person."

"I was afraid of that. Can't you meet him some other time?"

Sarah shook her head. "How often is he in Toronto? His business has picked up recently, and he's so busy."

"I heard he was in Greece last week solving a missing person's case."

"And now he's in Toronto to talk to me. Parkman's safe. I'm going to meet him, hear what he has to say, tell him my plans and then come back home." She got up, walked to the closet, and pulled out her shoes. "Is my bike where I parked it last?"

"Still there." Aaron got up and walked to her side. "I guess there's no talking you out of this, is there?"

"Absolutely not."

"Even though Vivian advised you to stay away from Parkman?"

"Even though." She rested a hand on the door handle. "Parkman's safe. I know him. There's no danger with Parkman. I think Vivian warned me away because Parkman had something he needed help with, and that's why he wanted to meet with me at this late hour. Vivian's worried I will acquiesce, give in, and help Parkman one more time. When I tell him I'm out, he'll respect my wishes and let it go at that. We'll part ways with no hard feelings. The next time we see him will be over Thanksgiving or Christmas dinner with the family."

"I hope you're right."

Sarah stuffed Vivian's note back in her pocket.

"You taking a gun with you?" Aaron asked.

"No need. It's Parkman. Why would I need a gun?"

"Better to have one and not need it than to—"

"I know, I know. But this is different."

"Okay. If you say so." Aaron looked at his watch. "Almost eleven. You'd better get this over with. I'll wait up for you."

"You don't have to."

"Sarah, I can't sleep without you. Missed you for too long when you were gone. I will be up and waiting."

She leaned in and hugged him. They kissed long and hard. Then she pulled away, opened the door, and stepped out into the hallway.

"See you soon," Sarah said.

Aaron nodded and closed the door.

Sarah took the stairs, always eager to exercise the leg that took a bullet two months ago in Italy. She wiped off her BMW motorcycle in the underground garage and started the engine. It purred as it if hadn't sat for the last three months.

In her tenure as a vigilante, responding to the prophetic notes that came to her from her dead sister, Sarah had lost a lot of people. Esmerelda was gone. Drake Bellamy was dead. Dolan, and her cousin Russell. It was time for a change. It was time to stop.

If Aaron only knew another part of the reason she was quitting, he might convince her not to. He would want her to quit because she chose to do it for herself. He would say she had to quit for the right reasons.

Sarah swung her leg over the bike's seat, revved the engine, and pulled away.

Eventually, someone would get to Aaron or Parkman and hurt them because of her. Maybe even kill them. She couldn't live with that on her shoulders. She had allowed herself to fall for Aaron deeper than she intended, and now it was time to quit the vigilante business to be with him before someone took him away from her.

It was her time to be happy in a world filled with misery and pain. Her time to go to the movies, read a book, and listen to classical music on a Sunday afternoon with a hot cup of coffee. She'd earned it.

She paraphrased Vivian's note for Aaron because she couldn't allow him to read it word for word.

Vivian had talked her into quitting. Something was coming that Sarah wouldn't be able to fully recover from. Something was coming that was altogether too big, and if it didn't kill her, she would never be the same again. Whatever was coming represented darkness.

Now was the time to stop and take a chance at a new life. Anything other than that was to risk her life. She had thought about it long and hard and decided Vivian was right.

The last part of the note told Sarah to meet with a girl named Tam Rood. Once they met and talked, things would be okay. That darkness would go away. Sarah was to help Tam with her family issues through diplomacy and dialogue, not anger and weapons.

Talk to Tam and do not meet Parkman were the note's final words.

But she had to meet Parkman.

It was the right thing to do. Parkman deserved it.

Then she would locate Tam Rood.

After that, she would find out when Aaron was going to propose, and she would get on with her new lease on life.

Sarah pushed the bike harder, not willing to wait any longer on her new life, the whole time wondering if she was making a mistake by violating her sister's last message.

Chapter 2

OLIVER PAYNE GASPED AND sat up in bed as the sun broke through the thin orange curtains, warming his skin. Clammy sweat covered his arms and back, and his pulse beat to the rhythm of a jogger. Another nightmare, another horror, relived in his nightly ventures after four months of freedom.

He took a deep breath and closed his eyes. This was freedom, this was peace. It had ended months ago when he escaped her.

Having to remind himself that he made it out alive was a daily chore. The car accident, the beating at the office when he stayed late one night, and the cardiac arrest were all brought on by his ex-wife. The carefully planned attacks had escalated over time.

None of the events of aggression had been accidents. Violeta knew the route he drove home. She knew what street he would be on and when he would be on it because she was on the phone with him the whole time that night.

Then a car, minus the driver, was pushed into his way as he rounded a blind corner. Airbags deployed, and he cracked a couple of ribs.

The beating after work was unprofessional. The two skinny idiots, meth-diet punks, pretended to rob him, but it wasn't his wallet they were after. It was him.

When he woke in the hospital, Violeta offered fake platitudes.

But that was all four months ago, and he was free of her and all her insane fantasies. Her wild goals of being one of the super-rich and her determination to get there at all costs. Even if it meant removing him. The one person she claimed stood in her way.

He didn't put it past her that she was still hunting him. Even though they were separated, she needed him for the business to thrive. With him gone, she was stymied. But if he were dead, it would all fall into her hands.

For his life, he ran. It was that or stay and eventually be killed.

She needed him to play along because he owned half the company's shares. Without him, a large portion of her finances was paralyzed.

But Oliver had different goals. He wanted to retire, relax, and play golf. They already had millions, with more residual millions coming in. A passive income. And he'd just had a mild heart attack. Even his doctors had agreed with him.

But to go against Violeta meant death. She had made that clear. The accident and the beating had been a warning. In the privacy of their own home, she told him in a hushed voice that he would do what she wanted or end up on the other side of the grass.

The sweet, kind woman he'd married had been replaced with a cruel dictator governed by money and the sin of greed.

He shook off the dream's last vestiges, rolled out of bed, placed his feet in his slippers, and headed for the small kitchen in the small, rented villa.

It was going to be another scorcher. The seething heat of southern Greece on the Aegean Sea came across as an angry, sweltering cape, something you wore outside and could only shed once you were under artificially cooled air. He made a point to set the air conditioner on high before he went out today.

He flicked the kettle on and headed for a shower. Another day in paradise, without anyone screaming at him. That part of his life was truly over. His wife was now his ex-wife, and she had no idea where in the world he was.

As the months passed, there was no contact from her. He needed time alone to heal the emotional scars. Her manipulation knew no bounds, and when she drank, it was worse. The alcohol loosened her tongue and added an element of extremism to her already austere and rigid ways. He was belittled, ridiculed, and asked about his affairs, even though he had never cheated on her.

Before leaving her mad world, a world of irrelevance, he had planned his exit for months, the entire time, his stomach was a bag of knots. But he had done it. There was enough money in his secret American bank account to live like a king for a very long time while Greece was mired in its current economic crisis. If Greece went bankrupt and reverted to the drachma, he would become richer as prices would drop everywhere.

After his shower, he grabbed his coffee and sat outside under the grape vines suspended along the pergola above. The air was crisp and clean, the sun already beating at over eighty degrees Fahrenheit. The pool to his left invited him, but it would have to wait until the afternoon. It was barely past eight in the morning. He reveled in his luck to be in this Greek paradise and away from Violeta's prison. Every day he thanked God for his freedom from her madness.

They had built a retail empire together in Northern California. At first, it was one store, then another, until they had five. Keeping stock in their basement for the five stores made sense as they could buy in bulk and drive down suppliers' prices.

By the time they hit their tenth store, they had rented a warehouse and began wholesaling to their own stores. Because of their buying power, they could sell off stock to other stores and competitors in their industry, cheaper than those stores could buy it on their own. It was simple mathematics and applied capitalism. It didn't take more than fifteen years before Oliver and Violeta were worth millions.

But he was happy to let that all go. Everything became all about the money for Violeta, but for Oliver, there was no meaning in that.

And Violeta wanted more. She always wanted more. And she drove him to his first heart attack. He pleaded with her that their goal of one day reaching the hundred million dollar mark in investment portfolio was over. The few million they had and their existing monthly income was enough for him to retire, heal his body, and enjoy life before it was time to go to the prize in the sky.

Violeta flew off the handle. She would have none of it.

Now more than ever was the time to expand, she had screamed. Slow down in their sixties, she had said, not their fifties.

But now he was living a slower life, and she was still in California, wondering what the hell had happened to him. He had five million in a bank account she was unaware of. She had twenty million and the entire business just as she wanted it. He could live with that. He only hoped she could as well.

He couldn't live with not seeing his daughter. Not being able to protect her from an abusive mother bothered him to the core of his soul. But he had to run to get out from under Violeta's sick umbrella. He had to hide. Maybe in a year, he would contact his daughter. Maybe then he would be safe from the retribution of any kind. She would be eighteen in a year. Time for her to move out of her mother's hell.

Violeta would rather see him dead than allow him to divorce her, and Oliver knew that.

"Crazy bitch," he said out loud.

He brought the coffee cup to his lips and smiled.

Free from her. Free from the rat race. Free from her demands. Free from her affairs. Her spending junkets in New York. Trips to Europe. Free from all of it. Just free.

That's all he needed, and he got it in Greece.

After his coffee, he cleaned his cup, put the kitchen back in order, and turned the air conditioner on. The walk into town was more than an hour. He would walk in before it got too hot. After his massage and shopping at the Wednesday farmer's market, he would take a taxi back to the villa for an afternoon rest.

"What a life," he muttered to himself as he picked up his backpack and slipped a water bottle into the side pocket.

The villa was eight hundred a month, cash. No questions, no receipts, and no one knew who he was or his location. He didn't know any Greek except for the common greetings, so he didn't have to talk to the locals who hardly spoke any English.

The little village he lived in, Agios Adrianos, was four kilometers from Nafplio, the capital city of Greece, before Athens took the title. In the small village, he had no phone, and the only internet connection was in the name of the British couple who owned the rental property. His name was only on his passport, hidden in the nightstand by his bed.

It had become the perfect scenario for peace and calm.

After exiting the small villa, he walked to the gated driveway, unlocked the chain, and started down the long driveway leading to the village's center.

He moved slowly, watching the fenced areas of the other homes, and the passing vehicles, keeping a vigilant eye on who might be watching him.

Last week one man appeared to be watching him. An American tourist with a toothpick in his mouth and a camera had taken his photo. Oliver was sure of it. But this man was good. He turned and snapped a few more shots of the Greek Orthodox Church and was met by a lovely woman who could have been his daughter. If Oliver didn't know any better, the woman was paid to appear as arm candy for the day.

But that was once, and it was a week ago. Nothing had happened since, and he hadn't seen the man with the toothpick again.

There was being paranoid, and then there was being safe. It would be years before Oliver would let his guard down. If he felt for a second that he was in trouble here, he would leave and head to Istanbul or maybe Egypt. Anywhere to disappear and stay hidden to protect his new peaceful and calm existence.

At the center of the village, the sun already beating him red, he nodded at the small convenience store owner, turned left toward Nafplio, and continued walking, watching his back.

A small Greek police car's engine turned on beside him, the driver watching as he walked by the car. It idled for a moment, then revved. Oliver wanted to turn around and look at what the driver was doing but refused to draw attention to himself.

More than a minute later, the police car cruised by slowly, got to the corner ahead, and turned right toward Nafplio.

It was either an omen of bad things to come, or his nerves made him crazy about every little detail around him.

Any other police car passing anyone else would mean nothing to them.

It had to mean nothing. It was just his nerves.

Chapter 3

SARAH BRAKED AND TURNED her bike into the ruined warehouse's parking lot off Keele Street, north of the 401 in Toronto. Demo crews had been at work since she was here last. The parking area was cleaned and swept, and the front of the building, where most of the bomb's damage struck, was half gone, cleared away so the rebuilding could begin.

She marveled at how she made it out alive that night. The Leap Year Killer had a gun on her. The bomb detonated outside, and the building fell down around them. All this happened while the leader of one of the toughest street gangs in Toronto was on the premises, looking for her. It was a crazy night. The same night her cousin died saving her on the roof of a hotel downtown.

These were some of the reasons that convinced her to quit. They came to her in flashbacks, images of carnage and death. All the people she had killed in the name of right and wrong. All the innocent people who had died because they were simply involved with Sarah.

Continuing down the violent path she lived would eventually get Aaron killed. Of course, he was a confident black belt and owned a dojo. He could defend himself quite well, but that didn't stop a bullet. And it only took one of those to put you down.

She maneuvered the bike to the side of the parking lot, nearest the road, and cut the engine. The helmet came off easily. After setting it on the bike seat, she straightened her hair.

The last time she saw Parkman was in Italy months ago. It would be good to see him again, but she worried slightly that he would be disappointed when she told him her decision.

What could he possibly have to say to her? If it was a minor task, would she still do it?

He had done so much for her over the years, rescuing her in Hungary, coming for her in Toronto, and showing up in Italy when she needed him. And now she stood in the parking lot of the ruined warehouse where she almost died so many months ago, trying to figure out how to say no to him.

Her watch said it was one minute past midnight.

Maybe there was a credible threat. Maybe he wouldn't just drive up, park, and get out of his car.

Could he already be here?

She moved back toward her bike without a sound. Then around the bike to put it between her and the building.

At this hour, only emergency lighting and night lights were on at the building across the street. The only sound came from a random car on Keele Street.

"Sarah?" a man's voice called.

She turned toward the voice, icy fingers crawling along her forearms. The silhouette of a man stood in the parking lot of the building directly across the street from her. She had been out of action for over two months and beginning to enjoy the calm, the peace. Coming here in the dark, having her name called like that brought the life back in a palpable swoosh she could almost hear as much as feel.

Anger brewed on the inside. Feistiness.

"Who wants to know?"

"It's me, Parkman."

His voice seemed strained, like he was trying to whisper but speak loud enough for her to hear.

"You said to meet here," she called, matching his strained whisper. "Why are you over there?"

He gestured with his arm for her to join him, then turned and slipped behind a bush.

Something was wrong.

Parkman never acted this way. He wasn't one to be afraid, hiding in bushes and acting so covertly. Why not meet somewhere even more discreet, then? Unless something was wrong with Parkman, it had to mean there was a credible threat to him. If that were the case, she needed to hear what he had to say.

No noises came from the building behind her. No one was visible on the street. As far as she could tell, they were completely alone in this industrial area at this late hour.

She started toward him, crossed the street while checking her back a couple of times, and then stopped about ten feet from the bush Parkman huddled behind.

"You coming out to talk?" she asked.

At that moment, she wished she had listened to Aaron and brought a weapon.

The bushes moved, and Parkman stepped out, a long silenced weapon in his hand.

"What's that for?" Sarah asked. Everything in her body ordered her legs to step back, but she fought the urge. It was Parkman in front of her.

"We're in danger," Parkman said. He rotated the toothpick in his mouth to the other side. "Grave danger."

"Oh really," Sarah said as she raised her hands and looked around the empty parking lot. "Cause it looks to me like we're alone out here. If anyone's in danger, that would be me, as you're the one with the gun."

"No, no, not like that. It's about the client I took on last month."

"Tell me more."

She kept her eyes alert, watching Parkman's gun while making sure nothing moved behind him or in her peripheral vision.

Parkman spit his toothpick out, licked his lips, and looked down at his gun. "This crazy woman, Violeta, hired me to locate her missing husband."

"Are you saying you didn't find him, and now she's pissed?"

"No, I found him." He met her gaze.

"Then what's the trouble? Isn't that what private investigators do? Locate missing people?"

Parkman nodded vigorously and moved a few more steps away from the bush. He angled his head around Sarah, looking at something on the road.

"What? See something?" Sarah asked and looked over

her shoulder.

He shook his head when she turned back around. "This woman asked me to hurt her husband."

"Some people deserve it. What's his sin?"

"Too many details to get into right now. But from what I can gather, this is just a case of Violeta not allowing anyone to leave her employ."

"Her husband worked for her?"

"You could say that. They ran the business together, but she always saw him as an employee doing what she needed. Now with him gone, she's paralyzed. His signature is needed for a multi-million dollar deal. Alive, he won't sign. Dead, the business is all hers."

"Are you saying you found the missing husband, and when she wanted more from you, you terminated your services and walked away?"

"That's exactly what I'm saying."

"Oh, Parkman, haven't you learned anything?" She smiled at him. "I've missed you, but this isn't like you. You're never one to cower in the dark from a woman hiding in bushes."

"She has terrorized me ever since."

"What?" Sarah's tone belied her seriousness. No one gets to hurt her friends. Especially not Parkman.

"It was either a turkey or a chicken that was sacrificed in my apartment."

"How could you not tell what kind of bird it was?"

"The animal was torn to bits and pieces, and the blood smeared everywhere."

"Why is it that we haven't seen each other in months, and I haven't gotten a hug yet? Look around, Parkman, no one's here to get us."

Parkman unscrewed the sound suppressor on his weapon and slipped the pieces into opposite pockets on his jacket. Then he cautiously moved forward, his eyes aimed over her shoulders.

Sarah hugged him hard, feeling his nerves as he shook.

She pushed him back and stared into his face, concern in hers.

"Wow, what has gotten into you?"

His eyes watered. "Whoever Violeta hired is maniacal. They have been in my apartment, office, and car several times. They won't let up."

"Have you contacted the police?"

"There's nothing they can do. Nothing conclusive is ever left at the scene. I made a list of people who hate me, starting with the most recent names, and the police visited Violeta, but she was the crying woman who only hired me to find her missing husband. The police bought it."

"Why tell me? Is there something you want me to do?"

"After I returned from Greece, this letter was written."

As he pulled a piece of paper out of his pocket, Sarah asked, "Did you enjoy Greece?"

He nodded and offered a half-smile. "I found her husband in a city called Nafplio."

"I know the name," Sarah said. "Aaron was there before I met him. You remember that story? Aaron was shot by the man who killed his sister."

Parkman stepped back, still holding the paper in his hands. "Man, the people we know, eh? So much violence, so much death. Sometimes I wonder …"

"Me too, Parkman." She stepped closer, closing the

distance between them. "Whatever you have on that paper of yours, I have something I want to tell you first."

The sound of a car's engine moved closer than Keele Street. Together they turned and watched as a four-door Jaguar drove by, its windows down. The driver didn't appear to look their way, and the vehicle didn't slow down. After it passed and continued along the road, no longer posing any threat, Sarah looked back at Parkman.

"I'm quitting," she said.

There, it was out. When she told Darwin and Rosina back in Italy, they were very happy. In their experience, only luck stood between the great divide between living or dying in such a violent life, and eventually, luck ran out. Aaron had seemed happy with her decision, too.

But she was concerned with how Parkman would take it.

"Sarah," he said. "I'm surprised."

"And …"

"And cautiously happy. I would have never guessed you would quit."

"When I was missing for two months in Italy, everyone assumed I was dead and buried in an unmarked grave. Even you and Aaron thought I was gone."

Parkman nodded.

"Since I've been back in Canada, I can count how many people know I'm alive and well. There couldn't be a better time for me to walk away and leave that life behind. I can see how helpful I was in the past and even convinced myself that nothing would stop me. I've still got that tenacious streak. I'm just going to use it on Aaron and you." She leaned up and kissed his cheek. "You've been with me throughout most of it, and I wanted to thank you for that."

Parkman looked down at the paper in his hand and met her eyes again.

"Sarah, I don't know how to tell you this."

"Parkman, I'm still the same Sarah. I can handle it, whatever it is. Just spill the beans."

"Violeta knows you're alive."

"The woman who hired you? How and why does that matter to me?"

"That crazy woman had my phone tapped. She heard everything when you called, and then I called back to tell you I was coming up to Toronto this week."

"Wow, she's quite the handful."

"That's not all."

"I'm listening," Sarah said, her stomach twisting at the anticipation of what she was about to hear, concerned that it would pull her back in against her will.

"Four days ago, I was jumped two blocks from my house. They wrapped a bag over my head and dragged me into a van, where they drove me out of the city."

"Parkman, what happened?"

He looked down at his shoes. "They stripped my clothes off and tied my legs open wide, then they …" His voice caught on phlegm. He coughed, swallowed, looked up, and started again. "They warned me. Because I didn't help locate a hitman for Violeta to deal with her husband, the fact that I know about it is enough to hurt her. So I was warned that someone close to me would pay the price if I didn't come through for her."

"Who did they mean? Me?"

"Since they had been listening in on my calls, they only know of you, Aaron, and your parents."

"And you feel this is a credible threat? Do you really think this woman would go after my parents?"

Parkman shook his head. "No, I think she wants me."

"So why the games, the threats?"

"To intimidate me into working for her."

"Parkman, is there something you're not telling me?" She studied his face. "What did they do to you in the van?"

"Sarah, you don't want to know."

"Whatever it was, I've never seen you this rattled before." Then Sarah thought about Vivian's note. "What's Violeta's last name?"

"Payne. Her name is Violeta Payne."

"Okay, because I received a note from Vivian warning me not to meet with you."

Parkman frowned. "What? Why me? I'm safe. If anything, you needed to hear what I had to say. This woman has threatened you and your family."

"Be clear about something, Parkman. Vivian knows I'm quitting. She told me to stay away tonight *if* I wanted to quit. You bringing me in on this Violeta thing only makes me want to find her and ensure she knows who she's dealing with. This kind of shit could pull me back in."

Parkman blew air out of his mouth. "I don't want to be your enemy. I'm here as a friend—"

"Parkman, stop it. We've been close too long." She sized him up. "Shit, what did they do to you? You're rattling around like a broken-winged bird in a cage. I'm so sorry, Parkman. I've never seen you like this before."

"It's okay. Just—"

"I asked you about the name because Vivian told me to meet a girl named Tam Rood. I thought maybe that was connected somehow."

Parkman's eyes widened. "No, no, it's not possible."

The Jaguar was coming back up the road, heading toward Keele Street.

"Relax, it's the same car." Sarah turned back to Parkman. "They probably forgot something at the office, and now they're heading home."

Parkman moved two steps back from her, watching the Jag.

"What's with the paper? Did Violeta write you a note, a threat?"

Parkman looked down at the paper in his hands and then at Sarah. His eyes had glazed over.

She glanced behind her as the Jag came even with them, its windows down as before.

"Sarah!" Parkman yelled.

He screamed so loud that she let out a small, startled scream and twirled to face him.

Parkman had his gun out. In the brief second, she stared at his face, she saw the look in his eyes, the determination to pull the trigger.

She had seen it countless times in the past. The decision was made. The gun would go off, and anyone in the path of the bullet wouldn't have to worry about guns anymore.

Sarah lunged sideways but didn't get out of the way in time.

Simultaneously, as Parkman's weapon deafened her with its report, her head jerked as a bullet entered her skull.

She hit the ground, her body still.

Isn't that ironic ... what a way to bow out, her eyes locked open, watching stars above ... *shot by my best friend.*

Her eyes shut slowly, the stars blinking out.

She floated off, her consciousness stolen by a tiny piece of lead.

***

Parkman screamed in a fury, ran around Sarah's unmoving body, and chased after the Jaguar, firing every bullet in his magazine.

In his demented charge, running, his gun hand bouncing, Parkman missed vital parts of the car, only hitting the trunk and a corner of the back window, breaking it out. The Jaguar's engine roared as it raced away and disappeared up the road, where it fishtailed onto Keele Street, narrowly missing another car, the driver of that car leaning on his horn.

Distraught, Parkman ran back to Sarah and untwisted her body, so she lay flat out on her back. The wound looked terrible.

Head wound. Lots of blood. Her breathing labored.

He yanked his cell phone out in a panic and almost dropped it. After dialing 911, he waited precious seconds, not breathing, staring at the blank expression on Sarah's face.

"Come on, come on," he said as he rocked back and forth over her inert body.

Someone answered. "911 Emergency. Do you require police, fire, or ambulance?"

"Ambulance," Parkman shouted. "Now!"

The line had already clicked away.

A man came on and asked what had happened.

"Gunshot wound to the head," Parkman gasped. "Adult female. Bleeding out. Need assistance now!" He gave the man on the line his location and set the phone down.

He had almost blurted *officer down* from his years on the police force. Sarah acted like a cop. She had been tougher than most cops he'd known and had done more for people than most cops ever had.

He slipped out of his suit jacket and laid it gently under her head, using one of the sides of the jacket to apply pressure to the wound.

Then he held Sarah's head and monitored her weakening chest as it rose and fell.

He cried, tears streaming down his cheeks, taking all the responsibility for Sarah's wound because she came to meet him.

"No, no, no, no, no, no …" he whispered over and over. "Please, Sarah, stay with me, stay with me. I can't live in a world without my Sarah. I'm so sorry I couldn't protect you."

Her chest stopped moving.

He stared at it for a breath. Panic charged the blood in his veins to boiling.

Her head safely on his jacket, Parkman set his hands on her chest and began to pump, spittle and tears mixing on his face as he shouted.

"Come on, Sarah!" He pushed on her ribcage. "You can't leave me here like this. Come on, Sarah, don't you dare die on me!"

He added more weight, pressing down on her chest in a fit of anxiety. He looked up at the sky and wailed like a wounded animal, all the pent-up aggression, fear, and anger mixed in one scream.

A siren broke through the still night around him. They were coming up Keele. Multiple sirens.

The ambulance dispatcher would've notified the police because of the gunshot victim call.

He stopped pumping her chest, leaned down to listen for breathing, then started pumping again.

"Sarah Roberts! Do not leave us!"

Tires screeched behind him. He didn't turn around. If it was the Jaguar again, then he deserved a bullet in the head for this. If it were the ambulance, then he would be shoved out of the way any second.

He bent to listen for breathing again, then got down and said directly into her ear, "You are not allowed to die. Do you hear me, woman? You're not authorized to go. I will fucking kill you if you die on me."

Rough hands eased him aside.

Two paramedics dropped down and started to work on her. Two uniformed officers were walking toward him. Another cruiser pulled up and turned off its flashing lights.

Parkman covered his eyes with his hands and cried.

Why hadn't Vivian warned Sarah? Then he remembered what Sarah had said. Vivian *had* warned her to not meet Parkman tonight. But Parkman was a friend. What could go wrong? Of course, Sarah would come.

He would hunt down the people responsible for this, and he would eat a bullet for Sarah when they were all dead.

No one hurt his Sarah and got away with it.

Not even him.

Chapter 4

"Excuse me, sir."

Parkman opened his eyes but didn't move. With his back against the wall of the building, legs drawn up, arms draped across his knees, he rested his forehead on his crossed arms.

One of the two paramedics whispered something to an officer close to him. Parkman assumed the worst. It had to be about Sarah, and they didn't want to tell him.

He wasn't ready to look up yet and face her dead body. He had no idea what a world without Sarah looked like.

The concrete under him was dirty. The remnants of a broken leaf half concealed a discarded cigarette butt.

If he raised his eyes, that meant he would have to see Sarah as they worked on her. He refused to allow the last image he would ever see of her to be a white blanket covering her face. That was something he couldn't live with.

"Sir, we'll have to ask you a few questions. Would you

mind coming with us?"

Parkman had to look up. He had worked with Sarah for years. When they weren't together, Sarah kept in touch. She was the sister he never had, the daughter he wished for. One day she would've married and had children. He had secretly wondered if she would pass her gift down to her children but had never talked to her about it.

He slapped his face. The officers stepped back and looked at each other, unsure what he would do next.

Sarah is a fighter. She would make it out of this. He had to stop thinking like she was dead already. The paramedics wouldn't be hooking her up and preparing her for the ambulance if she were dead.

"Sir, are you okay to stand?" the other cop asked, his voice deeper, more demanding.

Parkman nodded. "Yeah, sure."

"You're going to have to come with us. We will need to hear what happened. Are you armed?"

"Yes, I'm licensed." Parkman touched the butt of his weapon, and both cops reached for their holsters. "Relax, it's empty, and I'm pulling it out to offer it to one of you. You'll need it for testing."

The men attending to Sarah counted to three and then hoisted her onto a stretcher. The wheels came out from under it, and they pushed Sarah toward the back maw of the ambulance.

"She gonna make it?" Parkman yelled after them.

Neither one responded.

"The gun," the cop nearest Parkman said, his gloved hand held out for it.

Parkman dropped the weapon in the cop's hand and got

to his feet.

"Hey," he yelled at the paramedics. "What hospital are you taking her to?"

"Humber River Regional on Keele South," the cop answered. "Now, come with us."

After the ambulance took off, its sirens going again, the cops put Parkman in the back of their cruiser. The other officers rolled out tape to block the crime scene for further investigation. A whole slew of people would trample through the area in the next twelve hours investigating what happened here, adding homicide detectives to the equation if Sarah died.

"Take me to the hospital," Parkman said. "I have to be there when she wakes up."

"Just hold your horses, sir. We'll get you there in good time. She'll be on pain meds or in surgery for a few hours. There's nothing you can do for her there. The first thing we need to know is what happened here."

The cop in the driver's seat had thinning hair and was balding. Parkman knew the type. That kind that had been on the force for twenty-plus years ate take-out most of the time, which accounted for his large paunch, and was probably hanging on for retirement.

The passenger cop was younger, in his early twenties, just starting out, learning the ropes. He hadn't said much after the veteran officer took control.

Parkman identified himself as an ex-cop, now turned private detective. He had been working on a case where he had been threatened and came to Toronto to warn Sarah. He told them about the Jaguar and how he fired at it.

"Tell other cars on the street," Parkman continued, "to

look for a newer model Jag, probably green, but it was hard to tell in the darkness. The back window is blown out. There'll be bullet holes in the trunk, too."

"Didn't you get a plate number?"

Parkman shook his head. "If I had, I would've told you that already."

"Hey, I was just asking because you used to be a cop and were trained as one. That is one of the first things you look for and memorize."

"True, but Sarah was on the ground bleeding from a head wound. I thought emptying my weapon into the vehicle would've stopped it. I guess I wasn't thinking I would need a plate number."

"I'm just trying to do my job." The officer turned in the front seat and met Parkman's gaze. Parkman wondered how he could turn so well with that hefty paunch. "Now, I know you've gone through something terrible tonight, but we have to do this, and you, of all people, know we have to. There's the hard way or the friendly way. So keep it friendly."

Parkman nodded. "Fine. But let's do this on the way to the hospital. If Sarah wakes up, I need to be there."

The men in the front seat looked at each, a gesture passing between them.

"What was that all about?" Parkman asked.

"The only way you get to go to the hospital to check in on the girl is if you go with us."

"That's what I was asking."

"I'm saying that you were armed when we showed up. Your weapon is empty, and there are bullet casings behind the girl on the concrete. The paramedics told me the bullet entered from the back of the girl's skull. How do we know you didn't shoot her and then emptied your weapon to make it look like you were trying to hit a shooter in the street?"

Parkman clenched his jaw. Heat rose to his forehead. Cops or not, if the wire mesh weren't separating them from him, he would probably take a shot at the overweight asshole.

"Let me out of this cruiser," Parkman ordered. He needed a toothpick to calm down. Something flavored.

"Excuse me?" the veteran asked.

"I said, open the door."

"No," he chuckled. "You're not going anywhere. And with that attitude, I might take you to the station until we can get a better handle on what happened here tonight."

"I told you what happened!" Parkman shouted.

"That doesn't help," the older cop yelled back. "You say you were an officer of the law. You say it was a Jaguar, but you didn't get a plate number or a description of the driver, yet they had their windows down to shoot. You've given us nothing and told us everything."

"What is that supposed to mean?"

"When the paramedics got to you, one of them saw you bend down to the victim's ear and mumble something."

"I was telling her to stay alive."

The cop looked out through his windshield and watched as other cars showed up. "I was afraid you'd say that."

"What? Why?" Parkman clenched his fists. "You know, talking to you is maddening. How long have you been a cop, Rookie?"

When the veteran cop turned back, the streetlights outside reflected off his pate where the hair had thinned in the center of his dome.

"The paramedic heard you say, 'I will fucking kill you if

you don't die on me.' Do you deny saying that?"

"Why would I say something so ridiculous? I told her she *can't* die. Sarah and I talk that way. She has said to me if I were to die, she would punch my corpse. That's the way we are. I was telling her that she didn't get much of an option. It was either live or deal with me."

"You, too, must have some kind of weird relationship." The cop smiled through his words. "Fascinated on death much?"

A man in plainclothes, a tie, and a jacket knocked on the cruiser's window. Thinning hair lowered it.

"Yeah?"

The man bent down and looked in at Parkman. "This the shooter?"

"Not sure yet, but probably."

"Let him out. He's coming with us." The man pulled out a wallet and flipped it open to ID. "Homicide Detective Richard Joffrey. This is my case now."

Parkman's stomach twisted and dropped so far he thought it was filled with radioactive clay.

Why would homicide be involved if Sarah was still alive?

"Whatever," the veteran cop said. "Fine with us."

He opened his door and got out. Parkman waited a full five minutes while the two men talked ten feet from the cruiser. The younger partner sat in the passenger seat.

"Hey, sorry about what happened." He looked back at Parkman. "For what it's worth, I believe your story."

Parkman nodded, looked down at his hands, and pried at a thumbnail.

A moment later, his door opened, and Thinning Hair gestured for him to get out.

Parkman got out and stood beside the open door of the cruiser. He caught a sneer on the face of the veteran cop.

What a fucking idiot. Parkman was losing Sarah. It was his fault she got hurt. And this cop stood beside him, sneering. Everything in his soul begged his muscles to listen and strike at the cop's face, hard and swift.

Cops like that gave the force a bad name. It was men like him that reminded Parkman why he wasn't on the force anymore and thankful that he had his own private security agency.

"Come with me," Joffrey said, adjusting his jacket.

Parkman followed him to an unmarked sedan, where Joffrey opened the passenger side door.

"In the front?" Parkman asked.

"Of course. You're Parkman, right? Sarah's friend?"

"Yeah," he said as a wave of emotion swept over him at the mention of Sarah's name. This new guy sounded like he knew more than he was letting on.

"I'll take you to the hospital. Let's see what her condition is before you tell me what happened. Deal?"

"Deal."

"After that, I'll get you to write out your statement, and then we'll call it a night."

Parkman dropped in the front seat hard.

The detective got in, turned the car on, and started down Keele Street toward the hospital.

Parkman turned to him. "How do you know me so well?"

"You were in Toronto working a case with Sarah a while back. A few officers were killed in the mall on Yonge Street. Guys with white shit on their faces were hunting Sarah, and you helped see that case to its conclusion in a yoga studio.

I'm sure you remember?"

"Yeah, the Rapturites. How could I forget?"

"There's a lot of respect on the force and surrounding police departments for Sarah Roberts and Parkman for what you two have done for this great city." He turned to Parkman. "Not every cop has been briefed on your history, like those two back there."

"Makes sense." He looked out the window as they crossed a bridge spanning the huge 401 highway. "What did you two talk about?"

"That cop back there?"

"Yeah."

"The usual. He had an interesting theory about your involvement."

"I thought so." Parkman faced front, staring out the windshield, the grief for having pulled Sarah into his trouble almost too much to handle.

"You mind if I make a call?" Parkman asked. "Sarah's boyfriend should know."

"No problem, go ahead."

When Parkman pulled his cell phone out, he noticed Sarah's blood on his hands. He hadn't retrieved his suit jacket from under Sarah's head. It still lay on the concrete back at the scene. Inside the jacket was a note from his client, Violeta.

Shit, that is not going to look good for me.

Violeta was very clear about what would happen if the police found out what Parkman knew. He had tried to deal with it the proper way, but Violeta had disappeared under a layer of security at her mansion near Santa Rosa. He hadn't spoken to her in almost two weeks, but she had sent him messages through third parties, loud and clear.

He dialed and waited as Aaron's phone rang at his apartment.

"Detective Richard Joffrey, right?" Parkman asked as he waited for Aaron to answer.

"Yeah. Why?"

"Richard is often changed to Dick. You ever get called Detective Dick or Dick Dick?"

"Funny." Joffrey looked sideways at him. "Yeah, I do. Used to it now."

Aaron answered the phone.

Chapter 5

AARON CHECKED THE CLOCK again. Sarah should've called and let him know she was okay. He wondered how Parkman took the news that she was quitting the psychic vigilante gig.

Maybe that was what was taking her so long. Parkman's performing some last-ditch attempt to convince her otherwise.

Aaron set his cup of tea on the coffee table and walked to the sliding doors. They were open, the screen letting the cool night air inside the apartment. He stepped out onto the balcony and closed the screen behind him.

June in Toronto was always a good time, but it was even better now that Sarah was back from Italy, back from being a missing person for two months. It had been one whole week together, and he still worried when she got home late.

Sarah had worked her way into his heart, unlike anyone he had ever been with. He saw them making a life together, getting married, and having kids. Now that she was ready to retire from her day job, things seemed more plausible.

He had decided months ago to never stand in her way, whatever she decided to do in her life. To try to understand and support her in any way he could. But if the day ever came when she chose to quit, he wanted to be there and was willing to accept her for who she was until then.

The phone rang.

He turned and walked into the screen door.

"Dammit."

After bumping it off its track, it took an extra ring to get the screen door unjammed.

"Coming, Sarah," he yelled at the phone.

On the fifth ring, just before the machine picked it up, Aaron got to the phone.

"How did it go?"

"Aaron, it's Parkman."

His stomach dropped. "Why are you calling? Not that I don't miss you much, but where's Sarah?"

He pulled the phone away from his ear and checked call display.

Parkman's cell.

Parkman was talking when Aaron brought the phone back to his ear. "Did she show up?" he asked.

"I was just telling you—"

"What happened?" Aaron couldn't contain himself. He had lost his sister to a madman. Then he fell in love with Sarah and lost her for two months, the whole time thinking she was dead and buried in some field in Italy. To only have her back a week and …

"Can you meet me at Humber River Regional Hospital

on Keele Street?"

"Tell me what happened!" Aaron shouted.

There was a moment of silence where Aaron heard the background noises of a car on the road and his own breathing. For a second, he wondered if Parkman would hang up or if the signal would drop.

Then Parkman said the words that would haunt him for a long time.

"Sarah's been shot."

"How, how …" he choked and swallowed. "She was with you. What happened?"

"At the hospital. Come there. I'll explain everything."

"Shot where?"

"At the factory off Keele. You know the one—"

"No, I mean, where did she get shot? Stomach, arm, leg?"

"Head."

Aaron dropped the phone and ran for the apartment door, snatching his key ring off the clip on the wall as he went by it.

By the time he got to his car, he had to wipe his eyes in order to drive.

Chapter 6

OLIVER PAYNE MADE IT to Nafplio without another police car or officer paying any extra attention to him. The Greek sun beat down so hard that his shirt had pasted itself to his back, and he had finished half his water bottle.

The massage he had booked was going to be extra good this week. He had found out about Sugar Spell Spa by going to the twice-weekly farmer's market that assembled on a side street in Nafplio just off the main road downtown. Large colorful signs advertised the spa on the second floor of a building built over a small gas station across the street from the market.

When he looked into them, he discovered they weren't a dirty replica of the massage parlors back home. No, Sugar Spell Spa was a studio, clean and professional, exactly how he wanted it. The attendants were schooled and educated, and the owner, Lina, was one of the best masseuses he had ever had.

In the past, during years of traveling with Violeta for business, it was their regular routine to stop during business holidays and enjoy a massage in a local spa and then compare them to other spas from around the world. Oliver had been massaged in Budapest, Toronto, Vancouver, Los Angeles, Italy, and now Greece, just to name a few. At Sugar Spell Spa, Lina had now been crowned the best in the business and, due to the economic crisis in Greece, the least expensive. He would pay double—or even triple—what Lina charged at her spa for the kind of work they did there, but he was informed that would come across as disrespectful. Even tips were discouraged.

The streets got progressively busier as he neared downtown Nafplio, a bustling city with no outward signs of economic struggle. Retail stores were open, cafés had their outside chairs filled, and restaurants were always in demand.

He quickly surmised that the economic struggle in Greece was one of a political nature. The people had money because they didn't pay their taxes, so they were doing fine. It was the government that was in financial trouble.

He had heard countless times in his four months in Greece that it was considered a national sport to not pay taxes. There were entire islands that had never paid taxes, and still, the antiquated system the Greeks had for tax collection was years behind.

At times, around ten in the evening, he couldn't get a table in any of his favorite restaurants as the crowds were simply too large. It didn't seem like a country in trouble by a long shot.

Five streets converged at the city's center, with no traffic lights or signals. It was called suicide corners because drivers were supposed to enter at their own risk and, once inside, navigate through the pile of other drivers attempting the same thing. He had seen more than a dozen vehicles in the center of the intersection at once, and yet they all made it through after the required honking.

Sugar Spell Spa was a block away when another police car drove by. This time the little car had two officers inside. Neither turned to look at him.

"Paranoid," he whispered under his breath. "Just paranoid."

He hadn't done anything wrong. Leaving his wife wasn't a crime. Overstaying the ninety-day limit in the eurozone made him an illegal immigrant, but as far as he understood it, the Greeks didn't really care about things like that.

Isn't an illegal immigrant just someone who moved from here to there?

He passed the bustling Wednesday market, past the smell of booths where swordfish were sold, and eventually made it to the street the spa was on ten minutes before his appointment.

At the door to the spa, he hit the buzzer and waited. On this side of the building, the sun was relentless. No breeze, no shade. Nothing to quell its onslaught. The sun beat down, baking him in his clothes and making him yearn for the shower before his massage.

When the buzzer clicked and the door unlocked, he opened it, and a chill, like someone was watching him, fluttered through his shoulders. He turned around and examined the street behind him.

Vehicles were parked wherever there was a spot along

the edge of the road, close to the curb. Roughly a dozen cars to his left, a police cruiser with two men inside sat behind a small red Fiat. From where he stood, half in, half out of the door to the spa, it looked like the men were watching him. The way the sun reflected off their windshield, he couldn't tell for sure.

Why would they be watching me?

He stepped inside the spa and closed the door behind him, listening for the telltale click of the lock.

Maybe he should leave. Get back to the village, grab his things, and take a taxi to another city. Or grab a plane to another country in the eurozone.

Or maybe he was just being paranoid. What could Violeta do to him on Greek soil? He hadn't broken any laws in the States. He'd simply left his wife and took not even ten percent of the wealth they had together. If he was considered to be on the run, it was because his wife had terrorized and emotionally abused him.

Rationalizing it, he had nothing to worry about. Police cars were all over the city. Why, all of a sudden, did he feel they were all after him?

Maybe because of that American man with the camera that Oliver would swear had taken his picture about a week ago.

He started up the stairs, feeling like he had missed something. The idea that he was being watched may be ridiculous, but it was borne from somewhere. He was a businessman first. His decisions were derived through logic and reason. That was how he made it so long with a witch like Violeta.

If he felt the eyes of the law were on him, then maybe

they were. But not for any reasons he could come up with.

But for reasons, Violeta could come up with.

Lina opened the frosted glass doors ahead of him on the second floor.

"I was wondering what was taking you so long," she said, her usual smile changing his mood instantly. Lina was perpetually happy.

"I thought I saw someone I knew outside. Had to do a double take."

"No problem. Your room is ready. Just go in there," she gestured to the left, where a shower and bathroom were located. "Have a shower, and I'll meet you inside."

Oliver headed in while Lina walked back behind her counter.

The bathroom window looked down onto the street where Oliver had seen the cop car. Before disrobing, he slid the window open and stuck his head out.

The police car was gone.

"See," he said to himself. "It was nothing."

But he still felt he was missing something.

He prepared for his massage, entered the room in his gym shorts, the rule at Sugar Spell Spa, and lay down on the table. Lina entered less than thirty seconds later.

The massage was amazing, as he had expected. They talked about life, her boyfriend, Oliver's enjoyment of Nafplio, and Greece in general.

When she was done, she told him in her soft voice to relax, don't get up too fast. When he was ready, he could get dressed and meet her at the front counter.

The feeling that the police would be waiting for him when he stepped outside turned his stomach. The feeling of missing something still nagged at him, and he couldn't put his finger on it.

Violeta had to be up to something. Maybe he had underestimated her. If he had, she would make it hurt. But she wouldn't kill him. He didn't believe that she *wouldn't* hire someone to kill him, but she needed him in the short term. She needed his signature for a business deal and to sign over his shares and any other interest he held in the company.

She wouldn't have him killed, but she'd make sure he knew just how painful it was for her that he had left in the first place.

At the counter, he paid Lina, offered a small tip but not enough to be disrespectful, and set another appointment for next Wednesday.

Even though he tried not to think it, the thought of not being here next Wednesday crossed his mind.

She thanked him profusely, and he said his goodbyes, his muscles warm and jelly-like.

At the bottom of the stairs, once the door was open a crack, he stuck his head out and looked up and down the street.

No police cars anywhere.

Relief swept over him.

The thought of relocating made him feel better. Maybe in a week or two, he would move to another city, another village, and settle down. If that American man had found him, Violeta wouldn't be far behind.

Maybe he should've relocated already.

Across the street, at the market, he got enough fruit and vegetables for three days when he would return for the Saturday market. Enough for two stir frys, a couple of salads, and lots of cucumbers to cool him off by the pool to combat Greece's relentless heat.

When he looked across the street at Lina's spa, it all came to him in a flood. When he realized what he had done, his knees almost gave out. He moved to the side and sat beside two gypsy ladies with their children.

With his bags between his legs, he breathed in and out, trying to calm down.

He was a creature of habit, and Violeta knew that. Oliver would locate the local spa and have regular massages wherever he lived. Sugar Spa Spell had a monopoly. Lina's spa was the only one in Nafplio. If Violeta even suspected he was in Nafplio—with enough money, she could find that out as he didn't hide through a fake name or passport—she would hire someone to watch the local spas with a description of him.

That's why the cop watched him in the village that morning. They knew he would be walking out to Nafplio today. The two officers in their car parked up the street from Lina's door had been watching him.

Hell, they were probably watching him right now.

He looked up and felt the blood drain from his face as he scanned the crowd. No one seemed to pay him any attention. Behind him, where the farmer's market vendors parked their vehicles, no one was looking his way.

He needed to get home. Think on things some more. Evaluate the need to move. Weigh everything.

The combined adrenaline rush of his realization and the recent massage weakened his legs even more. He needed food, peace, and quiet.

A left through the throng of shoppers took him out to the

road. He flagged down a taxi and hopped in the back seat.

"Agios Adrianos, efharisto," he said.

The driver nodded and performed a U-turn to move away from the congestion of the farmer's market. Once they got through the suicide corners and started along the side road leading to the village, Oliver glanced out the back window.

Directly behind the taxi were three police cars, one right behind the other.

He spun around and sunk lower in his seat. He waited for them to hit their sirens, pull the cab over and yank him out, but nothing happened.

The driver maneuvered through a traffic circle and continued toward Oliver's village. In the rearview mirror, the driver's eyes watched the cops behind him, probably wondering what they were doing.

Oliver didn't try to look back again. They were either going to pull them over or let it go. Looking back did nothing to change that.

On the outskirts of the small village, the road turned to the right and became one-way. When leaving the village, there was another one-way on the other side.

The taxi driver turned onto the one-way and applied his brakes.

Up ahead, two Greek police cars blocked the road.

The driver muttered something unintelligible in Greek and stopped his vehicle.

He opened his door to get out.

"No, wait," Oliver shouted.

Either the driver didn't hear him, didn't understand English, or didn't care. He spoke to the officers who were approaching the taxi.

Someone knocked on the trunk. Then the back doors on each side of the taxi opened.

A young Greek cop, probably just out of high school, gestured for Oliver to get out. Oliver looked to the other side of the car, where another cop nodded and smiled.

"Go ahead," this cop said in English. "Everything be okay."

Oliver got out and stood beside the car. The taxi driver was arguing about something, most likely that he was trying to do his job and that this interruption was unheard of.

Two cops pointed at the driver's seat and yelled something back at him. The driver was suddenly convinced that he should just get in his car and leave.

A sour look on his face, the driver walked by Oliver, spit on the ground, and dropped into the driver's seat.

He shouted something else. The cop who spoke English a moment ago responded. The driver slammed his door and drove around the roadblock, squealing his tires in protest.

"Hey," Oliver yelled. "What about my things from the market?"

The English-speaking officer moved to stand in front of Oliver. He had thick black eyebrows, dark skin, and a five-o'clock shadow before noon. "He is keeping them in lieu of payment."

"What? Why? Who said he could do that?" Oliver had no idea what was happening and didn't like any of it. His legs shook, and couldn't be trusted to hold him up anymore. In a foreign country, with foreign police, doing things on their terms could mean anything.

"I told the driver he could keep your things," the dark-skinned officer said.

His mustache was graying, his temples lined by sun-damaged skin. He had the dark complexion of a Greek descendant whose bloodline had mixed with the Turks from the days when Turkey had occupied Greece.

He also had a hard edge to him that Oliver couldn't put his finger on. Something about his half smile asked the world to challenge him. The officer's eyes displayed intelligence far greater than his comrades, and his almost perfect English confirmed that. Oliver had met many people in his four months in Greece, but none who spoke English as well as the cop in front of him.

"My name is Kostas," the cop said. He didn't present a hand to shake. "We are cracking down on illegal immigrants. May we see your passport?"

Oliver turned to examine every officer standing on the road. In total, five police cars sat in the middle of the road, with eight policemen scattered about randomly. All for him. Not a single car had passed in the four minutes they had been there.

His taxi had been sent away with his purchases from the market. That meant only one thing. Kostas had an agenda, and Violeta most likely financed it. Kostas already knew Oliver wouldn't need his purchases, which meant this was all a formality for what was coming.

"Seems like a lot of wasted manpower for an economically weakened government to use on checking an American's passport." Oliver turned back to face Kostas, calling on his nerves to cooperate and allow him to appear calm and collected. "Wouldn't you think?"

Kostas's smile widened. His hand came out, palm up. "Passport, please."

"I don't have it on me. It's back at the villa I'm renting, in my nightstand drawer."

"What? You don't carry identification on you in a foreign country? What if something were to happen to you? A car accident? A mugging? How could we identify your body or even know where you're staying without an ID?"

He turned to his assembled men and blurted something out in Greek. The men laughed.

Oliver's insides shook so much that he was worried it would show in his extremities.

"Hop in my car," Kostas said, gesturing to his car with a meaty hand, his forearm covered in thick black hair. "We will drive you to your villa and take a look at your passport. Then everything will be fine, I'm sure."

Two officers rushed up and placed a gentle hand on each of Oliver's arms, guiding him to the lead car. He sat in the back as the other men reclaimed their cars. A moment later, the entourage drove through the village and up the long driveway to his rented villa.

The eurozone allowed a ninety-day stay every 180 days. Basically, three months were allowed inside every six months. Oliver was a month past that, which meant he would have some explaining to do.

Maybe he could offer them money. Enough to feed them and their families for a few months. Just enough to let him leave the country of his own free will. He could go back into hiding. Maybe he would forgo the massages in the next country and change his routine.

Or maybe Violeta had already paid these upstanding men a handsome sum, which was simply the beginning of a nightmare she had planned.

Her last words entered his mind. The threats of what she would do if he ever left her. The violence, the pain.

His mid-life crisis would be a bit different than most men's.

Chapter 7

PARKMAN WAITED IN THE visitor lounge after cleaning Sarah's blood off his hands and arms. The blood on his shirt had darkened. He figured the stain would serve as a constant reminder that it was his fault Sarah Roberts was killed.

Detective Joffrey sat across from him. Aaron had shown up five minutes before. Parkman talked to Joffrey but looked at Aaron frequently as he explained what had happened. He covered as many details as he could remember in an attempt to forget nothing and make the entire scene clear to both men.

"And you hadn't seen this Jaguar before?" Joffrey asked. "Tailing you? Watching you?"

Parkman shook his head.

"What is your relationship to this client that you say has threatened you?"

"I have to respect confidentiality here, but I'll tell you as much as possible." He chanced a side look at Aaron again, who had stayed relatively quiet since he arrived. "I did the job for this client. When the job was complete, another job was presented to me, one I couldn't take on ethical, moral, and criminal grounds. Said client became enraged. Swore she would change my mind. I didn't. The client harassed me through third parties, leaving no trail back to them. Then I was told that if I didn't perform the final task required of me, they would get to me by hurting my friends."

"Your friend, as in Sarah Roberts?"

Parkman nodded. "That's right. This client wouldn't take no for an answer. And they didn't like how much I knew about them."

"So they followed you," Joffrey interrupted, "and shot at you, hitting Sarah."

"Something like that. At least that's what makes the most sense."

"What do you mean, something like that?" Aaron asked.

Parkman turned and met Aaron's dark eyes. "I think Sarah was the intended target. I came to Toronto to warn her, to keep her safe."

"How did this client of yours even know she was alive?" Aaron asked. "As far as anyone knows, Sarah's still missing in Italy."

"I thought about that. There were too many coincidences. The client knew too much. It wasn't until last night in the hotel that I realized the client had probably tapped my phone. Which means they heard my conversation with Sarah when she called last week. They know I was trying to reach her. The client would also know if they're tracking my cell phone, exactly where I am, and when."

"Are you saying this is your fault?" Aaron asked. "That you were responsible for this?"

Parkman looked down at his shoes. "I can't live with that. The responsibility, to have to own that, would be too much." He looked up, wiped his face with his hands, and stared at the stained ceiling tiles above his head. "I came here as a friend to warn her. I shot at the fleeing vehicle." He looked at Joffrey. "I did everything right. Sometimes the ball just falls, and there's nothing anyone could do."

Aaron's head had dropped. He sat with his elbows on his knees, hands clasped.

"Aaron, if I could trade places with her, I would. You have to know that. You have to consider how many years Sarah and I have worked together. Getting to her was the last twist of negotiation my client needed. They don't understand that by doing this, they have sealed their own fate."

Parkman cleared his throat and looked around the waiting room.

"Something's bothering me," Joffrey said.

"What's that?" Parkman asked.

"Why would someone travel across the United States and enter Canada just to chase you down and shoot your friend? Why not just perform this task themselves, whatever it was they wanted you to do?"

"I don't know."

"What's the worst they could've asked of you? Kill someone? Torture someone? If what you're saying is true, and that client hired someone to trail you here, then why not use tonight's shooter to perform whatever it was they wanted you to do instead of taking out Sarah? You're no longer a part of it if they have a shooter. So what am I missing?"

Parkman shrugged. "No idea, but I will do everything possible to find out."

The double doors that led to surgery opened. A tall doctor, at least six foot three, stepped out, swept the room with his gaze, and stopped on Joffrey.

He nodded subtly, and the three men got up.

"Follow me to my office," the doctor said.

The pit in Parkman's stomach hardened to a lead ball the size of a shot-put. What would life be like without Sarah? How could he ever face her parents again? Or Aaron? Regardless of how this looked and the shooter's actions, everything appeared to be his fault, and he had to own it. Calling Sarah, and coming to Toronto to warn her, was a mistake.

Sarah had wanted to quit. Vivian even warned her to stay away from him tonight. When Sarah told him that, it hurt. Even Vivian knew he was a threat now.

And Sarah knew the name Tam Rood. Sarah was supposed to meet Tam and talk to her, and everything would be okay.

But Tam was in Santa Rosa with her mother, Violeta. How would Sarah meet with Tam in Toronto?

Unless Tam was here. Unless Tam was the shooter.

Would Violeta hire her own daughter to kill people?

Parkman took one more look around the waiting lounge before the doors closed. No one paid any attention. An old woman read her Kindle in a corner seat. Two young boys were stretched across three seats, sleeping, evidently waiting for their relative to get out of surgery. Six other people were in the area in various states of rest, all waiting for news on their loved ones.

Nobody looked like Violeta's henchmen. And Tam Rood was nowhere in sight.

"Parkman?" Joffrey asked. "You coming?"

He let the door fall shut behind him. The only reason he still protected Violeta with her client-privileged confidentiality agreement was that he needed to be the one to make her pay for what she did to Sarah.

No one else could be brought in on this.

The doctor's office was surprisingly neat and tidy. The desk was uncluttered, and a plastic human body with removable parts sat on the corner.

"Gentlemen," the doctor said, waving his hand at the chairs. "I'm in and out of surgery today, and I only have a few minutes, so please have a seat."

Two chairs faced the desk. Aaron grabbed a chair from the side bookcase and brought it over.

"How is she?" Aaron asked.

Parkman studied the doctor's face for anything that would reveal the harder truth as he sat down.

"To be honest," the doctor started, "she's not out of the woods yet."

"What does that mean?" Parkman asked.

A wave of relief swept over him. At least she wasn't dead.

"She's a fighter, that girl, but she has sustained a major hit to the head. What we call a TBI."

"Which is?" Aaron asked.

"Traumatic Brain Injury."

"How bad?"

"Not entirely sure yet. What confuses me was how she arrived."

Parkman frowned. "How are you confused?"

"When the emergency response personnel arrive on the scene with a TBI, they're supposed to try to get her eyes open, check for movement and verbal response."

"But she was unconscious."

"I understand, but that's what we do. When she arrives here, she's already supposed to be sedated with a tube running into her lungs to make sure she has enough oxygen so we can run a CT scan. Luckily for Sarah, she was breathing on her own, her blood pressure was relatively good, and her oxygen levels were high enough to perform the CT. Most of the time, with a gunshot to the head, that wouldn't happen."

"So what are you saying?"

"I was able to resuscitate her here. She was able to talk for a moment."

"Did she say anything important?" Joffrey asked.

"She kept saying a girl's name."

"Her own?" Aaron asked.

Maybe Tam Rood's name, Parkman thought. *Or Violeta. Sarah's gonna wake up pissed.*

"No, she kept saying, Vivian. Over and over. Something about Vivian being in her head. Vivian helped her to be dead."

"Dead?" Aaron asked, his voice an octave higher than Parkman had ever heard it.

"She's not dead now. We got the bullet out, and it's at forensics. Now I'm just trying to deal with the swelling in her brain. The problem with swelling is that the brain has nowhere to swell, with the skull keeping it enclosed. She's dealing with increased intracranial pressure, which isn't looking good."

"When will she be out of the woods?" Parkman asked.

"Hard to tell at the moment. I wish I could have better news. I'm sorry."

Aaron choked, like he was going to cry, but held himself back.

"What else can you tell us?" Joffrey asked.

"If and when Sarah regains consciousness, a variety of neurologically based symptoms may occur, such as irritability and aggression."

"Oh, don't worry about that," Parkman cut in. "Sarah is aggressive by nature."

The doctor frowned, then continued. "If everything works out and we get the swelling down, as time passes, the brain will approach physiological stability again, although neurons in the brain don't mend themselves. New nerves won't grow in ways that lead to a full recovery. But I can't even promise Sarah will come out of this. I just want you guys to be ready if the news isn't exactly what you expect it to be."

"So what are you saying?" Aaron asked. "Can you give us odds? Is it fifty-fifty or better?"

"It's more like eighty-twenty."

"That's not bad," Parkman said.

"Twenty percent chance she lives, eighty percent we lose her." He cleared his throat. "Certain areas of the brain are damaged. There's nothing anyone can do about that. Only time will tell how damaged Sarah Roberts will be if she pulls through, and it's not looking good at the moment." The doctor got up and headed for the door. "I have to get back." He stopped before leaving the room. "I'm sorry the news isn't better, but I think you must prepare for the inevitable. Call any relatives she has in the area and get them here before it's too late. In the meantime, I'll do whatever I can to save her."

The doctor shut the door softly as he left.

Chapter 8

As the five Greek police cars came to a halt in front of Oliver's rented villa, Kostas let Oliver out to unlock the gate. The residual massage oil on his back had cooled in the car, but out in the sun, his back was moist and pasted against his shirt.

What was the worst they could do to him? He had overstayed four weeks on an American passport. The worst would be to give him over to the American Embassy in Athens. Or they might take him to Athens themselves and see that he gets on an international plane, thereby leaving their country. There could be a fine of some sort. He would pay it and then head to London, England. Hide somewhere in Scotland. Violeta would spend the rest of her years hunting him down because an experience like this only strengthened his position by teaching him about routine and exposure.

He pushed the gates wide enough for the vehicles to

enter the property. Once Kostas and his men had parked and exited their vehicles, they followed Oliver to his villa behind the main house.

"This is a nice little place you have here," Kostas said. "I didn't know this was back here."

"Where did you learn such good English?" Oliver asked.

"I went to school in Athens, then traveled to New York for three years. When I returned to Greece, I became a policeman."

"So you've been to the States?" Oliver opened the door to the villa and moved inside. Kostas followed him in. "What did you think of it?" he asked as he moved down the hall to the bedroom and walked around the bed to the nightstand.

"At first, New York was overwhelming. It was so big."

The nightstand was empty. Oliver stopped and stared at the empty drawer.

"Then I got used to the bustle and hustle, as you Americans call it."

He tried the second drawer, but it was empty, too.

"During the second year, I got mugged. Then I asked myself what I was doing in the States. So I decided to fly home to Athens and begin my career."

Oliver walked across the bed and tried the other nightstand, panic settling in on his bones. It was empty.

His passport was gone. Someone had stolen it.

The last time he checked, it was there. No way he moved it and forgot. That wasn't like him. It was there, but now it was gone.

"You're not interested in my story, are you?" Kostas asked.

"No, yes, it's just …"

"It's just, what?"

"The passport isn't in my drawer. Someone must've taken it."

"Are you saying you don't have a passport because someone has stolen it?"

"Locks that way," Oliver said, the agitation coming through in his voice.

"You are aware that I am not the one who has stolen your passport, correct?"

"I never said you were."

"Though you talk to me with anger. You sound mad at me. Am I to understand you have no identification?"

"I have my American ID." He pulled out his wallet.

"That is not necessary." Kostas raised his hand to stop Oliver. "I only need to see your passport. Please, could you get it for me?"

"I don't have it." Then he walked over to the sliding access door to the outside and tried to move it, but it was locked. "Someone must've broken in when I went to the farmer's market this morning."

He moved to the kitchen and tried that window. Then the one in the living room, too. Both were secure. "I don't get it. Where could it be?"

Kostas stepped out of the open villa door and waved at his men. A moment later, three of them entered the villa.

"One more time," Kostas said. "Are you refusing to provide the Greek authorities with your passport?"

"I'm not refusing anything," Oliver retorted. "I don't have it."

"Then you cannot produce it. Gentleman, arrest this man for being in Greece illegally."

The man in the middle produced a white zip tie for Oliver's wrists as the three approached him.

"Hey, wait a minute," Oliver said as he backed up. "I'm an American citizen. Let me call my embassy. We can work this out."

Kostas had already exited the villa, and the three men weren't listening.

They grabbed his arms a lot rougher than before, turned him around, and wrapped the wrist ties on too tight.

"Hey, that's cutting off my circulation."

The older of the three cops said something in Greek to him. The other two chuckled and then shoved him toward the door.

Outside, they pushed him again. He got his feet in front of him just in time.

"What the—?" he shouted back at them. "You don't have to be so rough. I'm going with you. I'm complying."

Kostas stood by his car, arms crossed, watching as Oliver headed his way, the three officers bringing up the rear. Oliver detected the slightest of nods from Kostas, and then a second later, he was shoved again. This time two hands landed on each shoulder blade, thrusting him forward so fast that his head snapped back, and he lifted off the ground for a brief moment. Without the ability to brace his fall with his hands tied behind his back, he landed chest and shoulder first, his face rubbing along the stones as he skidded a few inches.

Breath caught in his lungs. Pain screamed from his face and knees, and his shoulder felt like it had popped out. Dazed and confused, he didn't have time to gather his thoughts before they picked him up again. Just as he got to his feet, they let him go.

He dropped in a heap, twisting his right knee so badly he was sure something tore. Oliver moaned, rolled onto his side to get off his tied hands behind his back, and tried to curl into a ball.

In the grand scheme of things, this was nothing worse than a high school fight. Scrapes and bruises would be all that was left days from now. But for Oliver, who hadn't had to deal with anything worse than a paper cut, minus the mild heart attack, this wasn't so much about the pain to his body but the pain to his ego, the humiliation.

He opened his eyes and looked up into Kostas's smiling face.

"You poor man. You tripped when my officers were only trying to lend a hand." He leaned down. "Come on, get up. As they say in America, we'll take you downtown and set things right."

Kostas grabbed his left arm and hauled Oliver to his feet.

His ear tickled as Kostas leaned in close and whispered something.

"What was that?" Oliver asked.

"Thank Violeta for this," Kostas repeated. "She wanted me to tell you at the beginning."

It was spoken so low Oliver was sure no one else heard what Kostas said.

"No, Kostas, I can double what she's paying you."

Kostas let go of his arm, walked around to stand in front of him, and shook his head.

"Attempting to bribe an officer of the law." He rubbed one index finger along the length of the other. "Tsk, tsk, tsk."

Kostas's right hand balled into a fist. Oliver hobbled on his feet, his bladder suddenly needed to vacate.

One second he blinked, the next, Kostas's fist connected with his left cheek.

He dropped to his knees, screaming as new pain seared in his already aching right knee. He fell sideways to the ground, bits of dirt entering his mouth.

Kostas kneeled in front of him. "You should never try to buy an officer of the law in Greece. That is very disrespectful." He shook his head. "For that, you will have many accidents."

Kostas motioned for his men to pick Oliver up, but Oliver didn't want to be moved. He moaned, twisted away from their grasp, and writhed in the dirt until finally, four men lifted him shoulder height and carried him like they were pallbearers at a funeral.

At Kostas's car, one of the men opened the back door and stepped out of the way.

Before they tossed him inside, Oliver dreaded the impact, knowing they wouldn't be gentle, but there was nothing he could do about it.

And he was right. Consciousness wavered for a moment after they had him in the back. The pain in his shoulder intensified. His knee had already begun to swell. Something wet trickled down his hands. It had to be blood from the zip ties cutting into his flesh.

The driver's side door opened, and Kostas got in, the car's shocks dropped and adjusted to the new weight.

Kostas turned the car on and backed out of the driveway.

"How did you think you could get away with it?" Kostas asked.

Oliver didn't want to speak.

"I talked to Violeta myself. She told me everything you

did, and then she made a generous donation to our police station in Nafplio and asked if we could find her husband. Oliver Payne, the man who raped his seventeen-year-old daughter and then fled to Greece to hide from the American authorities. I have mercy for horses with broken legs, so why not you, you disgusting animal."

A cold sweat covered his body. He shivered in pain. He had heard stories of what other prisoners did to people who raped a woman, not to mention what they did to men who raped someone so young. Telling Kostas he was innocent would do no good. Violeta had set him up even though he had never touched his daughter in any way.

"Of course, we found you at the local spa," Kostas said. "Were you scouting out other girls to prey on with your sick fetishes?"

"I didn't rape anybody," Oliver said, knowing it would fall on deaf ears. His lower lip had started to swell.

How could one woman do so much damage?

She needed him alive to sign over his shares to the company. He had to hope they wouldn't kill him. One day, he would be back on American soil, and when he got there, he would seek retribution. He'd figure something out. Violeta would pay for this.

"I just hope they don't kill you when we place you in the holding cell," Kostas said.

Oliver was a planner, a doer. He wrote an agenda for each day and fulfilled it. He was never lost.

But today, for the first time in his life, he felt more lost and scared than ever before, and he wondered if he would ever see a sunrise again.

Chapter 9

Joffrey stopped at the elevator. "I've got to go to my car for some paperwork. I don't expect you to come to the station right now as I'm sure you want to hang out here and wait to hear more, so I'll bring paper and a pen to get your statement while it's still fresh in your mind."

Parkman nodded. "Fine with me."

"All right. Give me five minutes."

The elevator door opened, and Joffrey stepped on, offered a sympathetic smile for Aaron, and the doors shut.

"What are you going to do?" Parkman asked Aaron.

"Wait around here. I've got nowhere to go until Sarah wakes up."

"What about the dojo?"

"My guys will open it for me in the morning."

Parkman put a hand on his shoulder. "You know my relationship with Sarah. You know I would die for her. I didn't do this. It was the culmination of a chain of events, and it may lie on my shoulders, but—"

"I know, Parkman." Aaron met his eyes. "If I thought you had shot her, or it was directly your fault, you would be on an operating table as well."

"Fair enough. I get it. Now, why don't you go down and fetch us a couple of coffees from the cafeteria? I'll wait here."

Aaron left without another word.

"Oh, and see if they have any toothpicks, okay?"

Parkman reclaimed his seat from earlier. He tried to piece it all together. Violeta didn't want her husband killed. She wanted him paralyzed. As long as Oliver could still sign documents, still use at least one hand. Parkman had been asked to break Oliver's back since he had him under surveillance in Greece. He was there. He could do it. Violeta stressed that Parkman was perfect for the job because he was already in position. Violeta had offered him a cool million simply to put a man in the hospital. Parkman had hospitalized many men in his time. Many men he had shot and killed. But he could never willingly attack another human being for a paycheck. Violeta warned him not to disobey her. That had been her mistake.

Parkman had learned from Sarah years ago how to handle people who thought they could strike fear in his heart. He would rather fight whoever or whatever Violeta tossed at him than hurt an innocent man.

But he had no idea the crazy woman would go after Sarah.

Violeta said she would use her own daughter to paralyze Oliver, but Parkman guessed Tam refused. And since the world of mercenaries and hitmen wasn't a place familiar to Violeta, she had requested Parkman help find someone to replace him. Someone with fewer scruples. Someone who could actually finish the job.

Parkman refused again and ceased all contact. Then the attacks happened. Then the letter.

The letter that was inside his jacket pocket back at the crime scene. Unless it had been picked up already.

The door opened, and a doctor came out to talk to the young boys who had been sprawled across chairs sleeping.

After a moment of hushed tones, the older boy's face hardened, and the younger boy wept. They walked away, holding each other. Even the doctor shed a tear as he watched them leave.

Parkman checked his watch. Joffrey had been gone more than five minutes now. Aaron would be back at any moment.

He had a decision to make. Tell them all of it, everything, and get their help in arresting Violeta or going after her himself.

If Sarah hadn't been hurt, he might've offered Violeta up to the police, but now that Sarah was fighting for her life, especially when she wanted to walk away from the violent life, it had become personal. He wanted Violeta Payne all to himself.

The elevator doors opened.

Detective Joffrey stepped off and headed his way.

"Where's Aaron?" he asked.

"Gone for coffees."

"You think he's getting three?"

"Can't be sure."

Joffrey handed Parkman a pad of paper and two pens.

"You know the drill. I need your statement. Write it out as best as you can. Be as detailed as possible. And write so I can read it."

"Okay, but I'll need a few hours."

"I don't think any of us are going anywhere anytime soon. While you get started, I'm going to find that doctor. I have a couple of questions for him."

"Did you catch his name?" Parkman asked.

"The nameplate on his office door said Jacob, so I'm assuming he's Doctor Jacob."

"Shit, missed that. I'm usually observant enough to catch that sort of thing."

"I'll be right back."

Joffrey walked off as Aaron showed up with two coffees.

"I didn't know if you take cream, sugar, or both, so I left it black."

"Black's fine. Nothing for the detective?"

"Forgot. He can go get his own when he comes back."

Parkman sipped his coffee and then set it down.

"I'm going to start writing my statement."

"I'm going to veg until doc comes back out with more news."

Parkman wrote as legibly as he could, adding everything he could recall. At times, he had to wipe his eyes. He had asked her to meet him at the ruined building across the street and then, on purpose, met her in the parking lot of the industrial building, so if they had been followed or his cell phone traced, his pursuer would see Sarah's bike and assume they were on the other side of the street.

He had no idea the occupants of the Jaguar were the enemy. The driver didn't even turn to look at them as he drove by.

Parkman shot his head up and looked at the wall across from him.

"What?" Aaron asked. "What is it? You remember something?"

"Unless it wasn't the Jaguar."

"What?"

He turned to Aaron. "What if the shooter had been waiting across the street, listening with a parabolic mike or something? They waited until the Jaguar passed and then took the shot. Sarah and I would've assumed the shot came from the Jag."

"Won't the investigators look across the street for evidence of a shooter?"

"Not necessarily. They might, especially if they suspected that was a possible scenario. But based on my statement, they would assume the shooter was in the Jag."

Detective Joffrey entered the waiting lounge. He walked up to Parkman and took the pad of paper from him.

"Hey, I'm not finished. There's lots more."

"I know. Just checking something."

"Ask me if you need clarity. I know what I wrote."

Joffrey studied Parkman's words for a moment longer, then lowered the pad. His jaw muscles clenched like he was grinding his teeth.

"Parkman?" Joffrey said.

"What?"

"What kind of gun do you carry?"

"A Glock 22. Why?"

"Doctor Jacob pulled the bullet out when Sarah arrived. It was in relatively good shape."

"Which means?"

"It has to undergo testing in the lab, but upon visual inspection, it looks like a .40 S&W bullet."

Parkman looked at Aaron for support, then back to Joffrey. "So the gunman used the same ammunition I use."

"The first responders called me when I went down to my car ten minutes ago."

Discomfort at being questioned this way angered Parkman. Was Joffrey trying to say that Parkman shot Sarah?

"And? What did they say?"

"They located the Jaguar you shot at already."

"Good."

Joffrey shook his head. "Not good."

"Why?" Parkman asked. It came out curt, angry. His patience was thinning.

"The man driving it works three buildings down from where you and Sarah were. He had a baby in the back seat because his wife had recently died of cancer. As he drove by your location, he claims he thought he heard a firecracker go off, which startled him and made him duck his head. Just before he passed your location, he said he saw a woman with long blonde hair fall to the concrete in front of a man with a gun in his hand. Then the gunman tried to take him out, too."

Some of the anger at feeling like he was about to be accused of shooting Sarah turned to sickness. He had acted on instinct. He was convinced the shooter was in the Jaguar. At the time, there had been no doubt. But even going over the situation again, before Joffrey told him this, he already thought the shooter set him up to think it was the Jag.

They aimed to take Sarah out and make Parkman go to prison for murdering an unsuspecting member of the public driving a Jaguar. The baby could've been hurt or killed. He could almost hear Violeta ordering this reckless task.

"The baby had to get splinters of glass removed from her ear because you blew out the back window. The father is being treated for shock as we speak."

Parkman raised a hand to cover his mouth. He didn't know what to say. Aaron put a consoling hand on Parkman's shoulder.

"The officers have a theory," Joffrey continued.

Parkman didn't say anything as he held back warring emotions.

"They think you waited for the car to drive by, shot Sarah, and then emptied your weapon at the fleeing vehicle."

Parkman found his voice. "Why would I do that?" he said. "Why the fuck would I shoot Sarah? Huh? You tell me that?"

"Calm down," Joffrey said.

The remaining people in the waiting room sat up straighter and watched them.

"They think you shot Sarah because of the note found in your jacket pocket at the scene."

Parkman's stomach clenched. For a second, he thought he would throw up on the detective.

"I just checked your handwriting against what's on this note," Joffrey said. "From what I can see, you wrote it. Care to explain?"

"What's the note say?" Aaron asked.

"That Sarah would die with a bullet to the head," Joffrey offered. "It was signed by a woman named Violeta, but it's Parkman's handwriting. Are you trying to set this woman up? Were you trying to kill your friend? Come on, Parkman, tell me what's going on. No more bullshit, or I will lock you up and charge you." Joffrey stood in front of Parkman, handcuffs in his hand. "You want to put these on now or later?"

Aaron removed his hand from Parkman's shoulder.

Chapter 10

OLIVER PAYNE DIDN'T WANT to move a muscle. Everything ached. The Greek police had placed him in a small, dirty holding cell without a bed or anything to sit on. The toilet was seatless, and there was no toilet paper to speak of. The damp room stank of mold and past occupants' urine and feces.

They had clipped the zip ties off his wrists. Only in the last ten minutes had the blood stopped oozing from the cuts.

Luckily, his shoulder hadn't popped out when he hit the ground. His knee was intact after twisting it but had swollen to double its original size. He looked down past his fat lip at the dirt clinging to his skin, stuck on the leftover massage oil. It spread out like he had layered butter on himself and then sprinkled cinnamon.

His passport was missing, and all he could surmise was Violeta had someone steal it before the police showed up. He guessed the police already had his passport as they were probably the ones who stole it in the first place.

Within days he would be on a plane, heading back to the States, where he would hire a lawyer and leave Violeta the hard way. Walking out had been easy. Coming to Greece and living here for four months had been fun. But this was the coward's way out. He knew it and could live with it. But Violeta had pushed too hard.

He would go for dissolution of the company, and he would want his share in cash. Either she would have to find a way to buy him out, or the company would go up for sale.

She didn't want that. But what she wanted any more wasn't of importance to him. Tam would be eighteen in a few months. She'd understand sooner or later what her mother was like.

A door clicked open down the hall.

"What now?" he asked out loud.

The lock clicked on his door.

"Mr. Payne, you have a call."

He had to take it. Maybe it was Violeta willing to work things out. His first step had to be to get out of this holding cell. If that meant befriending his ex-wife, then he would.

He rolled to his side, wincing at the pain. Without letting his swollen knee touch the ground, he got up on his good knee and pushed with his hands.

"Ah, shit," he whispered.

"What?" the cop asked.

"Split open the cut on my wrist again." He met the cop's eyes. "The cut from your zip ties."

The cop shrugged and stepped out of the doorway to let Oliver pass.

He escorted him down the hall, where a phone dangled from the wall. The cop gestured to it and stepped behind another door. Metal doors barricaded any thoughts of escape in the back of the Greek police station, which pleased Oliver. That meant they didn't have to bind his wrists again.

He picked up the swinging phone. "Hello?"

"Enjoying the comforts of home, darling?"

"Do you know what they did to me?"

"You stayed past your allotted time. In their eyes, you're an illegal immigrant."

"How did you find me?"

"I have my ways."

Oliver wanted to reach through the phone and strangle her. "Stop with the bullshit, Violeta. I want out. I am out. Leave me alone. You can have the business, everything—"

"No. It's not that easy." Her tone darkened, the lightness gone.

"Why not?"

"It's black and white. You're either with me, or you're not."

"I know. I've heard your speeches about yin and yang and right and wrong a thousand times—"

"Are you with me?" she asked.

He thought about his answer. He was supposed to be friendly, with the aim of being released from this hell hole. But she told them he had raped his own daughter. She had become foreign, enemy territory. She had started a war, and he couldn't just surrender.

"Obviously, I am not with you. I should've seen your delusional side years ago. How did I miss how fucked up you are?"

"Then you're not with me," she said, almost to herself, barely above a whisper.

"Are we getting anywhere here? You keep saying the same thing. What do you really want?"

"I want the business. Not just a controlling interest. If you're not with me, then I want it all."

"Fine. Take it. Leave me alone."

"I need signatures from you. Lawyer meetings. This isn't something we can agree to over the phone. You have to return to me and sign everything."

"Get me out of this Greek police station, and then send me the documents. I'll sign whatever you send."

"Not going to happen."

His hand tightened on the phone. It always had to be her way.

"Why won't it happen? Isn't that what you want?"

"You come here to the States. It'll take weeks, if not months, to transfer everything. I have a rather large deal in play right now. Before everything is signed over to me, I need you to sign off on this other deal, and I can't send those documents to Greece."

"Sounds like you have a lot going on. Well, enjoy yourself with it. I'm not coming back to the States. When I leave Greece, I'll be in Britain or Australia. Good luck finding me again."

"A moment ago, you offered to sign if I sent you the documents. Were you lying again?"

"If you were amicable, willing to work with me, I'd make it happen at my end. But because it has to be your way, I'm done with you. There's no negotiation. It's not open for discussion anymore." Without cautioning himself, his voice rose a notch. "That's why I left you, Violeta. Don't you get it? Now that we're separated, I don't have to do it your way. You don't have any control over me anymore. It's not always cut and dried. It's not always black or white. Sometimes there are gray areas. Once you realize that, you will understand that you can't keep acting like—" Oliver stopped talking. He heard nothing on the line. Not even her breathing. "Violeta? You there?"

The guard opened the metal door to his right and nodded at the phone. Oliver replaced it in the cradle and limped past the guard, favoring his swollen knee as he headed back to the holding cell.

Your move, bitch.

What would she do to get him back to the States? How far had he pushed her? How much could the Greek police be manipulated? Maybe she could get him beaten or even killed in a shifty Mexican jail or some uncivilized country. But Greece?

All he had ever wanted was peace and quiet. He was willing to let his old life go. Willing to leave the wealth and the company in her hands. Why couldn't she just leave him alone?

And what had Violeta told their daughter? That her father doesn't love her anymore?

In Violeta's world, there was never a gray area. You were either on the team or off the team. You were either in the water or out of the water, in the fire or out. She didn't believe in fence-sitting of any kind.

That meant there was only love or hate. Now that he was the enemy, he would be hated.

To stay under Violeta's financial umbrella, his daughter

would have to hate her father, the enemy. She would have to hate him so much as to be in collusion with her mother. It was a matter of survival for Tam now. Or death.

There was no in-between with Violeta, and there never had been.

He realized that he had just answered his own question.

How far would Violeta go to get his compliance to return to the States? Whatever it was, she would find a way to make him come home, even if it was against his will.

Or she would have him killed, which would be easier than obtaining signatures for everything.

Yes, his death would solve her dilemmas as their wills were specific.

In the event of death, everything is transferred to the surviving spouse.

Everything.

Chapter 11

VIOLETA PUSHED THE BUTTON down, ceasing the sound of her ex-husband's whiny voice. She had heard enough. Oliver had two options, and he had made his decision. There was a right answer and a wrong answer.

Because he willingly chose the wrong answer, what happened next was on him. He did this to himself. She had to protect her interests and further her aims. There was no other way to operate. No other way to live.

Oliver Payne had declared himself her enemy. He had deemed them at war and was in an active state of retreat. Once he left Greek police custody, he would either go back to the States to work with her or he wouldn't, and she was betting on the latter.

That meant he had to be forced to return. Against his will. Something she could make happen without remorse since this was all his fault anyway. Why have pity on the enemy? She would easily squish a mouse if it intruded on her home. Oliver was nothing more than the nuisance a mouse could cause. The only difference was a mouse wouldn't hurt her financially. Oliver had the potential to cost her the new wholesaling deal if he wasn't back within a week.

She picked the phone up and dialed Nafplio's Hellenic Police station, the same number she had called earlier to let them in on the rapist immigrant living among them. When they answered in Greek, she asked for Police Captain Elias Kostas.

A moment later, he came on.

"Good afternoon, Captain Kostas."

"Mrs. Violeta Payne, what a pleasure to be speaking with you again. I want to personally thank you for your kind donation to the Hellenic Police and also your tip that your husband had overstayed his allotted time in our country."

"Kostas, who is listening in to this conversation?"

"Excuse me, ma'am. No one is."

"Then let's stop with the platitudes."

"Platitudes?"

"I didn't just give you a tip about my husband. I told you what he did to our daughter. But he can't be tried in a court of law in Greece for that crime. He needs to come home."

"I understand you just discussed this with him."

"I did."

"I'm to assume he does not want to come willingly?"

"That is correct."

"Well, ma'am, I can take him to the airport, but once there, I can only, by law, advise him to leave the eurozone, effectively deporting him. This means he could fly to many different countries. Unless, of course, you or your authorities could supply us with extradition papers. I'm sure that would speed things up in getting Oliver back to the States."

"There's no time for that." Violeta looked out the sliding doors at the view of vineyards facing the eastern sun, trying to calm herself for what she was about to say.

"Excuse me, ma'am?"

"I'm willing to make another contribution, another *sizable* contribution to your wonderful police services."

"Oh, you are too kind, Mrs. Payne."

"I would need assurances that Oliver is delivered to the Athens airport and put on a plane for Los Angeles."

"But Mrs. Payne, as I just said, that is beyond my control —"

"I know what you just said," she cut in. "But there is no other way. He has to be delivered back to the States."

"I'm sorry, but I think—"

"Tell me your banking information."

"Excuse me?"

Through the line, Violeta heard him clear his throat and then cough.

"Your personal banking information. I want to donate half a million American dollars to you, personally."

The captain was quiet for a moment. Violeta waited. Whoever spoke first lost. Violeta knew the rules of negotiation, which translated to Violeta's rules of engagement. She wouldn't accept a negative response but would say *no* until her tongue bled.

Finally, Captain Elias Kostas found his voice.

"That would be very kind of you, Mrs. Payne, but I'm not sure I could accept such a donation personally."

"Let me ask you something."

"Go ahead."

"Have your colleagues ever taken you out for a beer?"

"Oh, yes, all the time."

"What about a friend taking you out to dinner?"

"Absolutely."

"Am I your friend?"

"Yes, ma'am. A good friend."

"Then let me buy you a drink. Let me buy you dinner. But since I'm not there, I have to transfer the money to you, and since I won't be there for a few decades, if ever, let me buy you hundreds of dinners over that time. Would that be okay?"

There was another pause, shorter this time.

"I guess, if you put it that way, then everything is okay with accepting a personal invitation for dinner from you. A few thousand dinners are unorthodox, but—"

"Once you email me your banking information, wiring number, and routing number, I will send you half a million dollars. But if you could do me, your friend, another favor, it would be worth another half a million dollars' worth of dinners."

"What kind of favor would that be?" Kostas asked.

"Make sure my husband makes it to Los Angeles in the next few days."

"But as I said a moment ago, it's outside my legal borders—"

"Then do it on your day off, in civilian clothes. One friend to another. You do favors for your friends, don't you, Kostas?"

"Well, of course, but he will protest. How do I ensure he doesn't walk off the plane at the layover in Amsterdam or

Frankfurt? I couldn't possibly fly with him the whole way."

"Break his legs."

"Excuse me?"

"I said, break both his legs, so he doesn't walk anywhere."

"Uhm, ma'am?"

"If that's not enough, break his spine. Paralyze him, so he has to come home for proper care. Don't worry, when he gets here, his loving family will take care of him."

Silence again from Kostas.

"After what he did to my daughter," Violeta started, not willing to wait for the Greek policeman to lose this battle of silence, "Captain, if you don't break his legs, when he gets here, I will. But I'm willing to pay you one million dollars to do it. Make it an accident. I don't care. Accidents happen all the time. Have another prisoner do it for a hundred bucks. Think of something."

A key slipped into the lock at the front door. Violeta turned in her chair as Tam entered the house.

"You have two to three days to complete the job and get him on a plane." She turned in her chair to avoid letting Tam hear the next part. "Once you have Oliver in a wheelchair, send me a picture, and I will send the money. Make it happen, Captain Kostas. Don't make me an enemy."

She clicked off the phone before he could reply.

"Tam, you're home. How was it?"

Tam appeared forlorn, sad. Like the day when she was ten, and her hamsters all died. Or when her first crush broke up with her at fourteen, only three years ago.

"Well, you have a tongue," Violeta said louder. "Use it to communicate. Tell me what happened in Toronto."

Tam kicked off her shoes and moved toward the couch. She sat with her legs up and rested her head on her forearm.

"I screwed up," Tam said.

"You? How?"

"I shot Sarah. I think I killed her."

"What?" Violeta flew out of her chair in anger. She slammed the phone table with both hands and gritted her teeth. Tam reared back, fear replacing the sad look on her face. "You had one task," Violeta mumbled the words. "I gave you everything. The tools to track Parkman, the money to handle your one simple task. I even gave you Parkman's own gun to use with his prints on it. All you had to do was use his weapon when he was in the vicinity and get him arrested for the worst crime you could come up with. No one instructed you to shoot Sarah."

"I know, Mom," Tam pleaded. Her eyes already glazing over. "I tried. My plan was perfect."

"Explain to me what you *tried*." The last word came out with as much disdain as she could muster.

"I followed him to a warehouse in Toronto. I set up across the street and waited. Sarah showed up. I saw them talking. I wondered what to shoot at. How I could trap him? Then a car drove by, and an idea formed."

Violeta crossed her arms to make Tam work for it. She closed herself off, making Tam convince her she did the right thing.

"I fired a warning shot as the car passed, going the other way. It made Parkman think the shooter was in the car. I thought it was perfect because Parkman shot at the fleeing car himself. There would be no need to use the gun to frame him. And the police even picked him up at the scene."

"Then what went wrong? How did you kill Sarah?"

"The warning shot." Tam got up from the sofa and retreated a couple of steps from her mother. "I don't know how it hit her, but she took the bullet in the head. I saw Parkman pumping her chest."

"You little piece of shit," Violeta shouted. "I have paid for your private school. I have paid for your training at the gun club. We are proud Americans, and we have the right to bear arms. I will retire in Texas, mark my words." She uncrossed her arms and advanced on Tam. "You passed all your tests and impressed the marksmen at the range with how good of a shot you are. So tell me, how did you kill someone when you fired a warning shot?" She raised her voice to a screech. "Tell me!"

She stopped in front of Tam as the kitchen wall arrested Tam's retreat. Violeta's hand tingled with the anticipation of slapping her insubordinate daughter.

"Sarah jumped into it. Sarah dove toward the bullet. It wasn't my fault."

Before Tam could break down sobbing, Violeta slapped her, the crack of skin on her skin loud and biting. Tam's face shot sideways, hair jerked with it. She placed a hand on her reddening cheek and slowly lifted her head back to face Violeta.

"You have disgraced your family," Violeta deepened her voice. "You have failed us. It is you and me against the world, and you have potentially fucked all that up."

Tam shook her head. "No, Mom. Please, let me finish."

Violeta raised her hand again but kept it suspended, palm open, waiting for her daughter to sink deeper into the hole she had created for herself.

"I used Parkman's Glock. When they check his gun and see it had been fired recently and the bullet in Sarah's head matches his make and model, he will have more to explain." Tam's shoulders hitched with sobs as she started to cry. "I tried to serve you. I tried to do the best I could."

Violeta lowered her hand. "In the coming days, we will see just how much you have served me. Remember, you are either Tam Rood, my daughter, or turn your name around, which spells Door Mat. I walk *with* you, or I walk *on* you. Understood?"

"Yes, Momma."

"Yes, Momma, what?"

"Yes, Momma, I understand."

"Now get the fuck out of my sight before I slap you into a coma. I have to figure out what to do next."

Tam scurried past her mother, crying as she ran up the stairs. It made her smile. Her daughter had to learn the rules of life, and there were only two. Work for Violeta, or work against her.

Work against me, and I will crush you.

Her husband was about to learn that very lesson.

Chapter 12

DETECTIVE JOFFREY HAD AGREED to give Parkman a chance to explain before he took him downtown to process him. Parkman had to convince Joffrey of a conspiracy against him or wait for Sarah's recovery from behind bars.

They tried to locate Doctor Jacob but to no avail. A nurse found an empty room where the trio could talk.

"Yes, I wrote the letter," Parkman started. "But under duress."

Aaron stood by the window, leaning on the wall, watching the sunrise.

Detective Joffrey sat on one of the two beds in the room while Parkman paced the floor.

"What duress?" Joffrey asked.

"Okay, understand, this will be very hard for me, but I'm going, to be honest with you here."

"I hope so."

"Unless it comes up in the course of your investigation or ends up in court, I don't want any of this repeated outside this room. Deal?"

"Fine," Joffrey said. "It's your business unless it becomes mine."

"Aaron?"

He turned from the window. "Parkman, you've known Sarah longer than I have. You're a trusted member of her family. Whatever happened to you is going to bother me deeply. Once Sarah's better, we'll fix whatever's going on. Just do what you have to do with the local cops, and we'll deal with this shit after. But don't ask me about confidentiality because you never need to. You know I have your back. I always will."

It warmed Parkman's heart to hear those words from the man he respected as Sarah's choice. She would do fine with him.

"Whoa, what's this about fixing things after you're done with the local cops?" Joffrey asked.

"No disrespect, Joffrey," Aaron said, "but I don't have a lot of respect for the lengths law enforcement go to. You got your thing to do. I get it, and I will stay out of your way. But I do my thing a little differently."

Joffrey twisted on the bed to better face Aaron. "And what exactly is your thing?"

"Okay, guys," Parkman interrupted. "Aren't we here to discuss what's going on with Sarah?"

"My thing is everything yours isn't," Aaron said.

"That's a lot of things."

"Guys." Parkman raised his voice.

Aaron looked back out the window. Joffrey turned to

Parkman. The morning sun cast an orange glow on Joffrey's face.

He stared at Parkman as he spoke to Aaron. "Maybe one day I'll get to see what it is you do, Aaron."

"Stick around long enough, and you'll see it."

"Got it. Now, Parkman, you have the floor."

"I was instructed to locate a man. I did that. Took pictures, went to the hotel, and sent them to the client. I was supposed to fly home the day after—"

"Where were you? What city?"

"Nafplio."

Joffrey frowned. "Where's that?"

"Greece," Aaron said. "Been there. Bad experience, bad memories, but a nice hospital."

"Was that an example of you doing your thing?"

Aaron turned from the window. "Something like that."

"Okay, guys," Parkman jumped in again. "Seriously. Fuck."

Joffrey raised a hand in capitulation.

"Why didn't you fly home?" Joffrey asked.

"I did fly home."

"You said you were supposed to fly home."

"Yes, I was supposed to fly home as the job was complete, but the client asked me for another service."

"What was that?"

"Bring the man I located with me. Willingly or unwillingly."

"And?"

"I refused. Even if the man agreed to come. I'm a private investigator, not a human delivery man." He brushed something off his shirt, straightened the bottom, then continued. "If I returned the woman's husband, I would receive a bonus of about a quarter of a million dollars."

"Wow, this woman really wants her husband back," Joffrey said.

"She's quite rich and very demanding. I'm assuming people do what she asks of them without question, or she finds someone who will. That's why her husband leaving her is not *allowed*." He used air quotes on the last word. "Again, I refused. Then she asked if I wanted a cool half a million bucks."

"And you agreed, right?"

"She wanted me to put her husband in a wheelchair to force him to come home for special care. He wouldn't be able to run from her anymore. But his hands would still work for signing documents as she has a deal pending that won't go through without him."

"Oh man, hell hath no fury, and on and on."

"I flat-out refused. I was informed that I either work for her or I don't. That sounded reasonable, so I told her I don't. Then she tells me, now get this, that I was either a friend or an enemy and that I had to choose. Since I would not be doing her bidding, I was declared an enemy. She told me to expect what enemies get and hung up."

"What did you get?"

"Harassed for a week before I was jumped, tossed in a van, and taken to a warehouse where they stripped me and did things that I'd rather not say here and that have no value in furthering your investigation."

"Oh, shit, sorry to hear that," Joffrey said, a look of concern on his face.

In all his years as a cop, Parkman could determine a false

look, a mask, when he saw one. At that moment, Joffrey seemed real, sincere.

"I'm sorry, Parkman." Aaron had turned from the window and now faced him. "You should've called Sarah and me. We could've helped."

Parkman shook his head. "You were missing Sarah. She only showed back up a week ago." He walked over to the other bed and sat down. Joffrey spun around to face him. "When I was held captive," Parkman continued, "they made me write that letter in my own handwriting. The whole idea was to set me up to take the fall. I only kept the letter so I could show Sarah their intentions. They relieved me of my Glock 22 at that time."

"It's amazing how fast they got to Sarah," Aaron said. "No one knew she was alive until only a week ago."

"Sarah called me once she got on Canadian soil again. She told me she would surprise you at that dinner at The Keg."

"Oh shit."

"Exactly. They decided to hurt Sarah in some way to make me do it. They had a letter saying so in my handwriting, and they had my gun. They followed my every move, and finally, once I escaped their tail, or at least thought I did, I came here to warn Sarah."

"Let me get this straight," Joffrey interjected. "Are you saying they used your gun on Sarah, made you write the letter that was in your jacket, followed you to Toronto, and shot her just so you could take the fall?"

"Yes, that's what I'm saying. But add that they expertly waited for the Jaguar to drive by, so I would think the shooter was in the car and attacked an innocent party. That should at least get me jail time. They had this planned from day one. I either do what the client says or go down hard. Although, the more I think about it, the more I don't think they intended to hit Sarah. They don't need me. Maybe they thought they could recruit her."

"Why not just use the shooter to deal with the husband? Why not leave you out of it?"

"I did as much research on the family as I could. Their daughter is a seventeen-year-old marksman. One of the best at the range she shoots at. My guess is she was the shooter, but mommy won't ask her daughter to go after daddy. Might cloud her judgment at the last minute. My guess is mommy hasn't told the daughter everything."

"That's a lot of guessing," Joffrey said. "Especially that a seventeen-year-old would follow you across the country just to fire a warning shot."

"I don't know what else to think."

The door opened. A nurse pushing an empty stretcher entered. "Oh, I'm sorry, I thought this room wasn't being used." She picked up a clipboard and scanned the page on it.

"It's empty," Joffrey said. "We were just leaving."

All three men filed past the stretcher and headed back to the waiting area.

"I'll find Doctor Jacob to see if he has anything new," Aaron said.

"We cool?" Parkman asked the detective.

"For now," Joffrey said. "Sarah's and your reputation here in Toronto has bought you the benefit of the doubt. I'm going to want to look at this client of yours soon, though."

Parkman wondered how that would look for his business. The public wouldn't ever hear the inner details. All they'd see is that his agency has an open-book policy on who hires him.

In the waiting room, a younger doctor was just finishing up with an older woman and man, assuring them that their daughter would pull through.

Parkman moved past Aaron, waited until the doctor was free, and then stepped in. "Hey, Doc, you think you could get Doctor Jacob out here to let us in on Sarah's progress? Maybe we could get to see her soon?"

The young doctor frowned. "Who are you asking about? A lot of our doctors just did a morning shift change."

"Doctor Jacob. That's his office right there." Parkman pointed at the brown door twenty feet away.

"You must be mistaken. That's Doctor Alvarez's office."

The young doctor stepped away, but Parkman grabbed his arm. "One second."

The doctor looked down at Parkman's hand, then back up to meet his eyes. "I have rounds to do."

"I understand, but I asked you about Doctor Jacob. Have you seen him?"

"I haven't even heard of him. I've been here for seven years, and there's no Doctor Jacob on staff that I know of."

Fear gripped Parkman's stomach, and his knees felt like they would unhinge. How much more could he take? And what could Violeta be up to now?

"What about Sarah Roberts? She's a gunshot victim, brought here about six hours ago. Can you find out what her condition is and let us know? We would like to see her."

The doctor flipped a couple of pages on his clipboard and looked back up. Joffrey and Aaron were crowding them now.

"Maybe check with admitting. She must've been

moved."

"Moved? How's that? She was in surgery."

"I don't know, but on my rounds, there's no Sarah Roberts here, and no gunshot victims were brought in during the previous six hours. I'm sorry, but according to these pages," he held up the clipboard, "the name Sarah Roberts isn't on them."

Chapter 13

Violeta made her decision. She wasn't sure if the Greeks would come through for her. She wasn't sure if Sarah would be alive or not. There were too many unknowns. Having her daughter feel alienated wouldn't serve her at the moment. She needed as many allies in her camp as she could get.

She knocked on Tam's bedroom door. "Honey? Can I come in?"

This was a disgusting formality. Violeta only ever asked if she could enter when she needed Tam on her side. Everything was a negotiation, closing the sale. There was nothing else. This was her house. If she wanted to enter a room at will, she would. It didn't matter who was behind the door or what they were doing. But in this case, she needed Tam to be receptive and ready to make up for her failure.

"Tam?"

"Yes, Momma?"

"May I come in?" Violeta asked. She shook her hands to get the nasty feeling of having to ask off her skin. It just felt wrong.

"Yes, come in."

Tam was at her desk when she opened the door, drawing pictures.

"What are you drawing?" Violeta asked.

"Landscapes. My usual."

"Can I see?"

Tam set her pencil crayon down and moved far enough to the side for her mother to look over her shoulder. The picture was of a farmhouse surrounded by a white picket fence. In the background sat a red barn. To the right of the barn, Tam had drawn the base of a gallows with a hangman's noose above it.

"Why do you obsess over the Salem witch trials?"

"It's a fascinating time in our history. When I was in Toronto, I thought of heading down to Danvers, Massachusetts, where some of the famous trials took place. It's called Danvers now, but back then, in 1692, it was called Salem Village."

"That's nice, Tam. Maybe next time you're on that side of the continent, you could tour those areas." She cleared her throat and moved back from Tam a few steps. "There's something I want to talk to you about." Violeta moved farther into the center of the room, spread her feet, and crossed her arms, tilting her head back just enough to look down her nose at her daughter.

Tam placed her picture in the middle of her desk, set her pencil crayons to the side, and then twisted in her chair to face her mother. "Yes, Momma?"

"How would you like to regain your honor with me?"

"I would love that very much, Momma. I'm not your enemy, even if I make a mistake."

"Let me decide who my enemies are and who aren't. Making a mistake as profound as this one could have, and still might, hurt this family deeply. Which ultimately hurts me. And what are enemies good at? Hurting their adversaries. So understand, your actions are grave and could have long-lasting ramifications."

"I understand, and I'm sorry, Momma. What can I do to fix it?"

"Locate Sarah's parents."

"What?"

"They reside here in Santa Rosa. I caught something in the news a while back about there being a supposed attack on her parents, but they were dealt with in time." Even though Violeta knew about Caleb and Amelia Roberts, Sarah's parents, from the bug in Parkman's home phone, she figured the lie of hearing about them on the news would convince Tam. "After that, her parents sold their house and moved here. According to one of the Sarah Roberts fan websites, someone heard her parents live in Santa Rosa."

"Really, right here in our city?" Tam looked surprised.

"That would make sense, as Parkman is a long-time family friend," Violeta added for Tam's benefit. "He moved here about that same time and started his agency. So I think they're here and I want you to find them. Once you do that, report back to me. But you have to do it quietly. If anyone discovers what you're doing, you will have failed me again. In order to regain your standing with me, you have to do it alone. The only resource I will offer you is money. You don't get any outside help. Understood?"

"Understood."

"I will give you two days to locate them and two more days to inform me of some of their daily routines, providing they actually do live in Santa Rosa. Agreed?"

"But, how do I go about—"

"Figuring it out is your job. Are you willing to do what it takes to make it in this family?" She raised her voice. "Are you willing to regain your honor?"

"Yes, Momma."

"Say it."

"I agree to the task you have set for me, and I am doing it to regain my honor with you."

"You won't fail?"

A twitch had started under Tam's left eye. Violeta wondered briefly if her daughter hated her and only spoke the words to placate her. Then she discarded the idea. Tam knew her well enough to not go against her. Tam would end up dead in a river somewhere with her hands, feet, and head removed if she ever had mutinous, rebellious ideas against her mother.

"I won't fail, Momma."

Violeta clicked her heels and stomped from the room.

Tam's voice trailed her. "When should I start?"

"Start now. Get it done. Don't let me down again. Locate Sarah Roberts's parents because I have a special message for them." She laughed and added to herself, "One they can take to their grave."

Chapter 14

Captain Kostas entered the corridor that led to the station's holding cells. He paused in the doorway, rubbed his chin, and wondered how to handle this delicate situation.

Could Oliver be trusted after what Kostas's men had done to him?

"Open up Oliver Payne's cell," he called out in Greek.

The door's lock clicked. Kostas moved to the door and opened it. Oliver lay sprawled on the floor. He rolled his head toward Kostas, blinked twice, then rolled his head away.

Kostas retreated, moved down the hall, and grabbed two chairs from the front office without locking Oliver's prison door. Oliver wouldn't try to run, especially not with that nasty limp.

When he returned, Oliver hadn't moved.

He set the chairs on the floor, one beside Oliver and one by the open door.

"Get up," Kostas said. "We have to talk."

Oliver stretched his legs and adjusted his hands on his stomach but didn't move or attempt to get up. Kostas leaned back in his chair and waited. After a minute, he decided to start talking.

"I just talked to your wife—"

"Ex-wife," Oliver interjected.

"Right, ex-wife. We have a problem."

"Don't you mean I have a problem?" Oliver swiveled his head to look at Kostas. "Are you here to kill me or let me go?"

"Neither."

The Oliver that Kostas had met coming out of the taxi on the edge of Agios Adrianos had been replaced by a demure soul, capitulating to the negative, allowing his darkest thoughts to overcome him. He had entered Kostas's life as an American wishing to resolve the lost passport conflict. He had answers and solutions. But within twelve hours, Oliver had turned into a dejected waif.

"What did she do to you?" Kostas asked, bewilderment in his voice.

Oliver rolled over, got a knee under him, and lifted up off the floor to sit on the chair. He stretched, twisted, and settled into the metal chair before addressing Kostas.

"If you only knew," he whispered, barely loud enough to hear.

It reminded Kostas of the words spoken by a man on death row. Or a man about to go to prison for decades.

"How many women have you raped?" Kostas asked.

Oliver frowned and leaned back in the chair. "She lied if she told you that I had raped someone."

"You raped your daughter."

Oliver's face changed, and his brow wrinkled. He leaned forward, elbows to thighs, and rested his face in his hands.

"That's the information I received," Kostas said. "That was why my men were rough with you. We don't take kindly to that sort of thing."

Oliver didn't respond.

"Your ex-wife has asked me to send you home."

Oliver looked up and met his eyes. "That's beyond your realm of duties. I'm not a lost puppy. Yes, you can deport me, but I choose to fly to the UK."

"You're expected to be flown home as a cripple." Kostas paused to let it sink in. "Your wife has offered a handsome sum to break your legs and, if that doesn't work, to break your spine and send you home paralyzed."

Tears crept down Oliver's cheeks. Kostas could only imagine what Oliver was going through.

"Do you understand what your ex-wife has ordered here? She wants you paralyzed for the rest of your life. My goodness, man, what did you do to that woman to generate such hatred?"

"I'll never be rid of that evil woman, will I?" Oliver wiped his cheeks and then rubbed his hands on his pants. "If you do what she's asking, my life will be ruined, over."

"You needn't worry, Mr. Payne, we will not take part in paralyzing you. But I am a man of justice, and I will do whatever it takes to seek it. When I heard you had raped your daughter and fled your country to escape justice, you angered my men and me. Knocking you down was as far as we were willing to go, but trust me, I wanted to hurt you somewhat worse." Kostas got up, spun his chair around, and sat back down, resting his forearms on the back of the chair. "Because I seek justice in a world without much of it, I have a proposal for you. But I need to know I can trust you."

Oliver seemed to think it over. Then Kostas realized he was trying to find his voice in a world where he was lost, abandoned, and about to be crushed.

"Go … ahead."

"I want you to get in a wheelchair, cover your legs in a blanket, and fly home in a few days under doctor's care. I'll have a female police officer fly with you, posing as your nurse."

"Why would you do that? Wait, why would I do that?"

"For the sake of justice. I get what I want, and you get what you want."

"I'm listening."

"I will need the money your ex-wife is offering my police station to perform her dirty deed. It will cover costs for myself, my officer who would travel with you, and other payments that may arise due to our arrangement. She has requested pictures of my compliance. Once the pictures are sent to Violeta and the money transferred to my account, I will have proof of her illegal activities and her full intent to cause you grievous bodily harm. I will then produce a full written statement in English describing all of my actions and the actions of my men for your authorities in the States. My officer will protect you when you land in Los Angeles, and I will already have informed the authorities there of what is going on. If you are okay with this, I would like to get started immediately."

"In order for this to work," Oliver said, "you wouldn't be able to keep the money she sent you."

"I understand that. She is sending one amount to the police station as a donation. The other amount goes to my personal account. It is the one in my personal account that I will surrender. The donation is just that, a donation. That is the money I will keep and use. You only need one money trail to make this work."

Oliver wept quietly, without sobs. "Why would you do this?"

"I have an ex-wife. We have two boys. She has always allowed me access without question, even though our relationship failed miserably. I have seen those boys thrive because of our mutual support and love. My ex-wife may hate me, but she has not taken it out on the boys. What your ex-wife is doing isn't just criminal, it's barbaric. And had it not been me, she may have gotten away with it. Had it not been me, you could very possibly have been paralyzed by now. This is your chance to have her arrested for her crimes and your chance to move on with your life in peace without having to hide from her. Will you agree to my terms?"

"Without question."

Kostas got up from his chair and walked over to Oliver, his hand outstretched.

"Shake my hand like a man. Keep your word, and you will be past this mess in under a week."

Oliver took his hand, his grip as diminished as his fortitude, his hands soft and moist from tears.

Kostas brought his other hand around, in the shape of a fist, and sucker punched Oliver, knocking him off his chair.

"You'll thank me later," Kostas said. "Gotta make this part look real."

He dropped down and continued to punch Oliver until he

was bleeding. Every man could take a beating. If that was the worst Oliver got, he was getting off easy compared to what his ex-wife wanted to do to him.

Kostas just wanted to make Oliver's reunion with Violeta as authentic as possible, not to mention how much he despised the Payne family for lying to him and using him in their family drama.

It wasn't Oliver's fault. But Kostas didn't care about fault.

He only wanted the stain removed from his police station.

Chapter 15

"THERE'S GOT TO BE a mistake," Parkman said as Joffrey jumped past him and stopped the doctor from walking away.

"Get your hands off me," the doctor shouted. "I'll call security."

Joffrey flipped open his badge. "I'm Detective Joffrey with Homicide. Earlier this morning, a woman named Sarah Roberts was admitted to this hospital for a headshot wound." He lowered his badge and dropped it in a pocket inside his jacket. "We spoke with a man who identified himself as Doctor Jacob. He informed us of her diagnosis at the time. I even met with him a second time just recently. So there is a Doctor Jacob at this hospital, and a Sarah Roberts is being tended to. Just because you don't know about it doesn't make it not so."

The young doctor had taken a step back as Joffrey berated him.

"Is there a problem here?" A hospital security man walked up behind Aaron, who had been rendered speechless.

"There's no problem here," Joffrey said as he offered his badge for the security guard to see. "We brought a gunshot victim in hours ago, and this doctor says she's not here."

The security guard looked at the doctor, who had backed up against the wall. "Is this patient they're looking for one of yours?"

"She's not even on the rounds list. I've never heard of her or the doctor they claim to have spoken with."

"Well, gentlemen, that's not my area of expertise," the guard said. "I would just like you to keep your voices down as it is very early in the morning. If you're unsure where your family member is, you could always check down with admitting."

"Fair enough," Joffrey said. "We'll do that."

He took down the young doctor's name and then led Parkman and Aaron to the elevator.

At the front reception desk, Joffrey again produced his ID and asked to speak with Doctor Jacob.

The woman behind the Plexiglas typed something into her computer.

"I'm sorry, but I don't have a Doctor Jacob on staff. Is he a visiting doctor?"

"Look up Sarah Roberts. She was admitted around one in the morning with a headshot wound. We want to know how she's doing."

The woman typed again. After a moment, she asked, "Sarah with an h at the end or without?"

"With," Parkman said.

The woman shook her head. "I'm sorry, nothing here."

"Check again," Joffrey said, becoming increasingly agitated.

What the fuck is happening here?

After typing once again on her keyboard, she turned to them. "There's no one in our system that has been admitted within the previous six, or even twelve hours, with that name or variants of it. I'm sorry, maybe it was another hospital they sent her to."

"I want to talk to your superiors," Joffrey said. "I want your boss. Who is in charge here? What kind of hospital is this?"

"Sir, please keep your voice down. My boss arrives after nine this morning. Most of the supervisors arrive then. You can speak with them—"

"Fine."

Joffrey stepped away from the counter before saying more.

"It's got to be Violeta," Parkman said. "She has done something with Sarah."

Aaron wandered off, walking aimlessly.

"Hey, Aaron, where are you going?" Parkman asked.

Aaron spun on one heel, the other came around in a roundhouse until it connected with the brick wall beside him. He lifted off his foot and kicked with the other one.

Then he turned and faced them, the anger that fueled those kicks evident in his tormented expression.

"We must find Sarah, and we had better fucking do it before anything happens to her." He looked directly at Joffrey. "Or you will see a demonstration of what I mean when I say I do things my way."

"Now, Aaron, calm down," Joffrey said. He stepped

toward him. "We'll figure this out."

Aaron now stared at Parkman. "You said the name Violeta. Who is that? And if you think she had something to do with this, that's where we start."

"Violeta has been the one orchestrating all this shit from the beginning. This has to be her. But I don't think she'll kill Sarah. She would want to use her. A dead Sarah isn't good for anybody."

"I agree," Aaron said.

Chapter 16

THE DREAMS ACHED LIKE a river of lava burning her skin. And it wouldn't stop undulating the pain in her head. The pain itself even ached and throbbed.

Movement rendered her stomach weak, reminding her of car sickness or drinking too much and then lying down. Her abdomen clenched, but she forced the contents of her stomach to remain where they were.

She tried to open her eyes, but the light she detected through her lids changed her mind. She breathed in deeply, feeling her chest rise and descend without pain. Only minor muscular discomfort was different from a stab wound, broken bone, or bullet hole.

How would I know that?

Mentally, she cataloged the rest of her body, working systematically from her feet to her head. Her feet moved freely, but her ankles were bound.

Strange.

There was enough play for her knees to rise an inch, but that's where they stopped. Moving her torso left and right confirmed no broken hips.

Then what happened?

Her hands were fine. Each finger moved to her relief. She hated broken fingers.

Have I had them broken before?

But her wrists were bound, which equated to anger. Who did this and why? Was she drugged? Whoever it was would pay dearly.

She paused in her thoughts, listened to her inner voice, and wondered where the anger came from. There seemed to be a buried darkness deep inside her, surfacing. The kind of darkness that would give psychotherapists issues.

Like a pro wrestler, her shoulders were flat on the mat, or whatever she lay on, neither one could move. Something bit into the top of her chest, just below the collarbones, like a strap of some kind.

She rolled her head, which was free of restraints but was governed by padding on either side as if large pillows locked her head in place.

Her mouth dropped open, and she tongued her teeth. All there.

Something moved around her. She desperately wanted to open her eyes, but it was still too bright.

She tried to detect if anyone was close and if they would do anything to her.

While she waited, she tried to remember the last time she was awake, what had happened to bring her here. Sifting through scattered memories, she got to her sister. She had parents. Something about a cop who was their neighbor. He babysat her when she was younger, but she forgot her age. Her police officer turned babysitter was a horrible man. Twisted. Made her do things. Lost her virginity to him. Became depressed. Started pulling her hair out and became a victim of trichotillomania.

How would I know a word like that?

She wondered how much hair she had left.

Then she tried to remember her name. Nothing came up.

Who am I?

Her stomach twisted with anxiety.

What's wrong with me? What has happened?

The lights went out overhead.

She fell back under.

***

The light again.

A voice to her left. A male voice. On the phone. Responding at intervals to periodic questions.

He said her condition had improved.

What condition? My hair condition?

The man said they'd talk after. Shuffling feet. A chair. Someone close.

She opened her eyes, fluttered them, then tried again.

Still too bright.

"Here," the man said. "Let me get that."

A moment later, the light disappeared, and darkness greeted the backs of her eyelids.

She opened her eyes to slits. An engine hummed nearby.

"This," she tried to say, but it came out sounding like the

hiss of a snake. "Sucks." To her ear, that sounded like she only said, *ucks*, which was an improvement on the hissing.

"Good to see you're waking. We have a lot of ground to cover in more ways than one."

She rolled her tongue around her dry mouth, positioned it in the center, opened and closed her mouth, and tried to talk again.

"What happened?"

That sounded relatively normal.

"I was going to ask you that very question."

She got her eyes open enough to stare at the roof.

Where am I?

Gently, she rolled her head until her cheek touched the padded retainer and looked up into the face of a man in his forties. He had a wonderful, pleasant smile, and his eyes were a pretty blue, but his two-day beard growth scared her. A professional doctor wouldn't come to work like that. His hair was thinning and unkempt, and he wasn't wearing a white coat like other doctors. He wore a black T-shirt with the name of an eighties alternative band, The Violent Femmes.

"Where the fuck am I?" *What compelled me to ask like that?*

Something bumped the bed. An engine that hummed nearby revved.

"What is this place?" she asked.

"Let's start with the basics, shall we?" The man moved away from her field of vision. "You've bumped your head rather hard. I need to ask you a few questions, and then I'll answer yours."

"Wrong."

"Excuse me? What do you mean by wrong?"

"Answer mine first, or they'll be a fee at the end of the program."

He chuckled. "A fee? What program?"

"I don't know why I just said that." She swallowed. "But it sounded right. Am I someone who gets their own way?"

"I imagine so."

"I don't sound like a nice person." She stared up at the ceiling. "Is that why I have a head injury? Did I upset someone?"

"I would say something like that happened."

"Can you tell me my name?" she asked.

"You're not aware of it?"

"No, I just like asking stupid questions when waking up from a head injury to fuck with the doctor taking care of me." She closed her mouth. "Sorry, there it goes again. It's like a first response." Then, her voice lower, more to herself, she said, "Maybe it has something to do with the babysitter."

"Pardon?"

"Nothing. My name?"

"As I said, my questions first. Then yours."

"Talk in circles like a jerk, and I'll start calling you Doctor Circle Jerk. How would you like that for a new name?"

Again, the doctor let a small laugh escape.

"Hey, do I have any friends?" she asked. "I'm not sure I would like me."

"You have friends."

"I win."

"What?"

"You answered my question first, so I won. It's one

nothing now. Go ahead. Your turn.”

“Can you remember anything recent, anything personal? Like where you live, a boyfriend’s name, the car you drive, or are your parents alive? Anything?”

Her emotions welled up when nothing came to mind other than her parents. Then her eyes welled up.

“Why don’t I listen to you first,” she said. “Tell me a little of what happened here, and we’ll piece it together.”

Something bumped the bed again. This time her entire body shifted.

“What is going on? Are we moving?”

“We’re in a large vehicle on a highway south of the Great Lakes.”

“What? Why? Do I live down here? Where are we going?”

“We’re taking you home.”

“Where’s home?”

“Santa Rosa, California. We should be there in a few days.”

She rolled her eyes to study the roof again and tried to think about the name. “Santa Rosa means something to me, but it doesn’t feel like home. Why’s that?”

“You’ve been shot in the head.”

She lifted up against the restraints, stressing them. Her chest didn’t get far, but her wrists rose a full inch. “What are you talking about? Who and when? Did I shoot back? Because if I didn’t—”

He stepped into sight. “Calm down.” He placed a gentle hand on her shoulder and eased her back.

Her body loosened, but a subtle pain rose inside her head, like the beginning of a migraine.

"I think I'm getting a headache. I need something for it."

"Soon. Right now, you're lucid. We need to talk."

"About what, sadist?" She averted her eyes. "How come I feel like a good person on the inside, but on the outside, my mouth has its own agenda? Have I got some kind of Tourette's?"

"Not that I'm aware of, but I love how lucid you are. Just relax and listen to me for a second."

She waited, moving slightly with the susurrations of the vehicle.

"With the injury you've endured, you may experience dizziness, headaches, weakness, nausea, trouble sleeping, and you could encounter abnormal levels of fatigue."

"Great. Sounds like a ball of fun."

"I want you to know what to expect with a head injury. These things can be common when a bullet enters the skull like the one that hit you. You seem to have memory issues, but that's hardly permanent. It's not like in the movies. Most of it will come back to you. It's called Retrograde Amnesia. Also, you could experience difficulty understanding others and go through periods of poor concentration. Until you're back to a normal routine in months to come, I suggest you keep daily activities to a minimum."

"Noted. I'll start keeping all activity to a minimum right now." She paused. "There. Look at me. Quite reduced in what I can do secured to this bed-like thing in a large moving vehicle."

"The straps are so you don't roll off the bed when the vehicle turns. As soon as you can stand and walk, which I think we should try in a few hours, the straps will only go on when you go back to sleep. I can't have you rolling off the bed and bumping that head of yours again."

"Anything else I should know?"

"Yes, overall, it could take a few months for all symptoms to clear up, but the one I think you're experiencing the most is tinnitus."

"Why do you say that?" She rolled her eyes to look at him. "Actually, what is tinnitus?"

"You shouted out in your sleep. I wrote some of it down but stopped when it got violent."

"Tinnitus gets violent?"

"It's a fancy word for a perception of noise in one ear or both, or simply noise inside the head."

"You mean schizophrenia? Am I a paranoid schizo?"

"No, you're not *hearing* voices in your head, just noises. Foreign noises. Ones that aren't normally there. They'll go away, though."

"And you think I have this already?"

The doctor moved away and clicked something.

"What are you doing?"

"Preparing a syringe to help you sleep and get rid of your headache."

He entered her field of vision again, a small syringe in his right hand.

"You sounded like you were talking to someone when you were under," he said.

"Really?"

"A full conversation. You asked questions, then I assume you received answers in your head because you responded as if you had. I only heard what you were saying. It was like listening to someone on the phone. A couple of times, you got quite angry. I was worried."

"How bad was the bullet hole? Is my brain okay?"

"There wasn't a lot of damage, which surprised me, but the bullet only started the injury. You have a second head injury on the back of the skull where you must've fallen after being shot. The two combined jostled your brain around, causing it to make contact with the inside of your skull, which knocked you out. There was some swelling, but you're out of the woods now, and by the sound of your speech, the only lasting issue will be a temporary memory loss."

He plunged the needle into her thigh. She didn't protest as she was already feeling drowsy again.

"Who shot me?" she asked.

"I was hoping you would know that."

"What's my name? Say my name." She forced her eyes open and found his face above hers. "Sorry, that sounded sexual."

He brushed the comment off. "Your name is Sarah Roberts."

At the sound of those two words, she felt alive, rejuvenated. She loved her name and knew she lived that name with honor. It was a feeling she couldn't deny.

The fear of missing memories made her feel weak. She tried to remember what fear meant to her and how she lived with it daily, and all she got was False Evidence Appearing Real. That's what fear meant. Then she recalled another one. Fuck Everything And Run.

She smiled. It wouldn't take long before her memories came back. And when they did, she would locate the people responsibly and render consequences. The memory loss was a temporary situation. One that allowed her to heal.

Then an image of the shooter floated to the surface like it

was buried under an ocean of sand, and a tide of synapses pulled away and uncovered it.

The man's gentle face. His concern. The gun in his hand.

She dove out of the way, but it was too late.

His name came next. That man would have to die for shooting her. She would burn his name in Hell and tattoo it on her memory so as to never forget her mortal enemy.

His name became synonymous with pain. Even though something felt wrong with it, she shouted his name in her mind so she would remember it when she woke again.

Never forget this name. Make him pay for what he did.

Parkman.

Chapter 17

Violeta went to bed angry, displeased with her daughter and her husband, but she woke elated.

Elias Kostas had agreed to the full deal. Later today, due to the time difference in Greece, which would make it evening for them, he would personally see to it that Oliver's spine was severed in the lumbar section. He should retain movement of his upper body for the rest of his life, but he would be paralyzed from the waist down.

That pleased her.

See how it feels, Oliver, to have someone wipe your ass for the rest of your life.

She made coffee, read the morning paper on her iPad, and waited for Tam to join her with reports on Caleb and Amelia Roberts.

It had cost her a lot of money to manage this, but it was all coming together. Violeta was either a good manager or a bad manager. There was no in-between. Managing came down to delegating, organizing, and meeting deadlines. She had delegated what needed to be done, found the right people to do the tasks, and organized everything to come in on time, therefore making her not just a good manager but an exceptional one.

Soon, everyone would be in Santa Rosa, and she could get the signatures she needed from her soon-to-be-dead ex-husband, watch as Parkman was arrested in Toronto, and finally deal with Sarah Roberts when she showed up in Santa Rosa.

An uncharacteristic wide smile parted her lips before she sipped more coffee.

Ahh, it's good to be so in control.

"What's the smile for?" Tam asked. She stood under the alcove in the front foyer of the house. "It looks pretty on you, Momma. I'd love to see you smile more."

Violeta set her coffee cup down, adjusted her burgundy robe, crossed her legs, and looked up at Tam, the smile gone.

"What have you discovered?"

"Sarah's parents live here in Santa Rosa, like you said, but I haven't found an address yet."

"How long before you will acquire their address?"

"I'm heading downtown to the government buildings, where I will do my best."

"No, you won't."

Tam moved farther into the living room. "I'm sorry?" She frowned. "I thought that's what you wanted."

"I do."

"Then why did you say I won't?"

"You won't do your best to get an address. You *will* get

one. Understood?"

Tam nodded. "Understood, Momma."

"Good." She sipped from her cup and extended it to her daughter. "Fill this up for me."

Tam walked across the room, grabbed the cup, and left. Violeta waited, her iPad on her lap, and counted in her head. The time it took to walk to the kitchen, pour the coffee, and return wasn't more than fifteen seconds. At seventeen seconds, Tam returned and set her full cup on the table beside her. Five seconds longer, and Violeta wouldn't drink it. That was enough time for her daughter to poison it. She always had to be watching, cunning enough to manage the people in her life but also smart enough to thwart their efforts against her.

"I'm leaving now," Tam said. "To complete my task."

At the front door, she paused.

"What is it?" Violeta asked without looking up from her iPad.

"I just thought you'd say goodbye before I left."

"Fine, goodbye." She looked up. "Just remember, you're in a state of regaining your honor right now. As far as I'm concerned, you're no better than the man who vacuums our septic tank or cleans our pool. Not until you have located the Roberts's house. Then, and only then, do you reenter this house as my daughter. Understood?"

"Yes, Momma."

Violeta waved her hand dismissively. "Now, off with you. Do your job."

Tam stepped out and closed the door behind her.

Violeta smiled when she was alone again. Tam needed this. She had to earn her life. She had character to build, and nothing good ever came easy. Nothing valuable was ever formed without extreme pressure and erosion. Break Tam down and build her up under pressure. Maybe, when Tam was in her mid-twenties, she would finally make it to womanhood and thank Violeta for all that she had done for her, the sacrifices a mother makes for their offspring.

Violeta set her iPad down and picked up the cordless phone. She dialed the number by heart.

The two men she employed had turned out to be reliable. She had found them on the street while out late at night with her bodyguards. Ex-cons with no place to live. She had given them an apartment, a phone to contact them, food, and all the alcohol they wanted, plus a thousand dollars each. It boggled her mind how they thought a thousand dollars made them rich.

She had them do the Parkman job a week after they were well situated. It had been easy. Pick him up. Disrobe him. Drive to an empty warehouse she owns and do crazy things to him. She let them decide what crazy things they wanted to do. Their job was to take his gun and make him write the letter that would incriminate him in any court of law. If any of this saw the light of day, Parkman had been harassing her, she would claim. Even wrote a letter to make it look like she had authored it.

And now, a new job had come up for her two little ex-cons.

After dialing, the phone rang on and on at their apartment.

They had better not be drunk or high.

She hung up and tried again. No one answered.

Leaving her coffee behind, Violeta headed for the

kitchen, where she used her cell phone to call her driver. Her bodyguards had an address on the edge of town they needed to visit with her.

Bring extra security men. And bring brass knuckles.

Two ex-cons may need a beating to remember who was in charge.

Chapter 18

PARKMAN WAITED OUTSIDE THE hospital with Aaron. Detective Joffrey was doing his own rounds as he met with nurses in surgery, doctors working on the floor Sarah was supposed to have been on, and several hospital officials.

No one had seen or heard of Sarah Roberts. Joffrey had used his influence to hunt down all the ambulance drivers on staff before shift change but could not find the two who had attended the scene on Keele Street where Sarah had been wounded.

The only four people who could confirm that a shooting actually took place were the two first responding officers, Parkman and Joffrey.

But now they had no victim.

Detective Joffrey walked out the sliding doors and joined Parkman and Aaron. He shrugged and made a face.

"I tried. Nothing. She either disappeared, or she didn't

come to this hospital."

"No, no, she came here." Parkman shook his head. "Explain Doctor Jacob to me, then. No, they knew about her, and Doctor Jacob was tasked to keep us away, keep us busy."

"I agree," Aaron said. "We start here."

"It ends in Santa Rosa," Parkman said. "It started there, and it will end there."

Joffrey raised a hand to block the morning sun and squinted at Parkman. "I don't have jurisdiction in the States. We aren't going to California."

"The hell I'm not." Parkman moved past him and stepped into the shade. "You don't have a victim. All that talk about my bullet was bullshit. The note was in my handwriting, but none of that matters because Sarah isn't here. All you have is me shooting at a Jaguar, and no one got hurt. Cite me, take my weapon, charge me if you want, but I'm not a flight risk. When I'm free tonight or tomorrow morning after my arraignment, I'm going to California—"

"And I'm going with him," Aaron added.

"And I suggest you come, too," Parkman told Joffrey. "Take a week off. A leave of absence. Call in sick for a week. I don't care but come with us. Follow this to its conclusion so you can see for yourself what is going on."

Parkman could tell Joffrey liked the idea, but then he shook his head.

"I can't. I just can't go to California to solve a Toronto case. I have too much going on."

"Bullshit. You want to see what's happened to Sarah as much as we do. In fact, Sarah has done a lot for this city. I bet if you told your superiors what you wanted to do, they would call the Santa Rosa authorities to tell them you're coming."

"You're right about one thing, Parkman."

"What's that?"

"I really don't have much on you right now. Finding that letter in your suit jacket pocket was an illegal search of a private citizen's personal clothing. Sure, there's blood on you, but whose? At this point, I don't have a victim. And yes, you shot up a Jaguar, but that'll have to be investigated further before charges can be laid if any." Joffrey paused to let a man pushing a woman in a wheelchair pass. When they were out of earshot, he said, "I could press charges because you admitted to shooting at the car—"

"No, I didn't," Parkman interjected. He looked at Aaron, "Did you hear me confess to anything?"

"Nope."

"Okay, then I have to investigate further. You're free to go for now. But I have to advise you to stick around. I'll need a number to reach you at, and where will you be staying?"

Parkman gave Joffrey his cell number and Aaron's home address.

"You do know I won't be sticking around, right?" Parkman asked.

"I'm just doing my job." Joffrey put his pen and pad away. "But if it were me, I'd go find out what happened to my girl. Then begin a massive lawsuit against the hospital or anyone else who had anything to do with this."

They shook hands, and Joffrey departed.

"Now what?" Aaron said. "We have to find Sarah. This is insane. I can't lose her again."

"Do you have extra keys for Sarah's bike?" Parkman asked.

Aaron nodded.

"I'll drive you to the bike at the warehouse on Keele. You follow me in my car, and together we'll go to your place and lock it all up. You'll get your passport. Then we go to the airport and get a ticket to San Francisco. We could be in Santa Rosa tonight or tomorrow morning if everything works out. It's time to break this thing open wide."

"What if Sarah turns up at another hospital or somewhere else in Toronto and needs me?"

"She won't. And if she does, Joffrey's here. Worst case, she shows back up at your apartment and calls you. Then just fly back to be with her. But I don't think any of that is going to happen." Parkman shook his head. "Whoever took her will have no purpose but to move her to Santa Rosa to do Violeta's bidding. That's why they tailed me here. That's why we were shot at. It all makes sense, and Violeta has enough money to buy the mayor."

"No jokes about the Mayor of Toronto," Aaron warned. "I've always loved Rob Ford."

Parkman nodded. "No problem."

"And you have to tell me everything about this Violeta person."

"There's one thing to be prepared for."

"What's that?"

"Be prepared to fight. She is never without security guards. Often two or three flank her wherever she goes."

"Don't worry. I'm prepared to have some fun. It's been too long."

What Parkman didn't tell him was to be prepared to never see Sarah again.

Once Violeta was done with Sarah, there was no way she would let her live. With enough security, the kind of criminals Violeta sent after Parkman, and the things they did to him, Sarah didn't have much of a chance with a bullet wound to the head.

Unless Parkman and Aaron got to her first, which Parkman doubted.

All they would find in Santa Rosa would be Sarah's body.

Chapter 19

Kostas knocked and opened the cell door. He had a metal bed brought in with a new mattress and a softer chair for Oliver. He had even located a couple of English books at a tourist store in Nafplio's main square for Oliver to pass the time.

"Enjoying the books?"

Oliver grunted a yes.

"The bed has to be better than the floor."

"It was."

Kostas held up the envelope in his hand. "Looks like we have everything we need to make this work."

The fat lip had split under Kostas's fists. One of Oliver's eyes had blackened and swollen nearly shut. He complained of two loose teeth, but Kostas assured him that dental care in America would be better than in Greece and to wait until he got home to deal with it.

"I was at the hospital and got all the necessary documents. X-Rays, letters, legal transfers, everything. Even your passport is here. You're officially a paralyzed American male, on your way back to your hometown of Santa Rosa, California, via the Los Angeles airport, from Athens, with a two-hour layover in Zurich, Switzerland. How does that sound?"

"Like I'm going to be sick."

Kostas set the envelope down on the bed. "Why's that? This is your opportunity to set things right and move on with your life."

"I know, but I never thought I would return to that place. Also, I have to ask. You had my passport all this time, didn't you?"

"None of that matters now as it seems this is the only way to handle your ex-wife. Your other plan wasn't working out too well for you. Eventually, Violeta would find you in Britain, Argentina, or India, wherever you decided to go, and she would send men to paralyze you. A life on the run." Kostas looked Oliver up and down and shook his head. "You're not cut out for that."

"Knowing that doesn't make going back any easier. But I will."

"In fifteen minutes, I want to set you up in the wheelchair, cover your legs and take the pictures. Then I will fax the hospital documents to your ex-wife and send her the pictures. Once the money has been transferred, I will freeze the assets in my personal account as evidence and contact the authorities in the States. You will already be in Athens, awaiting your flight by that time. As long as everything goes as planned, you'll be in Los Angeles in thirty-six hours."

"Have you come up with a plausible story about how I got paralyzed?"

Kostas nodded. "It's in the envelope. Read it, study it. The story stays the same until Violeta is arrested in the States." He headed for the door.

"Can you offer me an abbreviated version?"

He turned at the open door, leaned on the doorframe, and smiled.

"You were mugged on the back streets of Nafplio by a drunken group of twenty-year-olds. After a few punches, you fought back. They pushed you to the ground, which accounts for your shoulder and knee injury, and knifed you in the back with a homemade knife. What do you Americans call it, a shiv? Three stab wounds, to be exact, one of them severing your spinal cord, the other two cutting off any chance of you ever walking again. Then they left you for dead. How does that sound?"

"Like a nightmare."

"Good, then it'll work." He pointed at the envelope. "Do some reading. The wheelchair and camera will be here soon. We have a performance to put on, and I'm counting on you to be the show's star."

Oliver grabbed the envelope off the bed and opened it.

Kostas closed the door. The lock clicked audibly, echoing off the steel walls. An uncontrollable shudder rolled through his shoulders.

What he would do to see Violeta's reaction when the police arrested her and Oliver stood from his wheelchair.

Maybe he would get Oliver to film that moment.

He had to consider that Oliver wouldn't go through with it. If he didn't, the worst that could happen would be that his female officer would fly back alone, and Kostas would keep the money in his private account as it wouldn't be needed for evidence.

A part of him wished Oliver chickened out.

Kostas would be richer for it.

Chapter 20

If asked, Sarah would be one of the first to shout out how much she loved to sleep. It was comfortable, warm, and without pain.

Waking brought on the nightmare. The headache, the lost memories, the constantly moving vehicle, and the deadpan stare of the lone doctor caring for her.

She rolled her head slowly to avoid increasing the pain on the inside and found him eating some form of microwavable pasta. Today's T-shirt was from another eighties alternative band called, The Cure.

A doctor wearing a shirt like that made her smile.

He turned to her. "Ahh, you're awake."

"What day is it? How long was I out?"

"You've been asleep for almost two days now."

"Really? How close are we to Santa Rosa?"

"We'll be there in five hours."

She frowned. "With a head injury, is it okay that I'm sleeping?"

The doctor wiped his hands with a napkin and swallowed what was in his mouth. "Oh yes. The myth of trying to keep people awake in case of concussion is only that, a myth. It was in the times before we had a CT scan and an MRI. Doctors in those days didn't really know what was happening inside the skull like they do today."

The smell of the doctor's pasta pained her stomach. "I'm hungry. Got anything for me to eat?"

"Of course."

The doctor got up and banged around near the front of the glorified ambulance. Sarah took in as much as she could. It was bigger than an average ambulance. Similar in size to a large UPS truck but fitted nicely with a small sink and several cupboards filled with medication. A traveling motor home for doctors.

As the doctor warmed her food, she listened to the engine and the sounds of the road. Trust was an issue for her. How did she really know where they were? Or where they were going? Who were these people? If they were real medical personnel transporting her back to her parents, wouldn't they have just flown her to California?

If they weren't who they said they were, then who was she dealing with?

"Tell me something," Sarah said.

The bell sounded on the microwave. The doctor retrieved the dish and brought it over to her. He swung a tray in place from beside her and set the bowl down on it. Then he inclined her bed and unstrapped one wrist so she could eat.

"Consommé. Good for the stomach. Now," he rubbed his

hands together, "what is it you wanted to know?"

"How come my wrists and ankles are secured to the bed?"

"I already told you that. We're in a moving vehicle. Sudden braking, turning corners, regular movement on the road could cause the sleeping girl to roll off her bed."

"I understand, but why the wrists and ankles? Why not a strap across my hips and thighs? I've been a prisoner before. This feels more like I'm a prisoner than a patient."

The doctor turned back to his food. "It is what it is. I have no idea why you're bound as you are. Maybe the bed you're on only came with binds in those positions, so that's all we could do." He sat down and swiveled his chair to face her. "But I assure you, you're not a prisoner. When you're ready, we can unstrap you and get you walking around to exercise those legs."

"I'm ready now."

"After your soup." He looked away.

The doctor was right. She needed food. She needed to get her energy up.

She couldn't escape the back of this moving hospital on an empty stomach.

Chapter 21

PARKMAN AND AARON HEADED toward the security gates at the Toronto International Airport with their plane tickets and boarding passes. It had taken an extra day and a half to get tickets to Los Angeles unless they had wanted long layovers, one of them being overnight.

No word had come in on Sarah. Even Detective Joffrey had come up empty.

"How did the call go?" Parkman asked as they got in line behind dozens of other passengers waiting to go through security.

Aaron had used his home phone, which both of them were pretty sure wasn't bugged, to call Sarah's parents and update them on what had happened to Sarah.

"I assured Caleb that we'd find Sarah." He turned to face Parkman. "Her father puts a lot of trust in us."

"How did he sound?"

"Hardened."

"What do you mean by hardened?" Parkman asked.

"How many times has Sarah been in trouble or gone missing, then resurfaced? Caleb reminded me of the time when they had been kidnapped and taken to an abandoned airstrip, where they were locked in a tiny portable shelter. Sarah was also taken, as was a woman named Esmerelda and Dolan."

"I know. I was there at the end of that."

"He told me it was Sarah who had broken out and rescued them. They were all in the same boat, but Sarah swam to shore in an ocean crawling with sharks. At least that's how he put it."

"Somewhat true. That was Armond Stuart's people. Sarah ended up going to Europe after him."

"Didn't you follow her there, too?"

"I did. And good thing I did. We both barely got out of Hungary with our lives."

They reached the conveyer belt with its plastic bins. Aaron grabbed one for his backpack and one for his shoes. Parkman was flying without luggage, so he only needed one for his shoes.

An airport security guard asked them to remove their belts as well. Aaron walked through the metal detector first, then Parkman.

After they were through security, clamped their belts back on, and slipped on their shoes, they turned left toward their gate number.

"Caleb was worried," Aaron said. "But he put his faith in his daughters."

"That's what he said? His daughters, as in plural?"

Aaron nodded. "For me, it's not Sarah I'm worried about. For her to be out there, all alone and physically capable of handling herself, I'd be willing to brush it off, wait it out. But she won't be a hundred percent because she has a head wound. She can't protect herself. And what if the head wound blocks her connection with Vivian?"

Parkman hated the thought of anything happening to Sarah. It would be his fault. Coming to warn her hadn't been his only motivation. He had wanted to see her again. She had been missing for two months in Italy, and as soon as she was back in Toronto, Violeta had threatened her. He wanted Sarah to know that he took that sort of thing seriously and would stay in Toronto to make sure nothing happened to her on account of him.

But she got hurt anyway. And now she was missing again.

"Parkman!" Someone called his name from behind them. "Aaron!"

Detective Joffrey stepped around a group of slow-moving tourists.

"Joffrey?" Aaron said. "What are you doing here?"

"You two didn't think I would let this mystery slip past me, did you? I have to find out how this ends, just like a good spy novel or a thriller. There's good guys and bad guys, gunshots, kidnappings, and at the heart of it all, an innocent girl trapped by the villain or villains orchestrating it all. Too good to pass up."

He slapped Aaron on the shoulder and looked around the area, smiling wide at the other passengers waiting for the flight to start boarding.

Parkman wondered for a split second if Aaron would

knock the offending hand off him.

"Are you on our flight?" Parkman asked.

"Gate C9? Leaving at this horrible early hour and arriving in LA as the sun comes up? Yeah, I think I'm on your flight."

"Sounds like it."

"Wouldn't miss it for the world," Joffrey said. He removed his hand from Aaron's shoulder. "Come on, guys, coffee is on me."

Chapter 22

The doctor, if he was a doctor, removed her soup bowl and pushed the TV tray back to the side, away from her bed. At the far end of the vehicle, he set her bowl in a small sink, turned on the tap to rinse it, then flipped a button to turn on the kettle.

"Would you like a cup of tea?" he asked.

"I want to walk," Sarah said. "I need to get up and move around."

"Okay." He started back to her. "When you were asleep and having those conversations that you have, I exercised your legs. It shouldn't be hard to walk again, although it has been almost four days."

He unraveled the straps on her ankles first.

"Tell me some of the things I say when I'm out."

"About four hours ago, you talked about a man named Parkman and something about revenge. Whoever you were talking to sounded like they were attempting to change your mind."

"My conscience?"

"Could be."

He undid her other wrist.

"Anything else?"

"Not really. Mostly names, places. Once, you talked about a man named Aaron."

A memory surfaced. She felt warm and comforted by it.

"Aaron," she repeated softly. "Why is that name so special to me?"

"Don't know, but you just said his name as intimately as you did when you were under."

"I think I'm in love with that man." She turned and met the doctor's eyes as he unraveled the straps covering her shoulders. "Whoever he is. What else?"

He stopped moving. "Oh damn. I almost forgot."

The doctor slapped a red button on the inside wall of the vehicle. A metallic voice resonated throughout the interior.

"What do you need?" the voice asked.

"Stop, preferably at a gas station or convenience store. Sarah's going to do a little walking around."

"There's one coming up in another mile or so. I'll stop then."

The intercom clicked off.

"I can't have you wobbling on account of a moving vehicle. Wait another minute. Once we're stopped, I'll remove the rest of these restraints and help you up."

"Did I say anything more in my sleep?"

"I'll give you random words that you spoke clearly. See if it'll mean anything to you."

He picked up a clipboard and read from it. "You said someone told you about Greece, and a man needed to be paralyzed. The name Violeta and pain were clear. A sacrificed chicken and a tapped phone. That's about all of it." He looked down at the clipboard, then back up. "There was something else. You said something about a vineyard, and you miss your parents. Any of that help?"

"Not at the moment, but the name Aaron is a good name. I think he was in Greece once." The tires bit into gravel as the driver maneuvered off the highway. As the vehicle slowed, she bit her bottom lip.

"What troubles you?" he asked.

"I just hate that I can't remember anything. Pisses me off and scares me at the same time."

"It'll all come back shortly. I'm just surprised that the noises inside your head are full conversations. That's a version of tinnitus I've never encountered. I sure would like to find out who you're talking to."

He undid the final strap as the vehicle came to a complete stop. A door opened and closed, the driver's weight adjusting the vehicle ever so slightly as he got out. She waited to see if anyone else moved at the front.

Now she had confirmation that it was just the doctor and the driver.

"Here, wrap your arms around my neck. I'll help you up."

Sarah clung to him as she twisted sideways and slowly allowed her feet to touch the floor. Whether the Nike shoes on her feet were hers before or not, they looked good on her. And felt good.

There was weakness in her thighs and a subtle ache in the

calf muscles, but her legs were strong enough to hold her after days of not using those muscles to hold anything.

"Hey, doc, who's financing all this?"

The look on his face told her he didn't want to talk about that.

"I can't say."

"You can't say because you don't know, or you can't say because you're bound not to?"

"Look, Sarah."

She loosened her arm on his neck and stood using the side of the bed for support.

"You're getting the best medical care money can buy. You're safe from anyone pursuing you. You're on your way home. What else do you need to know? Just heal and get ready to be reunited with your parents, okay."

"I'm curious by nature. I like to know who I'm working with."

"We're not *working* together. You're healing. I'm doctoring."

"That's where you're wrong. We *are* working together. And if I chose to stop working with you, I would want to know who I'm upsetting."

She wavered on her feet, gripped the bed tighter, and steadied herself until the dizziness waned.

"I will tell you that the person helping you is anonymous and wants to remain that way."

"Fair enough."

Using the side of the bed and the wall for support, she walked the length of the ambulance. At the front, she turned around and walked back.

"We found this in your pocket," the doctor said. "Looks

like a letter you wrote to yourself. It's weird, though, because you warn yourself to stay away from a man named Parkman." He looked up as she made her way back to him. "The same man from your dreams."

"Makes sense."

He folded the paper and set it on the side counter.

When she returned to the bed, she decided her legs were good enough. She was ready to incapacitate him and escape.

A small bandage covered the area where the bullet had hit her, and the hair was shaved around the bandage. She had shaved parts of her head before. It didn't bother her. There was no lightheadedness or dizziness anymore, only mild weakness. And she was of sound mind, only missing a few memories. There was enough food in the back of the vehicle to keep her energy up until she got to Santa Rosa.

It was time to leave captivity.

One memory had cleared. The image of Parkman. She saw him lifting his gun and shooting at her. He lived in Santa Rosa. She knew that now with certainty. According to the doctor, she was five hours away, and they were taking her there. Which meant they worked for Parkman. He missed killing her the first time, so he sent a team to keep her alive and deliver her to him under the guise of taking her home to her parents to get well and rest.

She was nobody's fool. And she was not a wounded horse being delivered to its owner to be put down.

Even without the memories, one thing was abundantly clear in her mind. If anyone was being put down, it was Sarah Roberts who did the putting down. It would remain that way if she had her feet on the ground and not six feet under.

"Doc, I'm not feeling so good."

She made out like she would faint, falling backward, then correcting herself before bumping into the wall cabinet. He rushed to her side and grabbed her around the waist.

"Come on, let's get you back up onto the table."

She squinted and moaned, holding a hand to her temple. "I need something for my head."

"Okay, I'll prepare a needle as soon as you're lying down and strapped in."

Sarah broke out of his grasp and bent from the waist, leaning her upper body over the bed.

"No," she said forcefully. "Get me something now."

The doctor paused. After a second, he moved away and opened a cabinet where he retrieved a small bottle. He stuck a needle inside the top, filled it, and returned to her side.

"Where are you going to put it?" she asked.

"In your thigh. Then I'll help you back onto the bed before it knocks you out."

Sarah moved her thigh out toward him, widening her stance for balance.

The doctor bent over.

She lunged at him and wrapped both hands around the wrist that held the needle. In the moment of surprise, she spun his wrist at an impossible angle before he could react, shoved the needle's tip into the front of his thigh, and pushed the plunger.

"No!" he yelled as he stumbled away from her. "What have you done?" He bumped into the wall and leaned sideways, favoring the stuck leg.

Sarah stood back up to her full height. "Sorry, Doc, or whoever you are. But this ride is over. This is where I get off." She shoved him to the floor of the vehicle. He fell, but not before brushing his hand along the counter, knocking needle packages, small boxes, and the empty pasta container he'd used at lunch to the floor with him. "Actually, I meant, this is where you get off. Appreciate your help, but I don't need it anymore."

The doctor's eyes were already closing as whatever was in the needle coursed through his blood.

"Nighty night," Sarah whispered.

And the doctor was out.

She ran for the cabinet from which he had pulled the bottle and saw a dozen more like it. Following his procedure exactly, she had two needles ready for the driver in case the first one didn't work fast enough.

She headed for the door, turned the handle, and bumped into it.

Locked.

"Shit, now what?"

The door needed a key. She set the needles down and searched the doctor's pants. Empty but for a few hundred in cash, which she relieved him off.

Frantic that the driver would return at any moment and start driving again, she rummaged around the areas the doctor frequented but found nothing.

"Shit."

The door to the front of the vehicle opened. The modified ambulance's weight adjusted as the driver got back in.

"Think, dammit."

The engine started.

She stumbled along the side, skirted the sleeping doctor, and hit the red button just as the driver started moving the vehicle.

It stopped, the engine idling.

The metallic voice returned. "Yes, doctor."

"Help," Sarah said. "He went to give me a shot to help me sleep when he slipped and fell down. He's out cold, and I'm not tied up. I'm weak and dizzy. Don't drive with me like this." She sobbed for his benefit. "I think the doctor may have had a stroke, heart attack, or something. Please help us."

She waited at least ten seconds before the driver responded.

"Okay, here's how we're going to do this."

"Please hurry."

"I will only open that door if you're tied up. I will have a semi-automatic weapon with me. I will give you a matching hole on the other side of your head if you try anything. Got that?"

"Why would I try anything? Please, I think he's going into convulsions or something. We just need help."

The door opened at the front as the driver got out.

"When I open the side door, if you're not secured in that bed, I will shut and lock the door and not open it again until we get where we're going."

"I'm in the bed now. I will try to tie myself up, but I will still have one hand untied when you get here."

Sarah grabbed the needles she'd prepared and moved to the bed. The ankle straps were easy and fast. She positioned the left wrist strap to appear secure but left it loose. Then she hid a needle under her left hip. The right wrist stayed unlocked, and the strap for her chest dangled under the bed, out of sight.

A key slid into the door to the outside. A loud set of locks clicked, then, for a brief second, there was the sound of air being sucked out. It reminded her of the sound an airplane door made when the flight attendant opened it.

Sunlight blanketed the floor and wall as the driver pulled the door all the way open.

"Are we cool?" the man outside asked.

"We're cool," Sarah called back in a frail, weak voice.

"Okay, I'm coming in, gun first. I will shoot if you try anything."

The tip of a gun appeared, then the hand holding it. After that, the driver dipped his head inside, saw her on the bed, and lowered the weapon.

"Please," Sarah begged, making her voice sound hoarse. "Help him."

The driver was young, sporting a mustache and beard. He had to be mid to late twenties. She had expected someone older, more experienced. His cheeks were pockmarked, leftover damaged skin from a teenage acne problem.

He scanned her body from the door and frowned.

"I don't see a strap on your right wrist."

"I was unlocked to stretch my legs and walk with the doctor. When he was putting me back, I needed a shot for the pain." She dropped her head back to the pillow softly. "I guess you didn't hear the screaming. I was in so much pain that he stopped and fell onto the needle himself." She looked back up at him. The driver was at the end of the bed now, the gun near his stomach, aimed at the floor. "Lucky for me, I wasn't fully secure. How could I have reached the buzzer when you got back in the driver's seat if I had been?"

The driver studied her face for a moment longer. "Something's not right here."

"Look, please, just do something for him and then tie me back up. No problem. But I need a shot of whatever he's having." She pointed at the doctor on the floor.

The driver bent down to check the doctor's pulse while keeping an eye on Sarah.

"I don't think so," he said.

"What?"

"I tie you back up first, then tend to the doctor."

"Sounds fine to me. Do it your way. Just do something."

The modified ambulance's engine still idled. She couldn't recall if he had shut the driver's door or not. If he did, it was probably unlocked.

The driver cautiously stepped up to her chest area, the gun now aimed at her face.

"You mind aiming that thing somewhere else? You can still make me dead with a bullet in the chest, only less messy."

Once he got the strap, he tossed it over her shoulders and walked to the other side to secure it. He fit it into something, and a second later, the strap was pulled hard, locking her shoulders down.

"Hey, the doc didn't put it so tightly."

"Look, Sarah." His face popped up in front of hers. She could smell his breath and didn't like the taste of Doritos. "I'm not as trusting as him nor as stupid. He was hired because he was the best medical guy money could buy. He would never jab himself with that needle and plunge whatever was in it into himself. You did this, and you will not do it to me."

"Fuck you," she said in a clear voice. "I'm trying to help."

He leaned closer and examined her eyes. "You're fully awake. The hoarseness in your voice is gone." He roamed her face with his eyes. "You set this up and didn't expect I would come in with a gun, did you?" He lifted the gun up for her to see now that she was almost all secure. "That's why the side door is locked. If you ever took over back here, no one would get out. Smart, huh? That was my idea."

"Yeah, real smart. No one gets out."

On the word 'out,' she wrapped her fingers around the hidden needle, flipped it in a way, so the plunger was at her thumb, spun her arm in a wide arc, and rammed the tip into the back of the driver's right shoulder as he leaned over her, depressing the plunger all in one motion.

His eyes widened like he'd been stung by a bee. Or maybe it was shock at being bested by a girl who was almost completely secured with straps to a bed.

He brought the gun around and tried to aim even as his eyes drooped.

Sarah unlocked the shoulder strap, sat up too quickly to unlock her feet, battled a wave of dizziness, and then finished unlocking herself completely.

After holding the second needle with the intent to use it, the driver's eyes closed, and the gun slipped from his grasp. She picked it up and checked the driver's pockets. A wallet with ID and money. She brought it with her to the open side door of the modified ambulance.

"Enjoy the ride back here, boys. It's going to get bumpy."

Chapter 23

OLIVER PAYNE NEEDED TO get up and move around. His ass had numbed, and his legs ached from sitting in the wheelchair. They had changed planes in Zurich and had to wait for two hours. The only break he got was when Athina, his Nafplio police officer posing as a nurse, pushed his wheelchair into the handicapped bathroom and allowed him to stand up and walk around.

Since Zurich, he had remained seated. They were still over five hours out of Los Angeles, and his mind had numbed too.

"Athina." Maybe talking would keep his mind off what his body was dealing with. "Does your name mean anything?"

Athina was a hardened woman. Kostas had told him she had spent a few years in military service before coming to work at his police station. She had been through a lot and would serve as a capable companion on the trip to America. The chiseled face and buzz-cut hair almost made her look male, but her soft voice and ample breasts confirmed her sex.

"I'm named after the Greek Goddess Athina. My parents used the name because of Athens, too, our capital city."

"Athens?"

"Yes, in Greek, Athens is called Athina."

"When we land, is everything taken care of?"

"Yes. Relax. Sleep. Don't stress. It is almost over."

He closed his eyes and put his head back, but there was nothing to rest his head on.

Kostas had sent the pictures. Violeta, as promised, had sent the money. While that was happening, Athina had taken the two of them to the airport in Athens, where they stayed one night, in two rooms, at the Sofitel Airport Hotel right across the street from departures.

When they landed, Oliver would be driven to Santa Rosa, where he would be checked into a care home. Athina would stay with him until Violeta was arrested once the local authorities were presented with Kostas's evidence and Oliver's statement.

If this didn't work, and Violeta found out he wasn't paralyzed, she would get her two gorillas that never left her side to paralyze him for sure. A bonus hundred grand each would be all it would take for those bozos.

He hated what his life had become. He hated that he needed to enter the lion's den after escaping it and hoped he didn't lose his head.

And he hated his ex-wife.

He needed a plan if everything failed. He needed to take care of Violeta if she went after him and the cops weren't there to protect him.

Living like this wasn't an option anymore. Now that he had made the decision, living on the run wouldn't work. Whether he came out the victor or not, he was determined to see this to the end.

All he needed was a long sturdy knife. The kind sitting in the butcher's block on Violeta's kitchen counter.

A plan began to form.

Oliver smiled as he worked out the details, momentarily forgetting his discomfort.

Chapter 24

The driver had left the key on the outside of the ambulance door. Sarah closed the door, twisted the key, and dropped it in her pocket. She would keep the two men captive in their own modified ambulance just in case she needed them.

Why would I need people like that?

She had to start remembering who she was so her thoughts would be less confusing. Personality and strength weren't part of the temporary memory loss.

It was early morning, the air warm, and the sun crested the eastern sky. With her newfound money, she needed food and drink for the long ride ahead. She couldn't use any of the food in the back.

The keys were still in the ignition. She turned the vehicle off and pocketed the keys.

Inside the convenience store, she stocked up on energy

drinks, a loaf of bread, and baked goods. Not the healthiest diet, but one with lots of sugars to keep her going. Something bothered her about what she was buying. Maybe the old Sarah was a bit of a health nut.

The letters GMO entered her mind. She recalled something about being in Italy and how food had been modified. Or they were fighting against modified food. The memory stayed fragmented.

Weird.

The man in the line in front of her turned around twice. He had to be looking at her bandage and the shaved hair around it. She ignored him because saying anything here would draw unwanted attention her way.

At the counter, the clerk stared at Sarah's eyes each time she addressed her, trying hard not to look at the bandage.

Outside, she got to the ambulance, tossed her purchases to the passenger side, slipped in behind the wheel, and started it up. Relieved that the vehicle was an automatic, she put it in gear, aligned the mirrors, and hit the gas.

Within ten miles of the rest stop, a sign said Reno, Nevada, was fifty-five miles away. Reno to Santa Rosa was roughly another four hours.

She didn't know how she knew that.

She pushed the gas harder, wanting to make Santa Rosa by nightfall. Parkman's apartment was on a quiet street five blocks from downtown. She knew where she was going and what had to be done.

Something still bothered her about this guy Parkman. The name sounded friendly to her. But there was no disputing the image in her mind. That was clear. She had been there. It was as clear in her mind as if a photo was tattooed on her brain. The note the doctor found on her had said to stay away from Parkman. She saw his gun, heard the report, and felt the pain. But why shoot her? What could she have done to Parkman?

He must've been a friend, someone she trusted. That felt right.

Toothpicks.

What the hell do toothpicks have to do with anything?

Her heart swelled at the thought of Parkman's name, but she ignored it.

Maybe she wouldn't kill him. Maybe just a bullet in the leg. Make him limp for a while to remember what he did to her.

She had compassion. She could feel it. Deep down inside, she didn't want to hurt anybody. In a perfect world, everyone would love one another, and no one would go out of their way to hurt anyone else. But this wasn't a perfect world. There were horrible people bent on destruction and pain. Sarah had a unique ability to stop them because of the contact with her dead sister.

She hit the brake and pulled to the shoulder of the road. Someone had said something, but the cab was empty. Maybe it was the guys in the back on the intercom system.

"What?" she asked out loud as the vehicle came to a stop.

(*The note was my words.*)

"Who are you?" Sarah asked. A lump formed in her throat as she checked the mirrors through watery eyes.

(*I love you, Sarah. All will be given to you in time.*)

The words faded like an inward echo. Her ears hadn't heard a thing. The words had formed in her consciousness, but they weren't her words. The inner voice held a palpable difference. It made her think of watching a movie with a surround sound system. The action was on the screen in front of her, but the noises connected to the action were behind her. A disjointed feeling of thinking one thought and having another planted, rooted.

It had to be the tinnitus the doctor had talked about. Noises in her head. Foreign sounds.

Other words came to her. The name Violeta. Parkman had talked about that woman. Something about Violeta wanting to hurt her.

Maybe after she was done with Parkman, she would find out who Violeta was and why they were connected.

The memories were returning faster than expected. With five hours left on the road, she could try to remember as much as possible before she arrived in Santa Rosa.

Won't Parkman be surprised when he sees that she's still alive and now she's the one with a gun?

As she sat on the shoulder of the road, her vision blurred. The morning sun wasn't too hot yet. Maybe now was a good time to nap. She didn't want to push herself too hard.

She locked the doors and slid along the front seat, pushing her purchases from the store onto the passenger side floor.

A minute later, Sarah fell asleep dreaming of her sister, Vivian.

Chapter 25

Martin, Violeta's driver, pulled up outside a three-story apartment building that ran the length of the block. Each apartment had a small balcony, some dotted with barbecues. But not apartment 302.

Violeta's pet ex-cons were given enough furniture to sit and sleep on. Once they were situated, they had to earn their keep. She had promised to protect them as long as she could, but if things ever went awry, she had a plan in place to distance herself from them.

The lease was a month-to-month, and it was in her husband's name. Whatever these idiots got caught for, Oliver would be questioned, and Violeta would spill the beans. It was all his fault. Everything was. She had never met the two ex-cons, she would say, except in passing.

Her word—her rich and respected citizen of the community word—against two ex-cons living in an apartment paid for by her ex-husband.

Too perfect.

"Is Derek here yet?" she asked Martin in her customary curt voice. Employees were paid for what they did and paid well. She wasn't their friend, and this wasn't a popularity contest. Being mean for mean sake wasn't necessary, but neither was being nice for nice sake. They had a job to do and were paid for it. End of story.

"Yes, ma'am. He's on the third floor waiting for your direction."

"Fine. Take me up, then."

Martin got out and opened her door.

She sighed and exited the vehicle. She followed him to the front doors of the apartment building, where she inserted one of the many keys she had cut for the building.

On the third floor, Derek, her head bodyguard, waited in the stairwell.

"I thought I'd cover this exit so the ex-cons wouldn't leave without me noticing," Derek said as a way of explaining himself.

It irritated her when an employee prattled on like a schoolchild with an A on their report card. But they were a necessity in a world filled with stupid people.

"Good thinking," she said and then bit her tongue. "Now, let's go see what they're up to, shall we?"

Derek led the way down the hall. At the door to apartment 302, Derek listened a moment, then knocked.

Violeta stayed back a few feet, the apartment key in her hand.

Derek knocked again.

She handed him the key.

Derek unlocked the door and pushed it open hard. It banged against the wall on the inside.

Martin pulled his gun.

Violeta almost slapped Derek for making so much noise. Nothing like letting the entire neighborhood know they were there.

Both men moved inside the apartment. Violeta checked the hallway but didn't see any nosy parkers. She stepped over the threshold and closed the door quietly.

Something banged to her right. A door smacked open on her left. Both of her men were doing what they were paid handsomely to do. Root out the rodents.

"Hey, what the—" a male voice started, but the crack of a slap cut him off.

"Violeta, come to the bedroom." Derek's voice.

The smell got to her first. Something overcooked. Pasta, or macaroni and cheese, was splattered on the floor outside the kitchen door. A dark liquid had spilled and splattered around it. Like red wine. Or blood.

On her way to the bedroom, she passed the living room with a used couch and a cheap television. Beer bottles littered the floor wherever pizza boxes weren't scattered. A large glass item she thought they called a bong sat on a coffee table the ex-cons had fashioned out of boxes.

What kind of life is this?

She got to the bedroom door, covered her nose, and looked inside.

Both ex-cons were sprawled out on two separate mattresses, a naked woman with each man. There were no bed covers, and all their clothes were piled in heaps throughout the bedroom. Another glass bong was at the head of one of the mattresses. More beer bottles were scattered about, two of them lying on their side with large, circular dark stains on the carpet at the open neck of the bottle.

Derek had ex-con number one in a headlock.

"Let him go. He can't breathe and is no good to us dead."

Derek released him, and the skinny ex-con fell back to the mattress, his eyes wide in fear.

"You haff to unnerstan," he said, not bothering to cover his genitals. "We bin in the joint a long time. Then weeze on the street. You settin' us up in ere was kind an all, but we needin' some pussy, right."

"We all have needs," Violeta said from the door, then under her breath, "like a shower."

"Wha?"

"We all have needs, but mine come first. Do you know why?"

The two horrid females and ex-con number two hadn't woken up yet.

What did they take last night?

"No," he said. "Why?"

"Because I'm the one who pays for all this, that's why."

He nodded vigorously. "And we like the setup."

"Good. I'm glad you like it."

One of the girls stirred in her sleep, her skinny legs and bony body a testament to what meth did to people. Violeta would have to have a talk with Tam about drugs next week. Maybe she would visit this apartment with Tam next time and leave her behind for a night so the ex-cons could show her what life is like on the disgusting side of the world. One night with these two scum, drinking, fucking, and getting high, and Tam would realize just how good she had it at home, safe with her mother.

A new idea came to her. Maybe when Tam was eighteen in a few months, she would let these two deadbeats bed her down. Show Tam a real good time. After that taste got in her mouth, Tam would forever search for a clean, fine gentleman and never speak of her time with men like these.

Violeta decided to keep these vermin around for a while. Men like them could be useful, even if she wanted to use pliers on their limp penises to teach them a lesson. Men like this only learned from pain. Their hierarchy was built on it. The whole alpha male shit was how the other half lived. Acting macho and tough. Educated and civilized people weren't at company barbecues trying to impress each other with whose dick was longer. It was the uneducated and uncivilized who partook in such barbaric games.

But too much pain would render these ex-cons useless to her, and she needed them. Discarding them would be something to look forward to.

"Derek, Martin, get them up and dressed and bring them out to the living room. Leave the whores. I see the whores again, it'll be in the hospital."

She shifted her gaze to the living room and walked away.

Minutes later, her guards held one man by each arm, pants on. Ex-con number two looked half asleep, but he was on his feet, and his eyes fluttered, trying to open.

"Okay," Violeta said. "Here's what you have to do."

The one Derek was holding nodded so hard she thought he'd knock himself over.

"Before two o'clock this afternoon, I want both of you at Parkman's home address. Do you remember where it is, or do I have to remind you?"

The ex-con stared at the ceiling for a second, then clucked his tongue and swiveled his gaze to meet her eyes.

"I got it." He tapped the side of his head. "In here."

"Good. I need you to go and remove the little listening devices we planted in his apartment. I need all of them. You cannot leave even one behind. Understand?"

"You mean the little electronic bug thingys?"

Who knew these idiots would know that term? She thought listening devices were the better choice so they could avoid any further wasted time going back and forth.

Derek shrugged. Martin just held the other idiot, who remained semi-conscious.

"Yes, I mean the little bugs." It came out sounding derisive.

"What if he comes home while we're there?"

"Then knock him out and call me, but he won't. Parkman was last seen in Toronto, on the other side of the continent in another country, embroiled in another matter."

"Embroiled?"

"Look, can you do what I have asked you?"

"We can do that, right, Pete?" He slapped the other ex-con with his free hand but only got a short grunt in return.

Violeta had seen enough. "You're damn right you can do that." She stepped closer. Ex-con number one's eyes widened. "I spent a lot of money for this shit hole. The deal was you would do small jobs for me. You two fuckups agreed. I even said there might be periods when we could go months without a job, when you two were free to enjoy the apartment, the money, and the booze. No one said anything about drugs, and no one said you couldn't answer the fucking phone." She swallowed hard and cleared her throat. "So clean yourself up, get dressed, and go to Parkman's house. Eat his food. Wreck the place. I don't care. Just wait there until I call you. I need two people picked up later tonight or tomorrow, and I need you two ready to do the job, not drunk or high. Is that clear?"

His head bobbed. "Unnerstood."

She moved closer until she was only inches from his nose. The movement of Derek's arm told her that he had tightened his grip so the punk couldn't try anything.

"There are only two ways this goes down," she said. "One, you work for me and enjoy your life. Or two, you don't do what I say, and I will cripple you."

"Cripple? You mean like in speech?"

"Speech?" His logic was driving her insane. "What do you mean, speech?"

"You said cripple. Do you mean like a figure in your speech? Like, cripple us with money?"

"Are you trying to say a figure *of* speech?"

He nodded.

"No, crippled is not a figure of speech. I mean, literally cripple you. If you don't answer your phone when I call, someone will come to the apartment and break your spines with a Louisville Slugger. I will order them to beat you until they sever your spinal cord. How much you anger me will dictate how far up the spine is severed." She thought about Oliver and how he got jumped and knifed in the back. "Or maybe I'll have them use a knife."

"Um, ma'am, the spine is pretty protected. I used a knife on a guy once and had a hard time with the bones." He avoided her eyes. "It would have to be a lucky stab to paralyze someone with a knife. Maybe a sword." He looked at her. "But with a knife, you would really have to dig. It can be done, but a bullet is the best—"

"Oh, shut up!"

Derek shook the ex-con violently.

Maybe what he was saying made sense. That's why she used them because they had unique skills and knowledge. Could Oliver be paralyzed from a lucky jab by street thugs? Did Elias Kostas play her like a used fiddle to extort money?

So many things to handle in such a short time. Oliver would be here soon, and Parkman was probably on his way home. As far as she could tell from her inquiries, he hadn't been arrested in Toronto.

In the middle of the ex-con's living room, standing amongst their filth, the feeling of being overwhelmed caused her to waver.

"Ma'am?" Derek said. "You good? You cool?"

Violeta snapped out of it, blinked, then stared at the ex-con in Derek's arms.

"Get to Parkman's apartment. Do your job. Then wait there for my call. I may have another job for you. Now, clean this place and yourself up and get going."

The ex-con nodded that ridiculous bobblehead again.

She walked past him and tugged on Derek's arm. He leaned down closer to her.

"Bruise them, but make sure they can still work."

He nodded.

By the time she made it to the hallway of the third floor and quietly shut the door to the apartment, she heard the first blows.

She smiled.

Everything was coming together, after all.

Chapter 26

A BUZZER SOUNDED.

Sarah rolled in her sleep, her arm numb, then settled back down. Pins and needles coursed through her hand.

A car raced by. Then something larger. The ambulance shook with the vibration from the wind.

She opened her eyes. The buzzer sounded again.

What the hell?

A red light blinked on the dash near where the glove box was. She pushed the button.

A metallic voice said, "You can't keep us back here forever. We only have enough food for a few more days."

It all came back to her. The sun had moved higher, and her shirt stuck to her from the swelter inside the ambulance.

She sat up slowly, favoring her tingling arm. Before going too far, she opened a can of Red Bull. It was still a little cool. The loaf of bread was close. She opened that, set it on the seat beside her, turned the vehicle on, and merged into the light traffic.

The buzzer sounded again.

She turned on the radio, tuned it to a hard rock station, ate some dry bread, and downed it with Red Bull.

She had lost time, but now she was well rested. The road wasn't busy, the driving was easy. She settled back for the five-hour trip behind the wheel and thought about her horrible dream.

It didn't make sense. She had a glimpse of a crypt. She was inside the crypt, somewhere in Italy, sitting on the other side of a desk, talking to a crazed man. She thought his name was Soprano or something. Then she tossed bullets, live ammunition, into the open fire and ducked out of the way.

Why would she do such a thing? Where were these memories coming from?

There was a feeling that the memories weren't coming back disjointed and random but organized, leading her somewhere.

She caught a glimpse of another image: Parkman, crucified, tied to a cross in a church.

Because he had shot her in the head, that should have made her happy. But this image bothered her. Something about it wasn't right.

As if a TV screen turned on in her mind, she watched Parkman on the cross and saw herself watching him from the pews. No happiness accompanied the image. The girl standing by the pews, the Sarah she watched, was mortified, angry, and ready to murder people because of what they had done to Parkman.

That aligned with what she already knew. He *had* been a

friend. But since he had shot her in the head, she wanted to be the one to crucify him.

She checked her speed and mirrors. After another drink of Red Bull, she had one more piece of dry bread.

Could she have it wrong? Wasn't it Parkman who shot her? If not, then why did she see it happen in her mind? The image of him pulling his weapon and firing from point-blank range was real. Where did it come from if it wasn't real?

She pushed on, confident she knew what she saw and trusted it because it made sense. Parkman had been a friend. A dear friend who always had a toothpick in his mouth.

She smiled at the thought. It was something special to always remember him by.

But this dear friend had betrayed her and shot her in the head. He was working for the woman Violeta, and Violeta had hired him out of Santa Rosa. The memories were reforming, coming back to her, and just in time, as she would be in Santa Rosa soon.

One thing that saddened her more than anything else was that she could be so unloved that a friend would rather see her dead.

It was the ultimate hit to her sense of self that hate played such a strong role in fate. She was a good person. She felt that on the inside. A person of warmth with a big heart. Only ever willing to hurt others if it was needed to save someone weaker, the underdog.

Yet someone wanted her dead. Whether it was Violeta, Parkman, or both, trying to kill Sarah was an error.

Since she was still alive, she would continue her fight for the underdog. She would move forward without pause. If it were true, and her sister did talk to her as she had come to realize before she fell asleep, then she would listen.

There was nothing else left in life but to avenge the weak and help the needy.

Sarah had been weak once. She had been molested by her babysitter all those years ago. Being shot in the head made her weak again.

Sarah decided she would never quit. She would never stop fighting until her hardened heart turned gray and stopped beating.

And she would start her war on crime, her war on evil, with Parkman and Violeta. She would deliver the two men trapped in the back of the ambulance to Violeta's front door once she got the address from Parkman. They were only a problem for her if they got in her way.

As she pulled out to pass a slow-moving truck, she understood why she had seen an image of Parkman on a cross in a church and why she was in a crypt throwing bullets in a fire.

She had to crucify, kill, and bury him in a crypt.

Chapter 27

THE SUN WAS JUST rising in Los Angeles as the plane touched down at LAX.

As they landed and the pilot slowed the plane, Oliver's wheelchair vibrated, jostling his sore limbs.

He turned to Athina. "Because of the wheelchair, we deplane first. I need a handicapped bathroom immediately."

She nodded. "I'm ready."

The plane pulled up to the gate, and after a five-minute delay, the door opened. Athina wheeled Oliver off the plane and up the long tube that fed arrivals into the terminal. Signs informed them where to gather their luggage and where customs was, but Oliver pointed at the bathroom sign.

Once inside the restroom, alone, he got out of the chair and stretched. He splashed water on his face, used the toilet, and then danced around the small room to restart circulation.

"Could sure use a massage right about now," he

whispered to himself.

Someone knocked on the door. "You okay in there?"

"Yes, Athina. Be out in a minute."

He did a few more turns around the bathroom, got back in the chair, covered his legs in the red checkered blanket they had given him, and opened the door.

Athina stepped around the chair and pushed him toward customs.

Other planes had arrived at the same time, and the line to see a customs agent looked a half hour or longer.

Oliver sighed in despair, not wanting to spend more time in the chair than he had to.

Twenty minutes later, they stood before a customs officer. Oliver showed him his American passport and was waved through with an entry stamp.

Athina showed her passport and police badge and said she was simply transporting the injured Oliver back from Greece as a professional courtesy. Her visit to the States would be short as she was heading back to Athens as soon as Oliver was settled at the care facility in his hometown.

She was stamped and waved through.

With no luggage to claim, Athina pushed Oliver's chair past the luggage area, out the exit doors, and entered the main airport.

"We're supposed to meet two officers from the Santa Rosa detachment here at the doors," Athina said.

Oliver scanned the crowds until his eyes stopped on someone familiar.

He froze.

Standing ten feet away was the man from Greece. The man who had found him at Lina's Sugar Spell Spa had taken his picture.

The man who worked for Violeta.

Would Violeta try to take him in such a public place? Why not wait until he arrived in Santa Rosa? Unless she wanted her men to escort him there.

The man from Greece was with two other males. One younger, fit-looking man who had the build of a fighter. The other was in his forties and had the look of a professional.

"I think I see them," Athina said, pointing just to the left of the three adversaries.

The man from Greece swiveled toward him.

"Turn me around," Oliver said in a hushed voice.

"What was that?" Athina asked.

"Turn me around!" he snapped.

There was a moment of pause, and then the chair turned too slowly.

Oliver snuck a glance toward the man from Greece. He was looking right at him. But then the doors behind them opened, and more passengers departed from the luggage area.

"Go," Oliver said. "Push me that way." He pointed away from Violeta's men.

Athina leaned down close to his ear and asked, "What's going on?"

"One of my ex-wife's thugs for hire might have seen me."

"Would she send people here? To the airport?"

"Evidently."

After clearing the majority of the people waiting on family and friends to exit the luggage area, Athina turned his chair around and almost bumped into two men in suits.

"Oliver Payne?" the taller one asked.

Oliver nodded.

"We're here to escort you to Santa Rosa. You're in good hands now." He turned to Athina. "We'll take him from here."

She stepped around the chair and stood between Oliver and the two men. "I don't think so. I take him to Santa Rosa. Your escort. And I need to see ID."

The men exchanged a glance and then produced ID.

"Fine," the taller one said. "Have it your way. Follow us."

When they were underway again, Oliver whispered his thanks to Athina.

He wasn't leaving her side until this was over, and Violeta was arrested for what she had asked Kostas to do.

Or he would stand from the chair and kill her with his bare hands.

Chapter 28

"Parkman, you okay?" Aaron asked.

"Yeah. I just thought I saw Violeta's husband. Or ex-husband."

"How's that possible? Wasn't he in Greece?"

"The man I saw was scared, broken, and in a wheelchair."

Aaron scanned the crowd. "What makes you think it was him?"

"It was only two weeks ago that I took a hundred pictures of him, and the woman pushing his wheelchair looked Greek."

"Really?"

"It's just." He turned to Aaron. "That's what Violeta had wanted me to do. Paralyze Oliver."

"Over here," Detective Joffrey called.

He had pre-arranged a courtesy car from the local

detachment for their time in California. On the flight over, he had explained that his boss was personal friends with someone high up in the ranks with LAPD. A favor was called in.

A man in a brown suit jacket and jeans handed Joffrey the keys and pointed out the window at the unmarked cruiser.

"All yours. Just call this number when you're done with it. I'll come back here to pick it up."

"Got it. And thanks."

Joffrey pumped the man's hand.

Then the man turned around and walked away without addressing Parkman or Aaron.

"Let's get more coffee, and then we'll head up the coast to Santa Rosa. We've got over six hours in the car, and I only want to stop for piss breaks."

He walked away.

Parkman yearned for a toothpick. He'd had too much coffee.

And he wanted to get underway as soon as possible.

Sarah had been stolen from the Toronto hospital and was out there somewhere with a bullet wound to the head.

Hanging around to buy more coffee almost felt like time was running out.

Six more hours on the road.

He dreaded the ride and suddenly felt that they were too late. The only explanation for Sarah's disappearance was Violeta, and Santa Rosa was her headquarters. That meant that Sarah was in Santa Rosa and would have already refused Violeta's demands.

Which translated to Sarah was probably dead.

They were only chasing ghosts now.

Chapter 29

SARAH PARKED TWO CITY blocks from Parkman's apartment. Dozens of memories flooded back, assaulting her on the drive to Santa Rosa, reminding her who she was and what she did best.

She understood herself better and now knew why she had chosen the path she had lived up to now. Something about quitting the vigilante life and doing something else left her confused. After examining the gift of being able to talk to her dead sister, it had become a responsibility to do whatever she could to fulfill the prophecies in the notes given to her.

She couldn't figure out why she had wanted to quit but wasn't too worried about it now. Determined as she was, nothing would stop her from working with Vivian until she died.

The men locked in the back of the ambulance had buzzed her several times but fell silent when she hadn't answered.

Now, late afternoon, shadows lengthening, Sarah exited the ambulance, pocketed the keys, and placed the gun she had taken from the driver in the back of her pants.

In Parkman's quiet neighborhood, one car passed, and two kids rode their bikes along the sidewalk on the other side of the street. The ambulance was soundproof. That was the reason for the red button and the air-tight door. No one would hear the shouts of the two men locked in the back.

She strolled, nondescript-like, along the sidewalk until Parkman's building came up on the left. The early evening breeze cooled her. It moved hair around the wound on her head and tickled her scalp. The pain was mostly gone. The stitches in her scalp held tight under the white bandage. Maybe by next week, when the bandage came off, she would wear a hat for a while.

The building's side door stayed unlocked until the superintendent locked it at nine in the evening. She remembered this when visiting Parkman before she left for Las Vegas last summer. That felt like a lifetime ago. After dealing with a crazy loan shark in Vegas, it was a serial killer and a street gang in Toronto. Then off to Italy, where she spent too much time figuring out who her enemy was. The FBI, a mobster hitman, or an assassin known as The Ghost.

The Ghost.

She stopped three doors down the corridor on the first floor of the building and said the name over and over.

The Ghost ... The Ghost.

Why was that name so important to her?

A door opened behind her.

"Okay, Mom, yes, I'll get the right kind. Okay."

The door shut, and a teenager walked the other way,

headed to the side exit.

She kept moving. On the third floor, she eyed Parkman's door before she got to it. His hallway was relatively quiet. The only noise was a TV that played a car chase, complete with a police siren, in one apartment. The air was spicy with the smell of someone cooking Indian cuisine.

The thin carpet underfoot masked her footfalls as she approached Parkman's door.

Her old friend, the turncoat, hung on a cross, flashed in her mind. There was something about the image of Parkman crucified that still bothered her. Not in a religious sense, but more that she was reading the memory wrong.

And why hadn't Vivian talked to her again? No internal brain messages, no notes. Maybe the tinnitus was fading as she healed. Maybe she would never hear her sister's voice in her head again.

But then why not offer a note of some kind? Tell her what to do and where to go?

Could she be on the right path, so a note wasn't needed?

That had to be it. Whatever Sarah decided to do in the next day or so wouldn't need a letter or an internal voice unless she was going to do something wrong.

Her Parkman hunt was justified.

When she reached his door, the mental image of Parkman firing his weapon so close to her solidified what she was about to do.

One last look over her shoulder confirmed the hall was empty.

Before she could try the door or attempt to break the lock, someone coughed from inside. She edged closer to Parkman's door, her ear a couple of inches from the wood.

Muffled voices. Another cough. A nose snorting.

Someone was home. More than one person. Males.

Perfect. She could deal with Parkman right now without having to wait.

Gently, she gripped the door handle and turned the knob. It wasn't locked. She stopped at the tinniest squeak from the latch. She listened. Nothing from the inside.

She turned it until the latch disengaged, then listened again, but there was nothing.

After a ten-second pause, Sarah pushed the door and opened it slowly. It gave way to an apartment she was familiar with. The front area with its mat, the small hallway-like kitchen to the right. Beyond that was the dining area, then the living room. She knew to her left were the two bedrooms.

Someone was home but staying very quiet since she touched the door.

She stepped inside cautiously and eased the door back until it sat ajar an inch.

She rubbed her sweaty palms on her pants. She wanted the gun in her hand before exploring any more of the apartment but didn't want it slipping at a crucial moment.

Before she could pull it out, a skinny man dressed in dirty jeans and a stained white T-shirt stepped into the kitchen, set a can of Coke on the counter by the fridge, and turned to head back to the living room.

He stopped on the balls of his feet, pivoted, and looked back at her.

"Oh, hey, didn't know we had company."

It was so nonchalant and surprising, yet friendly and unobtrusive that she didn't pull the gun on him. She allowed her hands to dangle at her side, ready, waiting.

"I'm looking for a man named Parkman," Sarah said.

"You want to come in? Join us for a drink? We can all wait together. He should be here in," he pulled a cell phone out of his pocket and pushed a button, "twenty minutes."

She almost drew her gun when he reached for his cell phone, her reflexes still honed and tuned.

"Do you know where he is right now?"

The skinny man dropped his cell phone back in his pocket and said, "I understand he was in Toronto, but he's coming back."

"Who is it?" someone asked from out of sight.

Sarah guessed the second male was in the living room.

The man in front of her shrugged and moved away. "Suit yourself." From behind the wall, he added, "Come on in and wait or leave and come back later. Your choice."

Maybe she should wait. Having two men here would complicate things if she had to hurt Parkman. But coming back wasn't an option. What if these men were also here to hurt Parkman? Then she wouldn't get a chance to find out why he shot her in Toronto.

She walked through the kitchen, and just as she was about to enter the dining area, she remembered what Parkman had told her the night she was shot.

It was either a turkey or a chicken that was sacrificed in my apartment ... the animal was torn to bits and pieces, and the blood was smeared everywhere.

The dining table was covered in blood and feathers. Something was wrong that these men were waiting for Parkman in such filth. A sudden urge to flee crept through her. Who were they, and what did they want with Parkman?

She couldn't identify anyone Parkman would have allowed to hang around his apartment. He didn't associate with people like the skinny junkie she had just met.

But her memory couldn't be trusted.

Where's Vivian now?

When she turned the corner and looked into the living room, the skinny guy was there, along with the man who had spoken from behind the wall. He was just as thin but more like a meth-diet skinny, all bony and sickly.

The room was ruined, the sofa flayed, and a thick piece of wood stuck through the center of the TV. The walls had a dark crimson paint job, complete with feathers, which were part of the sacrificed chicken Parkman had mentioned.

But that wasn't what caught her breath in her throat.

Each man held a gun.

The meth diet guy's hand shook violently from either too many drugs or withdrawal.

"Come closer, bitch," Meth Man said. "We want to get a good look at you."

Sarah looked at the kitchen to assess the odds of diving back behind the wall.

"Don't even think about running. If we have to chase you, we fill you with lead instead of our dicks. Now come over here and make yourself comfortable, pretty thing. We'll hang out for a while, see what you look like on the inside."

Dive or move forward, dive or move forward ...

The meth diet guy lowered his gun more out of lost energy than exasperation. He set it on the coffee table and jumped up, then walked over before she decided what to do. Diving for cover hadn't appealed to her, with the head wound still relatively fresh.

His grip was surprisingly tight as he wrapped his hand around her arm above the elbow. He leaned in close and whispered, "My friend told you to come in and get comfortable." He shoved her toward Parkman's couch. "Do what he says, or the sex won't be fun for you. It'll be violent, and you don't want that. I'm sure you'd rather enjoy it, wouldn't you?"

She lost her balance as she hit the arm of the couch and fell, her arms out to protect her head from any impact. Going unconscious now would mean waking to a nightmare.

Her level of calm surprised her. How often had she been in situations like this in order to be only remotely worried? Or was this a form of apathy toward death?

The first man she had met in the kitchen set his gun down and surveyed her form lying on the couch. Both guns sat useless on the coffee table. He pulled his cell phone out and speed-dialed a number.

After a pause, he said, "We have a problem."

Chapter 30

Violeta held the phone so tight the plastic casing made cracking sounds from the strain.

"Can you say that again?" she asked.

"We have a problem. There's a girl here."

"A girl? What do you mean, a girl?"

"We were doing what you asked. The last bug was hard to find—"

"Hard to find?" The fury of hearing that sentence almost overwhelmed her. She got to her feet. "How could they be hard to find? You were the ones who installed them."

"I know, but we forgot where we put the last one. Anyway, we were just finishing up when a girl walked in."

"And you decided to call me?" Violeta started pacing. Her bodyguard peeked in from the hall. She waved him off. The door closed softly.

"What do you want us to do with her? Can we play with

her? Does it matter to you?"

"No, what you do with her doesn't matter to me. That's entirely up to you, but I want to know who she is first."

He pulled the phone away and asked the girl her name.

The girl's words were soft and quiet but loud enough to sail through the phone line and touch Violeta's stomach, causing nausea to rise in her throat. She sat back down before she fell.

"She says her name is Sarah Roberts," he said. "She's got a bandage on her head, too. That name mean anything to you?"

Tam had said she had killed Sarah. Sarah was supposed to be in a Toronto hospital recovering from the wound that would imprison Parkman. How could she have traveled so far with a gunshot wound to the head? Why was she here, in Santa Rosa, in Parkman's apartment? That probably meant Parkman was coming back too.

And her paralyzed husband, Oliver, was arriving from Greece today.

Was it odd that everyone would be in Santa Rosa on the same night, or was it a coincidence?

She didn't believe in coincidences. Everything happens for a reason. Or it didn't happen.

"Violeta, what do you want us to do with her?"

"No names, dammit!"

"Oh, yeah, sorry."

The door opened, and Tam entered the main living room, smiling as wide and devious as the Cheshire Cat.

"Do with her whatever you want to do. But you've only got one hour. Then report back in." She paused. "Oh, and Pete, make it hurt. Really hurt. Do you understand?"

"Yes, we unnerstand perfectly."

The line clicked off.

"Tam, you look rather happy for a girl who hasn't regained her honor yet."

An image of the naked skinny ex-cons in Parkman's apartment doing terrible and disturbing things to Sarah popped into her head as she set the phone down. She moistened her lips with the thought of those two spending a night with Tam to really teach her what a woman was for. Maybe those two idiots would come in handy after all.

"I found them." Tam grinned like she had one-upped her mother.

Her words incensed Violeta to no end.

Tam plopped herself down in the chair on the other side of the living room, sweeping her arm across the back like she owned the place.

An attitude like that would get her locked in the ex-con's bedroom for a week if she didn't watch herself. Violeta would tie her daughter to the bed herself and let the skinny dope heads ruin her for a future husband if she didn't control her attitude.

"Found who?" Violeta asked, barely able to hide her contempt.

"Sarah's parents, Caleb and Amelia Roberts."

"Where?"

Tam must've detected Violeta's tone as a threat. She lowered her offensive arm from the back of the chair and sat up straighter. She cleared her throat, adjusted her pants, and blinked nervously.

"They live on Olivet Road. There's a large vineyard behind their house." She gave her mother the house number.

"I parked out front and waited for one of them to leave so I could report some kind of activity for you, but they stayed home all day."

"Do you understand what the word *dead* means?" Violeta asked. Without waiting for a response, she got up from her chair and looked at the closed door. "Martin?" she called.

The door opened. "Yes, ma'am."

"Get Derek. I want to talk to both of you."

"Yes, ma'am. Right away." The door shut softly.

"You see that?" she asked as she walked to the front window. "That's loyalty. That's respect." She pulled the curtains shut and turned back to her daughter. The rage building inside had to be saved for Oliver, Sarah, Parkman, and anyone else she had to straighten out tonight, but Tam was coming very close to unleashing it and needing a straightening out herself. "Those men do what I ask when I ask. They never question authority, and they are rewarded for their efforts. Do you get how that works?"

"Yes, Momma. I get it."

Violeta narrowed her eyes. "No, I don't think you do, little girl. You're seventeen and still have no idea how everything works in the big world, do you?"

Tam remained silent. Smart girl. Violeta gave her that one.

"You see, normally, finding Sarah's parents' house would pull you back into the family. You would have regained your honor with me." She said the words as they pained her.

"Why normally? What do you mean?"

"You do know what dead means, right?" This time she waited for an answer.

Tam nodded. "Yes, Momma."

Violeta shook her head. "I'm afraid you don't."

There was a soft rap on the door.

"Come."

The door clicked open, and both bodyguards entered, dressed in their uniform grays, their suit jackets, Hugo Boss.

"Martin, you stay with me. We're going to meet up with my ex-husband tonight."

Tam gasped. Violeta pointed a finger at her without looking her way. "You stay right where you are. We're not finished." She lowered her hand.

"Derek, it seems we have a problem at Parkman's apartment."

"They're having trouble with the bugs?" Derek asked.

"I would've thought the same thing, but no. They got all the bugs. But while they were there, a girl entered and saw them. This girl has to be removed from the scene."

"What are they doing with her right now?"

Violeta snuck a glance at Tam and offered her a wry smile. "They're enjoying themselves. Taking out their manly pleasures on her." She looked back at Derek. "The girl's name is Sarah Roberts."

Tam sucked air in audibly.

"Don't move!" Violeta yelled at her. "We're not done." She turned to face Derek. "There won't be much left of Sarah by the time you get there. Wait for Tam at Parkman's apartment. She will be along shortly. Just secure the premises and wait for Tam. Can you handle this situation?"

"Absolutely, ma'am."

"Then go. I'll leave it in your capable hands. When you're done, come back here and watch the house. We're leaving to meet with Oliver."

He nodded, stepped back a few paces, turned, and exited.

"Martin, please, have a seat, relax. I have a mother-daughter issue to iron out, and then we'll leave to go see Oliver."

Martin sat on the chair by the door and pulled out his cell phone to pass the time.

"Now," Violeta said as she finally turned to face Tam. "Where was I?"

"Sarah's alive?" Tam whispered. "And in Santa Rosa?"

"That was why I asked if you knew what dead meant. Since you said Sarah was dead, and she's evidently not, you must not know what that means."

"But Momma, I said I shot Sarah, and I *think* I killed her. I didn't know one way or the other if she was dead."

"Oh, come on. Have the decency to not sit there and try to backpedal your way out of this." Violeta strode across the floor and stopped directly in front of Tam. "How dare you? In front of Martin, too. You disrespect me at every turn."

She lashed out, the back of her hand hitting Tam's cheek so hard, blood bubbled up on her lower lip.

"Martin," Violeta shouted. "Stay seated. This is my daughter. I will discipline her as I see fit."

"Yes, ma'am."

Tam held her lip and cried, averting her eyes to the floor.

"You came home and told me Sarah was dead. And now she's here, tonight of all nights. Well, guess what? Your father is back from Greece. I didn't tell you because it may come as a shock to you, but he was jumped by some street gang in Athens, mugged, and stabbed."

Tam gasped and looked up at her mom, her wide eyes glazed over. "Is he okay?"

"The Greek police sent a nurse back with him because the knife severed his spine. Your father is paralyzed from the waist down."

A flood of tears burst from Tam's eyes as she keeled over.

Violeta allowed her daughter to feel the pain for a moment. Then she kicked Tam's foot to regain her attention.

"Because you found Sarah's parents is the only reason I don't put you in a hospital right beside your father. But now you have to regain yourself, yet again. You lied. Sarah Roberts is not dead."

"Did you have anything to do with what happened to Dad?" Tam blurted out through her tears.

The defiance and anger on her face surprised Violeta. It almost made her step back at the expression of hatred in Tam's eyes. In response to the outburst, Violeta swatted Tam three times, back and forth, like sweeping at an errant housefly.

Tam's head swiveled with each hit. When she stopped, another blood spot bubbled up from a horizontal cut on Tam's cheek.

Violeta turned her hand over and saw the offending ring. It was the diamond ring she had taken off when Oliver left four months ago. It was back on as a good show of being the wife for his return tonight. She had forgotten all about it, and now Tam might need stitches.

Tam's hand came from her face, blood seeping down the palm along her wrist.

"How dare you," Violeta snarled. In a mocking, whiny voice, she said, "Did I have anything to do with what happened to Oliver?" She stepped back in case Tam decided to charge at her. "I'm not so powerful that I could hire a Greek street gang in a city I've never been to. The fact that you asked that shows just how much respect you have for me." The image of the two naked ex-cons came to mind again. Tam just committed herself to their arms. When this was over, she would order Tam to move in with the ex-cons as their play toy.

"If I had to regain my honor," Tam said, "because I thought I had killed Sarah by accident, and now Sarah is alive, then that negates me having anything to fix in the first place."

"No. That's not how it works. We deal with the information we have at the time. You had a job to do, and you did it." The blood was clotting fast on Tam's cheek. She wouldn't need stitches after all. But she would need to clean up as it now graced her neck and the collar of her shirt. "The information we have now is Sarah's alive, and that will cause new problems. Since we thought you had killed her, I want you to go to Parkman's apartment and finish the job for me. Don't worry. My men will have her unconscious by the time you get there."

"What are they doing to her?" Tam asked.

"Everything a pretty young girl like you shouldn't know."

"Are they raping her?"

Now it was Violeta's turn to smile like the Cheshire Cat. "In every which way possible," she whispered. "You won't be able to recognize her when my men are done, and Sarah won't be able to use her plumbing down there ever again."

Violeta was in the zone, exactly where she wanted to be. Sarah Roberts would soon be out of the picture. Oliver would sign the documents, and Tam would move in with the oversexed ex-cons, where she would also learn what it's like to be abused. And if anything stood in Violeta's way, she always had Sarah's parents as barter. This time next week, Violeta would have her business deal sewn up, her money transferred, and her vacation to Europe booked. Even her babysitter for Tam, two horrible dirty ex-cons, was all now arranged. She smiled. She was in control, after all.

You are either in control or you aren't. There's no middle ground.

"Get up, Tam Rood. Clean your face and change your shirt. Then drive to Parkman's apartment and see what my men are doing to Sarah. When they're done, muffle the shot with a pillow and let Derek handle the rest. You do that, your honor is right as rain."

Tam shot up out of her chair, walked past Violeta, a hand still on her wounded cheek, and left the room.

Violeta laughed out loud for effect. Tam had to learn. Violeta was in charge, and as long as her heart beat in her chest, Violeta would always be in charge.

"Martin, bring the car around. We're going to the private clinic on Petaluma Road to meet my asshole ex-husband. I understand they've registered him in now." Then she thought of something else. "Oh, and Martin."

"Yes, ma'am?"

"Bring my fashionable walking cane. The one with the hidden blade in it."

He frowned, wrinkling his forehead.

"I don't believe Oliver is paralyzed," Violeta added. "I want to find out on my own. His legs should be able to handle a knife wound if he can't feel anything down there. If he's not paralyzed, I may need the blade to protect myself."

"Your cane will be in the car, ma'am."

Martin stepped out and quietly closed the door.

Chapter 31

On Parkman's sofa, Sarah listened to the phone call. The skinny one had said the name, Violeta.

What is her business with me?

It had to be the head injury. She would remember a woman named Violeta. It was one letter away from Violent. Parkman had said her last name was Payne.

Violent pain.

Interesting.

The skinny guy set the phone down. He licked his lips as he stared at the wall, moistening them until they shone like a red stone brushed by a river's torrent. He glanced at skinny meth-diet guy number two and nodded so subtly she almost missed it.

Meth Diet licked his lips, too.

Was it a prison they escaped from or a mental care facility? She wanted to hurt them a moment ago. Now she wanted to kill them for the lip-licking shit. Whatever they were thinking shouldn't cross the rational mind of a civilized man in society. These men represented everything uncivilized in society.

"Okay," Sarah said as she sat up on the couch. Both idiots had left their weapons on the coffee table in front of her. They were an easy grab for them and too far for her, but she had another idea. "The way I see it, you guys have only two options."

They exchanged a wry glance, their ineptitude shining through their blank stares. Meth Diet's shakes had grown worse. If he dove for his gun, would he even be able to get a shot off with any kind of reasonable aim, even from five feet?

"Option one," she said. "We fight to the death. In which case, you both die here, in this filthy apartment." She waited for them to grasp what she was saying. Skinny guy number one leaned back on his arms and rested on his elbows on Parkman's living room floor, exactly where she wanted him to be. "Option number two. I hurt you bad. So bad that you'll be in the hospital for weeks, but at least you'll be alive. That's it. Pick now, or I will decide for you. Which one'll it be?" She finished with a talk show host flare.

Meth Diet blew air out of his mouth, his eyes widened with the shakes. "Oh, man, I like this one. She's gonna be awesome."

Skinny guy number one shook his head back and forth, looking down at the carpet. As if in a slow-motion picture, he lifted his head and glared at her, a newfound rage in his features.

"You got some balls for a chick." He licked those

already-wet lips again. "It's talk like that"—he rolled his head back and forth—"that get pretty young things like you killed by accident. We be fucking you simultaneously, making you scream, and then, oops, I held the pillow on your face too long." He grinned like he knew a big secret and glanced at Meth Diet. "Then we fuck you some more. Ain't that right?"

"Damn right," Meth Diet shouted. "The ass is always better after you're dead. The muscles give out and relax. Hey Pete, we could probably both fit in her ass at the same time once she's dead."

Sarah shrugged, fighting hard not to dive over the coffee table at Meth Diet for the absolutely horrific comment he had just made.

"Have it your way. Can't say I didn't warn you."

Sarah lifted her feet and placed them on the edge of the coffee table. Both men frowned and stared at her shoes. A second later, they lunged for their guns.

With brutal force, Sarah shoved. The table shot forward, the corner clipping Meth Diet just below the chin, indenting his throat. The other edge smacked skinny guy number one, Pete, in the chest, stunning him. When the table shot forward almost three feet, the guns dropped off the edge on Sarah's side.

But she wasn't interested in the guns. Too much noise.

The second the table connected with both men, she pulled her feet in, jumped from the couch, and hopped around Pete. While Meth Diet held his throat and tried to breathe again, Sarah pulled the broken TV off its stand and let it fall on top of Pete. The piece of wood still sticking out of the front of the TV landed squarely on the top of Pete's head. He grunted under the weight of the old TV but didn't have the strength to push it off.

Meth Diet took a large squeaky breath as Sarah kicked Pete in the ribs to weaken his resolve further. Then Meth Diet did the unexpected. He dove onto the coffee table, his hands dangling on the other side in search of a weapon.

With no choice left, Sarah pulled her own gun from the back of her jeans and fired at Meth Diet. The report echoed off Parkman's apartment walls, deafening her briefly. She kept the pressure on her finger in case another shot was needed.

A small hole had formed on the side of Meth's neck, and a river of dark blood pooled onto the coffee table. His body relaxed and dangled loosely.

Shit, where did I learn this stuff?

She hadn't wanted to kill them. Breaking their legs would've been enough, but they hadn't left her much choice.

Meth Diet jerked once more as his body succumbed to death. A moment later, he stopped moving forever.

She lifted the old boxy TV enough to roll it off Pete's face. He didn't look like he was breathing.

What the hell?

She bent to check for a pulse.

"Shit."

When the TV had fallen on his face, the piece of wood had punched into his throat. The weight of Parkman's TV did the rest. His grunt had been his last breath.

"Why do they always pick the wrong option?" she asked out loud.

With her gun back in her pants, she ran for the door. At the peephole, she looked out into the hallway to see if anyone had been alerted by the gunshot. Then she locked the thumb latch deadbolt and turned around.

The bedroom appeared to be nothing glamorous. Usual bedroom stuff. The office was interesting. Parkman's desk was ruined from the ransacking. Someone had taken a knife and carved the top of the wood to shit. Posters on the walls were all torn, some still stuck on the wall, faces grotesquely skewed with chicken blood smeared across them.

A locked filing cabinet had been wrenched open, files pulled out and torn to shreds on the floor.

Glass crunched underfoot. When she looked down, her own face stared back from a photo. She picked it up. The frame was broken, but it was a picture of her, Parkman, Dolan, and Esmerelda at the hospital after Parkman had saved her from a man named Armond Stuart, whom she later chased to Hungary then Italy. The image brought it all back. The days when Parkman was her friend.

Italy. The crucifix. The crypt.

What was it about the memory of Parkman on a crucifix that bothered her so much? She remembered Parkman as a friend, but the image in her head of the night she was shot was irrefutable. His gun was out. He fired. The bullet hit her in the head. He tried to kill her. There was no going back. Parkman was her mortal enemy.

She stared at Dolan and Esmerelda a little longer. If only they were still around. She cried, longing to see them, talk with Dolan, laugh with Esmerelda. They had been good people, taken from this world by men like the two in Parkman's living room. How many good people had to die for society to wake up and change its antiquated laws?

She couldn't fix the world. She couldn't save everybody

from themselves. But for every bit of good she did, there was change. For every bit, there was less bad. Altering the seesaw to her side had always been her agenda, bit by bit. At least since Vivian started talking to her all those years ago. Where had that inner drive gone? When she almost died in Italy? She had nearly died several times. Why was the last one any different?

Then it came back. Because of her love for Aaron and the internal clock, the need, the want to settle down, have a normal life and have kids.

She let the picture fall from her grasp, wiped her eyes, and took a deep breath. Would she really want to bring children into this world? Into a world where men like the two lying dead in Parkman's living room existed?

Would she deny the gift of being able to receive messages from her dead sister and her work saving lives?

No, not anymore.

Her purpose, her path, had been chosen. Talk of quitting was the only thing she would quit.

She turned to leave Parkman's office. A metallic noise stopped her. She put her back to the wall and pulled her gun out slowly, listening for the sound again.

Someone tried the door handle.

What now?

Sarah edged into the hall, gun first, barrel parallel with the floor.

The door handle twisted again until whoever was on the other side realized it was locked.

Then came a soft knocking from the corridor.

"Hey, guys. It's me, Derek."

Derek? Who the hell was Derek? Probably someone

Violeta sent to help clean *her* body up.

She moved closer to the door, unlocked the deadbolt, and got ready.

The door opened slowly. Just as it was almost completely open, Derek started inside, and Sarah dove at the door with her shoulder. Derek, caught unaware, got jammed between the door and its frame. Stunned by the unexpected blow, he stood long enough for Sarah to smash the door into him again.

Without looking to see if he was incapacitated or not, she ran a third time at the door. He had moved back after the second blow, but his face hadn't cleared yet. The edge of the door smashed into his cheek, knocking the other cheek into the door frame with such force that his eyes rolled back in his head, and he dropped to the floor like a heavy lump of wet mud.

She opened the door and peeked down the empty hall. She pulled Derek's dead weight into the apartment.

Once he was lying beside the two dead skinny guys, she touched her temple gingerly.

"You fucking three," she whispered, "have given me a headache. Damn, this one is really going to hurt."

She headed for the bathroom, hoping Parkman had some pain reliever in his medicine cabinet.

How many more people did Violeta have working for her? Would more show up? Were they waiting for Parkman as friends or foes?

The answers to all her questions lie with Violeta.

After finding a bottle of 400mg-strength Advil, she downed three and walked back to the living room.

Sarah stepped over Derek's unconscious form and found

Pete's cell phone next to him.

She hit redial.

A woman answered. "Are you finished with her yet? Come on, tell me, was it deliciously fun?"

Sarah caught her breath. Was this woman for real?

"Are you there?" the woman asked, her tone turning hostile.

"Your two meth addicts are dead. They're on Parkman's living room floor. Derek, the other man you sent over, is also out of commission. I'm coming for you, Violeta Payne, and I'm really fucking pissed."

She threw the phone against the wall, where it broke into pieces.

Chapter 32

AFTER ARRIVING AT THE clinic, Tam looked at herself in the rearview mirror of the Mustang GT her mother had bought her six months ago. She wiped her tears away, grabbed a Kleenex, and spit on it. She used the saliva to clean off some of the dried blood around the cut on her cheek.

With one last look at herself in the mirror, Tam got out, locked the car, and headed toward the main doors of the Reed Clinic, where her father was recently admitted. At least, that's what her mother had said. In minutes, she would be sure.

How could her mother expect her to drive to Parkman's apartment and kill another human being? What had happened that pushed her mother so far? She had never been this out of control.

Ever since Tam's dad had walked away, nothing had been the same. The level of violence had increased. The screaming, the drinking, and the irrational decisions turned her mother into everything Tam hated.

Maybe her father could help pull things back together.

The sun had gone down, but the air was still charged from the day's heat. A chill ran down her back at the thought of what Sarah Roberts was going through at that very moment with those two horrible men. Poor Sarah. She had been accidentally shot and then came home to Santa Rosa to her friend's apartment, only to be given to the junkies as a sexual treat. Tam didn't understand anything her mother was doing anymore.

At the clinic's front desk, a woman in her fifties, with graying hair and high cheekbones, hovered over a computer screen, one hand typing something.

"Excuse me," Tam said softly so as not to startle her.

Without looking up, the woman said, "Can I help you?"

"I'm looking for my father, Oliver Payne. I understand he was admitted here tonight."

The woman stopped typing and met Tam's gaze. "Oliver Payne is your father?"

Tam nodded. The expression on the woman's face looked as if she was surprised like Oliver had told her he was childless or something.

She pointed. "Down that hall, by the back exit, room 106."

"Thank you," Tam said as she started down the hall.

She felt the eyes of the woman on her back the entire way. Just before the door to 106, Tam glanced over her shoulder quickly and caught her still staring.

Weird.

Tam knocked on the door. Someone shuffled about behind the door. Then more shuffling. She knocked again.

"Just a second." Her father's voice.

Warmth coursed through her, but also fear of what he was now. What would life be like for him? Could her mother really have had anything to do with what happened to him? Even though she denied it in her flamboyant style, something told Tam she was in on it somehow.

"Come in."

Tam turned the knob and opened the door. Her father lay on a bed, a lamp on either side of the bed illuminating his damaged face. She left the door open wide and stepped closer to the bed.

"Oh, Daddy, what happened?"

"What happened to your cheek?" he asked.

"It's nothing," Tam said, self-consciously holding a hand over it.

A nurse stood by his side, a clipboard in her hand.

"I didn't expect you here," Oliver's voice was weak, reserved. "I thought your mother was coming."

"I think she's on her way, but I wanted to get to you first because she's done some horrible things—" Her voice caught in her throat.

"Come come, now, Tam. Move closer."

Tam shuddered with sobs and leaned into her father. A moment later, as his warm and loving arms wrapped around her, she cried uncontrollably, her body wracked with grief.

"How could she, Daddy? How could Mom be so mean?"

He pushed her up. "Come on, Tam. Tell me what you're talking about, okay, honey."

Tam wiped at her eyes, now swollen from all the tears.

"Mom hired a detective to find you in Greece."

"I know about that, honey."

"She said you could never leave her. She wouldn't allow it."

"Here I am," he said.

"Then she tried to get that private detective in trouble and tried to make me do her dirty work."

"What?" His voice took on new interest. Like he wasn't tired or lethargic anymore. "Really?"

"The man's name is Parkman. After he found you, he refused to do more. He quit working for her. So she went after him and his friend, a girl named Sarah Roberts."

"What has she done?" he asked.

The nurse set her clipboard down and leaned closer, but Tam didn't care anymore. Someone needed to know what her mother was doing.

"She hired two scary men to hurt Sarah. They're in Parkman's apartment right now doing horrible, disgusting things to her. Mom just ordered me to go to that apartment, and she wanted me to …" Her throat closed again with emotion. She swallowed and took a deep breath.

"She wanted you to what?"

"She told me to go and kill Sarah Roberts. She said that Sarah wouldn't be able to use her plumbing down there for some time." Tam gestured to her pubic area. "How could she hurt another person like that? And how could my own mom ask me to *kill* someone?"

"I know, honey. Come here."

He opened his arms, and Tam fell into them again. More tears worked down her cheeks, stinging in the cut, wetting her father's shirt.

The closet door opened behind her. She bolted up, thinking her mother had been listening in. Two burly men stepped out from hiding.

"What's this?" Tam asked, suddenly frightened. She looked at her dad as she straightened up. "Who are they?"

"Those two men work for the Santa Rosa Police Department."

"What's going on, Dad?"

"It's a long story and one I want to tell you, but first, I think these men will want to hear more of what your mom has been doing since I've been away."

Tam looked at the two men. They stepped closer, peaceful, calm expressions on both their faces.

"Can you tell us what's happening right now at this man's apartment?"

Tam laid it all out for them, covering as many details as possible, and ended with Parkman's home address. One man spoke directly to her while the other wrote furiously onto a small pad of paper he had produced from a back pocket.

"Did she do this to your face?" the officer asked.

Tam nodded.

"Okay, we're going to step outside for a moment, let you two get reacquainted. I have to call this in. We need to have officers respond to this address to see what's going on. Everyone okay with that?"

"What happens if Violeta shows up here?" Oliver asked.

"We'll be right outside."

They turned to go. Tam's stomach twisted with nausea.

Her mother was due at any second.

***

Violeta got Martin to pull the car up to the front entrance

of the Reed Clinic.

She had just spoken with Sarah Roberts, who was proving to be quite a formidable young woman.

We'll see how tough you are when I've got your parents tied up in their basement being whipped with my cane.

"Please wait outside the front doors, Martin. I can handle this on my own."

"Yes, ma'am."

Violeta opened the back door, set the silver cane down first, and pushed herself up as if she needed the cane for support. Before closing the door, she leaned back in. "Be ready if I come out fast."

"Of course, ma'am."

She shut the door and started inside. At the reception desk, a lone woman sat behind the large wooden counter, typing into a computer.

Probably playing solitaire. Lazy sod.

"Ahem," Violeta cleared her throat loud enough to echo off the corridor to her left. "Oliver Payne, please."

The woman didn't look up. She performed an exaggerated display of looking for Oliver, then announced, "Oliver Payne is in room 106 at the end of the hall on the right."

Without thanking her, Violeta turned and started down the hall, clacking her cane as she went.

When she was done with Oliver, the rest of the evening would be a special feature called Killing Sarah. The rest of the evening would be devoted to that endeavor. Everything Violeta did for the rest of the night would be to kill Sarah mentally, emotionally, and then finally, physically. After all the trouble Sarah had caused her, she deserved to perish horribly. Violeta had never considered herself a murderer, but times had changed. If what Sarah said was accurate, her ex-cons were dead, and her bodyguard Derek was probably dead, too. Sarah had single-handedly taken out her two very useful skinny ex-cons. She had plans for them to reform her daughter. Tam was supposed to spend the next month tied up in their apartment, but now Sarah Roberts had fucked that all up.

Violeta would have to go find some other wretched human beings to violate her daughter into submissiveness now.

The name Sarah Roberts became synonymous with a vile, putrid hate. Every time Sarah's name rang through her head, she wanted to spit, but she controlled herself. She was a lady and wouldn't spit because of that little whore.

Well, maybe I will spit ... on her corpse.

Voices emanated from one of the rooms ahead. She thought she heard someone crying. Her step faltered. Was this a trap? Should she have brought Martin with her?

But then she reasoned that she had done nothing wrong. All she did was pay the good Greek police to help escort her wounded husband back home for proper care. If anyone did anything illegal, it was Elias Kostas, not her. His word against hers. She would win as she always did.

She walked with more confidence. Let them try to arrest her. She'd be out by the morning, and lawsuits against the Santa Rosa Police Department would be filed by the afternoon. They had enough trouble in Santa Rosa with officers using excessive force recently. A thirteen-year-old boy had been shot in the street, apparently for holding a replica AK-47 in his hands. The police department of Santa

Rosa didn't need any more negative press at the moment.

As she passed door number 105, she could've sworn she heard her daughter's voice.

She stopped in the hall and listened four feet from the open door of room 106.

It was Tam. Tam Rood, the traitor, the turncoat. Tam Rood, the fucking doormat. The rules had been reinforced over and over. Once Tam earned her place and her right to be a part of the family, at eighteen years of age, she could legally change her name and become Tamara Payne. But now, she would never earn it. Forever, she would be an enemy of the Payne family, not a member. Forever, she would be a doormat, and Violeta would be the one to walk on her.

Tam said something about how her mother had ordered her to go to Parkman's apartment and kill Sarah Roberts.

How could she implicate me this way?

Violeta felt the color drain from her face.

Tam would die for this. There was no other way in Violeta's world. The brutal truth of it sunk in, and just when Violeta's resolve would expect to be weakened, the knowledge of Tam dying emboldened her.

A man spoke. He sounded official. He said he had to call this in and send officers to respond to Parkman's address. Tam was talking to the police, telling them everything.

Footsteps approached from inside the room. They were coming.

She turned her face away, leaned on the cane, and wobbled a step. Her arm shot out as she used the wall for support.

Her playacting would work in a clinic like this one.

Unless the authorities had circulated a photo of her, which she doubted as Tam was just now spilling the beans.

Five feet back, two sets of footfalls gained on her. Then the men passed her as she wobbled on her cane for another step. They didn't look back once.

She continued up the hall, aiming for the front entrance, and Martin dutifully waited in the car.

It was over. It was truly over. She would've never thought Tam would tell the police anything.

Violeta had to lock down and go into protection mode. Especially now that Sarah was in town and looking for her as well.

An hour ago, she thought she had everything sewn up. But her plan was unraveling like white sand through her palms with every word out of Tam's mouth.

As she stepped into the warm night, she decided then and there that she would hurt Tam in the most brutal way possible before killing her. Betrayal was the most heinous crime. Acid in the face would be too nice. Tam would just be ugly. A knife in the vagina might do the trick. Ruin her in the worst way possible. Use the tip of the knife to pull each eye out, then let her live blind, ugly, and unfuckable.

Violeta smiled as her thoughts grounded her. Tam Rood would learn just how far she had gone.

Once safely inside the car, she ordered Martin to drive.

He pulled out slowly to not attract attention.

"Take me to Sarah Robert's parents' house. I think it's time we have a chat." She gave him the address on Olivet Road. "Do you know what just happened in there?"

"No, ma'am. I was in the car."

"I've lost my daughter."

Martin drove the car and stayed silent.

"You see, Martin, you either destruct or construct. Be constructive in a relationship or destructive and break it down. Be responsible or irresponsible. It's quite easy to understand, really. You go left or right, up or down. There are only two ways about it, and Tam has chosen a way that is opposite to my own. Hence, she's not with me. I've lost her. Absolutely and completely."

She watched the houses flash by, some dark, some with lighted windows.

"Just like these houses," she added. "In some, a light is on. In others, the lights are off. Tam is like the others now. Her light is off. She's closed to me. It's over." She turned forward and looked at Martin's eyes in the mirror. "From now on, she is Tam Rood only. She is not Tam Rood, my daughter. She will never take my name. She will never be Tamara Payne. Understood?"

"Yes, ma'am."

Martin drove through the darkened streets of Santa Rosa while Violeta got increasingly sick to her stomach for what she had to do.

To her, someone was either alive or dead. Being alive meant regeneration, creating, beautifying. Dead meant rotting. That was it. There was simply nothing left for Tam to do but rot and decay. How could her own daughter be of a such duplicitous character to betray her? Violeta tried to suppress her rage by clenching and unclenching her fists. Tam's insidious cunning, trickery, and deceit would come back to haunt her. Violeta wouldn't take it lying down. Even if she ended up in prison, there were ways to reach out and punish those who put her there.

Sarah Roberts had to be added to that list. If Violeta was going down for something, it was Sarah's fault, too. Why did she have to come back to Santa Rosa? If Sarah weren't here, then her ex-cons would've got the bugs at Parkman's and left. She would've dealt with Oliver, got her new deal next week, and lived on, leading a happy life.

But Sarah came back, just like the fucking cat. How many lives did this Sarah Roberts have? It angered her that Tam had screwed up. Sending Tam to Toronto was a lesson she needed to learn. In the end, everything was Sarah's fault. She probably even faked getting shot so the shooter, Tam, would feel terrible for having hit her when it was only meant as a warning shot.

Sarah Roberts. Her new enemy. Her *only* enemy now.

And she was eight minutes away from Caleb and Amelia's house.

Won't they be surprised when they meet her?

They'll be more surprised that they have to pay the price for their daughter's actions.

***

When the two police officers left, Tam turned back to her father and examined the length of his body.

"Is it true?" she asked. "Are you paralyzed?"

Her father and the nurse exchanged a knowing glance. They knew something but weren't saying it. It was probably due to her age, and they thought they had to be delicate.

"Go ahead," Tam said. "Tell me what happened. Don't hold back. I'll be eighteen before Christmas. After all I've been through with my mother, you don't think I can handle what you have to say?"

Her father patted the bed. "Come sit down."

Tam settled in beside him. The nurse sat in a chair in the corner by a little table and opened a magazine.

"What I'm about to tell you might hurt your heart."

"If it's bad and it's about Mom, I'll be okay." Tam shook her head. "I'm so done with her. I'll move out before I do her bidding anymore."

Oliver clasped his hands together across his stomach. "My nurse," he nodded at the woman with the magazine, "is actually a Greek police officer named Athina. She escorted me back here and met with the two officers who were hiding in the closet because of some of the things your mother has done."

"I had figured that when they jumped out of the closet." She smiled at him and realized it was the first real smile on her face in months. "Go to any room in this clinic. I guarantee you won't find random cops hanging out in closets."

The Greek cop/nurse giggled in the corner, her eyes still on the magazine.

Oliver lifted his legs. "I'm fine, look. See, no pain. No paralysis. But we can't let your mother know until this is over. The Reed Clinic graciously allowed us to borrow this room until the Santa Rosa Police investigation is over."

"What has Mom done?"

"She hired the detective to find me."

Tam nodded. "Yeah, Parkman. I know that."

"Next, she told the local Greek police captain, Athina's boss, that I had done terrible things to you and that I had fled the country to escape justice. Since I was in the eurozone for more than three months, they picked me up."

"So she lied."

"Exactly. But that part isn't the issue. She then offered the Greek police captain money to hurt me."

"Is that what happened to your face?"

"Your mother asked Kostas to paralyze me."

"I knew it. When she told me earlier tonight that you were back and in this clinic, I asked if she had anything to do with it, and she lied to me."

"Kostas told her he would go through with it, essentially, he would break the law, so this could happen." He swept his arms around the room, pointing at Athina. "As soon as your mother comes here and sees I'm not paralyzed, we'll have her on tape, we have the money she sent to Greece as evidence, and we'll have everything for several different charges."

"What if she doesn't come here?"

"Oh, she will. She wouldn't miss this for the world. Athina is here to protect me from her or her bodyguards, and those two cops will be the arresting officers. Athina will give them her statement, and then she heads back to Greece tomorrow."

"But something isn't right. Mom's too smart to walk into a trap." Tam looked at the bedside clock. "And she should have been here by now." She looked into her father's eyes. "That means she could only be one place."

"Where, baby Tammy? Where would your mom go?"

"To Caleb's house on Olivet Road."

The nurse set the magazine aside and got up. She walked over and stood beside Oliver.

"Who is Caleb?" her father asked.

"Caleb and Amelia Roberts. They're Sarah's parents, the girl they're hurting at Parkman's apartment."

"Why would she go there?"

"Last resort." Tam got up and started walking in a circle. "Parkman's apartment is not an option. Coming here is done. She would've been here by now. The only place left is the Roberts's house." She stopped walking, turned, and faced them. "If this is all falling apart around her, she has lost you, she has lost me, and she would know that by now as I haven't shown up to kill Sarah as she ordered me to do. She will have to apply more pressure somehow. The only place left would be the Roberts's house, or give up. And Mom won't give up."

"We'll tell the cops when they come back. Maybe they could send an officer over to warn these people."

"It'll be too late, and it'll be my fault."

"Your fault? Why's that?"

"I found them for her. I gave her the address. I was trying to regain my honor with her. She told me I had to." Her voice was rising steadily. "It's not my fault. I didn't ask for this. Why would she hurt me like this? What have I done wrong? She's my *mother*. Shouldn't she—"

"Shhh," her father consoled. "It's okay, Tammy. We'll work it out."

She panted for a moment, staring at them. They really didn't know who Violeta Payne had become. They thought police officers would magically drop out of closets and cruisers and arrest all the dastardly people, and all would be well in the world. Would the world be well for Sarah Roberts ever again? How about Sarah's parents when Martin and her mother worked them over, maybe even killed them?

Everything fell squarely on her shoulders. If her mother

had taught her one thing, it was owning what she did and fixing it if she screwed up.

She had found the Roberts's home address. She had given it to the vile witch her mother had become. Tam and Tam alone had sentenced Sarah's parents to an unfair and undeserved fate, all because she wanted to *serve* her mother.

That meant Tam had to fix it.

She turned and headed for the door.

"Tammy! Wait!"

"No." She turned back at the door and recited the Roberts's address on Olivet Road. "Tell them to bring everything they've got available. I think mom's going to kill those people."

Tam ran for her Mustang, hoping she could stop what she had started, and wondered if she could live with the worst-case scenario.

If those people were badly hurt for no reason, or worse, killed, then Tam would only be able to fix something of that magnitude one way.

By killing her mother and then herself.

Chapter 33

Detective Joffrey turned onto Parkman's street. The car moved along slowly as they watched for a spot to park.

"From here," Parkman said, happy to be home, "we can call Sarah's parents to see if they've heard from her. I can get changed and take a shower if we have time. There are drinks in the fridge if you guys need anything."

"It feels like we've been in the car longer than on the plane," Aaron said from the back seat.

They passed a large vehicle that resembled an ambulance parked on the side of the road.

"That's a weird-looking thing," Aaron said.

Joffrey pulled in and parked seven cars up from the cross between an ambulance and a paddy wagon.

"Okay, guys," Joffrey said. "Watch your backs. Let me go first. I'm the only one with a piece. We have no idea where Sarah is or what Violeta has planned. That woman may even have Parkman's place under surveillance."

"Let's get in and out in thirty minutes," Parkman said. "We need to get to Violeta's, and we'll probably want to meet up with Sarah's parents to see how they're doing with Sarah still missing. That work for you guys?"

Joffrey said, "I think we should go to the local police station here in Santa Rosa and let them in on what we're doing here. Maybe they'll escort us to Violeta's front door. Especially if we find any listening devices in your apartment."

Without answering Joffrey, Parkman got out of the car, and the other two men followed.

At the side door of the apartment building, the trio entered and made their way up to Parkman's apartment. He pulled his keys, then stopped. The door had marks and scratches and was slightly dented inward.

"Oh shit," he whispered. "Someone's been here since I left." He stepped back and pointed at the door, so Joffrey and Aaron could see. "That's new. Look how the door is dented in a bit here and here."

Joffrey put a finger to his lips for silence. He tried the door handle. The latch wasn't engaged. The door slid open on its own.

All three of them stepped back behind the wall for cover.

Joffrey motioned that he would enter first as he withdrew his sidearm. He held up three fingers and lowered them one at a time. When the last one dropped, he faced the door and kicked it all the way open.

"Police!" he shouted. "We're coming in."

Parkman followed as Joffrey cleared the kitchen, Aaron close behind, his hands up, fingers flexing.

"Oh shit," Joffrey said at the far end of the kitchen.

"What?" Parkman asked.

Joffrey ran back through the kitchen. On his way by Parkman, he said, "Let's make sure the place is clear first."

He moved down the hall toward the bedrooms.

Parkman, followed by Aaron, stepped through the kitchen and turned to look at what Joffrey had seen.

"Oh, shit is right," Aaron said.

Three men were sprawled out on the carpeted floor. One was wide-eyed with a dead stare, blood caking the side of his neck from what looked like a bullet hole. The other one was just as skinny and also just as dead. Part of his lower jaw was broken, and his neck seemed the wrong shape and size for normal breathing.

The third guy was still alive, breathing, chest rising and falling slowly. His head was bloody on both sides. Maybe his jaw was broken, too.

"That third guy is going to need medics right away," Aaron said.

"Clear," Joffrey shouted from down the hall.

He entered the living room and stopped beside Parkman.

"What the hell happened here?" Joffrey asked.

"No idea," Parkman said in a daze.

"Recognize any of them?"

"Yeah. The guy who is still breathing. His name's Derek. Don't have a last name. Works for Violeta. This may be where they've been dumping bodies, so the police come calling on me."

"Let's call this in right away. You've been in Toronto and with me. Perfect alibi." Joffrey patted Parkman on the back. "Nothing to worry about."

Parkman pulled out his cell phone. "Yeah, but I'm gonna have to move now. Can't live here after this shit—"

"Freeze!" someone shouted from behind them.

Parkman recoiled as if slapped. His cell phone went airborne as he pulled it from his pocket. The phone hit the couch, bounced, and landed beside Derek's inert form.

Joffrey lifted his arms and tried to turn around.

"I said, *freeze*. Santa Rosa Police. Don't move."

They came through the kitchen behind Joffrey, Parkman, and Aaron. Without looking back, Parkman counted two, possibly three officers.

"We were told there would be three men here harassing a girl, and look what we find when we walk in. Three men who appear to be ready to leave."

The officers were right behind them now, but Parkman was sure they hadn't seen the bodies yet.

"I'm a police officer," Joffrey said. "From Toronto. We were just about to call you guys."

"Bullshit. Keep your hands up."

Parkman's left wrist was pulled down, then his right. Ties were clipped on his wrists. They did the same to Aaron, then Joffrey.

The cop behind Parkman pulled him back, which opened a line of sight to the bodies on the living room floor.

There were three Santa Rosa officers standing in Parkman's dining room. Their jaws dropped at the same time. The youngest one's face drained of blood.

"Oh, man, are you three in for a long night. Better call homicide."

Chapter 34

VIOLETA WAITED PATIENTLY AS Martin pulled to the curb three houses down from the Roberts's residence. It was fully dark now, with no sign of the day's sun on the horizon. Only its heat remained. Would she see another sunrise from her bedroom or the back deck? Or would it be from inside a jail cell?

Violeta set her purse on the floor of the car and leaned forward.

"This is something I have to do on my own, Martin. It won't be dangerous. At least, I don't think so. That's why I want you to leave and return after an hour. Go get something to eat, and have dinner. But before you depart, I want your gun, just in case."

"Are you sure you don't want me waiting out here?"

"No. It won't be dangerous. But if someone gets hostile, I would like a little protection. If I leave the premises earlier than an hour, I'll call you. But for now, I want your gun, and I want you clear of this place."

"Yes, ma'am."

He reached inside his jacket and then handed back his piece, grip first.

"I'm leaving my purse in the back. Keep the car locked."

"Of course."

She slid along the seat, slipped the gun into the pocket of her small jacket, grabbed her walking cane, and opened the door.

As soon as she closed the door, Martin drove off. She knew he would be back in an hour. She could count on him.

Two cars whooshed by, the wind cooling her. She needed fresh air, a breeze. In the back of the car, the more she thought about what Tam had done, the sicker her insides got. But Violeta was smart. She would play this out and, as an upstanding member of the community, she would lobby this fiasco until it disappeared. The public, a jury of her peers, would take her side if it ever came to that. She could overcome this, and she was up to the challenge.

Violeta had been the one trampled on. Her husband walked out on her. She was trying to raise a daughter on her own. No one could prove she told Tam to kill anyone. Certainly not her bodyguards, who wouldn't dare testify against her. They'd be complicit in a hundred different ways.

Another car whooshed by. It made her smile with delight. Everything would work out for the better. Tam was a seventeen-year-old sniveling, whining child. And when everything had calmed down, that child would be disciplined. Even if it took years, discipline wasn't dictated by age. A twenty-five-year-old Tam Rood could still be raped and beaten over and over. And who would come to the hospital room to save her and pay her medical bills? Her mother, because that's what moms do. They take care of their babies. Violeta would exact her revenge, torture her daughter, and come out looking like the hero by saving her decrepit ass every time.

"Oh, Tam, am I ever going to take care of you for this," she whispered to the wind.

She took a step forward, then another, until the Roberts's house was on her left.

She was in charge. This was her gig. Even if things seemed off-kilter, she was the one who could even it up. Only her. No one else had her tenacity, her ability to hold even the most tenuous piece of wool together in the crazy world she wove.

And people like Sarah's parents needed a little reminder of what discipline was. Sarah had hurt the cause. Sarah had disrupted the order of things. With the police heading to Parkman's apartment to find dead bodies, it would be Sarah who got arrested for murder, not Violeta. That part was easy to understand. How could Violeta control what two ex-cons did with their life? Actually, Violeta was suddenly sure she didn't even know any ex-cons. What could Tam possibly be talking about? She only knew a man named Parkman because he worked for her once. He had done a wonderful job in finding her lost husband, Oliver. Concerning her involvement, the rest is all filled with doubt. Reasonable doubt. The kind a jury would have difficulty with.

That meant Violeta would remain free regardless of people like Sarah Roberts and Tam Rood, two enemies who would get theirs in short order.

Violeta headed up the driveway of Caleb and Amelia Roberts's house, the knife in the tip of her cane securely hidden, the gun with at least six bullets in it, ready and willing.

Did it ever feel good to be in control again?

She couldn't wait to see the look in Sarah's parents' eyes when she told them why she was there and why she had to hurt them so badly.

"This is going to be delightful."

She rang the doorbell.

Chapter 35

OUT ON THE STREET, which the Santa Rosa Police Department had blocked off with vehicles, Parkman and Joffrey stood with one of the officers in charge, who had introduced himself as Gibbons. Aaron sat in a police cruiser two cars over, watching through the side window.

"Okay, you already explained how you came upon the bodies." Gibbons had a nasty cleft palate. Someone had done a hack job on his upper lip, and it seems he never returned to the plastic surgeon. The top of his mouth stayed open in the shape of the top part a small tent, exposing yellow teeth stained years ago by a bad smoking habit. As he had taken notes, he held a half-used cigarette between two fingers, the heater end extinguished. Parkman had asked about the cancer stick and was told the best way to quit was to suck on a dead cigarette. It made Parkman yearn for a toothpick.

"Tell me again what you think happened here," Gibbons

said.

"Your officers mentioned a woman was supposed to be in my apartment?" Parkman asked.

"What if they did? I can't tell you what they think they know or don't know."

Frustrated, Parkman said, "This is the work of a woman trying to defend herself."

"Now you're saying some woman did this?"

"Yes, Sarah Roberts. She would've come here looking for me."

Gibbons guffawed, then calmed to a chuckle. "You think a woman killed two men, smashed that big guy's face in the front door, and then just walked away."

"Absolutely. Sarah is quite capable."

"Whoa, I'd like to meet this woman."

"Look," Joffrey stepped closer. "This is serious."

The look on Gibbons's face changed. He clenched his jaws so tight the muscles on his cheeks stuck out. "You think I don't take my job seriously?"

"Right now, I don't." Joffrey stood his ground. "I'm with the Toronto Police Department and—"

"Long way from home," Gibbons cut in.

"There was an incident where Sarah was shot earlier this week. She was admitted to a hospital, and we think she's been taken here, to Santa Rosa, by Violeta Payne."

"This Sarah Roberts. Is that the same woman you spoke of a moment ago? You think she did all that," he gestured with his arm toward the building, "in your apartment with a gunshot wound after leaving an emergency room in a hospital on the other side of the country under suspicious circumstances?"

"You don't know Sarah," Parkman said, gritting his teeth.

"Okay, say you're right. After I take you three to separate holding cells for the night, or at least until I can sort this all out, what's her next play? Where're more bodies going to be piling up?"

"Two places need to be checked out," Parkman said. "Violeta Payne's home and the home of Sarah's parents on Olivet Road. She may have gone home to assure her parents she's okay."

"Hey, boss." One of the three officers who had originally entered Parkman's apartment held up a cell phone. "You're going to want to take this."

Gibbons looked over his shoulder, then back at Parkman and Joffrey.

"Don't go anywhere."

He walked over and took the phone. From where Parkman was, he couldn't hear him well enough to listen in.

Oh, Sarah, where are you?

This was a royal cluster fuck. He didn't know for sure if Sarah was even in Santa Rosa. Violeta could have wanted rid of those ex-cons and left them in his apartment for him to deal with. It was Aaron who had felt that it was Sarah's handiwork.

An ambulance pulled away with Derek, the lone survivor of the apartment carnage, its red lights blinding Parkman momentarily.

Ambulance.

He looked down at Joffrey's car parked on the side of the road and then followed the line of cars behind it.

The modified ambulance was gone.

"Joffrey, remember that large truck ambulance thing we

passed coming in?"

Joffrey turned that way, his eyes searching. "Yeah."

"It's gone."

"So." He looked back at Parkman.

"That was Sarah. She would've stolen an ambulance and left the Toronto hospital. She hates hospitals. I told her about Violeta and Santa Rosa before she got shot. She would've had enough time to drive here from Toronto."

"Crossing the border in a stolen ambulance?"

"Look, I haven't got it all figured out. But that was Sarah. I'm so sure I'm right, I can smell it."

Gibbons walked back over. "Okay, that phone call was a little game-changer."

"What happened?" Parkman leaned in, eager to hear if it was about Sarah.

"Officer," Gibbons motioned for a cop standing a few feet away. "Release their wrist ties."

The cop stepped behind them and cut them off.

"That was Oliver Payne at the Reed Clinic, where he has been waiting for his wife, Violeta Payne, for over an hour. They were the ones who alerted us that those guys," he pointed up at the building again, "who we found in your apartment, were there to work a girl over. He understood the girl's name is Sarah Roberts."

Parkman gasped and rubbed his face. He could sure use a toothpick.

"Oliver's daughter explained some of what her mother, Violeta, has been up to, and he thinks they're all heading over to Sarah's parents'. At least, that's where his daughter is headed. Two of my officers just confirmed that they were waiting for Violeta with Oliver as his ex-wife is a suspect in another crime."

"That's what we've been trying to tell you," Joffrey said.

"Okay, give me five minutes. I'll round up a couple of officers, and we'll all go over and make sure everything is okay. When we're done there, we'll go downtown because I want a written statement from all of you."

"Agreed," Joffrey said.

"But hurry," Parkman added.

While he waited, Parkman leaned on a cruiser and thought about what Sarah had told him when they met in Toronto. He thought about all that life had thrown her way. All the violence and killing, and he realized that maybe she was right. Maybe she should quit. After this, if they all made it through the night, he would offer his blessing. He would tell her he thought she should stop what she was doing and go live a peaceful life with Aaron.

Part of the reason was selfishness.

He couldn't take much more of the pain Sarah had to go through with the life she had chosen.

He loved her too much.

Chapter 36

"Coming," a man yelled from inside the house.

Violeta forced a pleasant smile. The door opened, and an attractive American male specimen stood under the inside light of the front foyer. The smell of something delicious cooking wafted out, reminding Violeta that she hadn't eaten since that morning.

"Good evening," she said. "Wow, does that ever smell good. What are you cooking up this evening?"

"Can I help you?" Caleb asked.

Straight to business. She liked that in a man. Maybe Sarah got her balls from this guy. Violeta reminded herself to watch him. If anyone tried any hero stuff, it would be a man like Caleb. That meant he needed to be hurt first. Or killed first if necessary.

"I'm sorry, I should've introduced myself. Sarah told me to pop by anytime when she was in town. I just thought—"

"You know Sarah? How do you know my daughter?"

Interrupting her only added to his eventual torture. Play nice, die fast. Disrespect her, and death becomes an excruciating agony where the only release is … death.

"Yes, Sarah and I go back to a year ago. She helped me with a little matter, and I told her I wanted to repay her somehow."

"Let me guess. She wouldn't take any form of repayment?" Caleb asked.

"Who is it, honey?" Amelia shouted from behind him.

Caleb hollered back over his shoulder. "A friend of Sarah's."

"Be polite. Invite them in at least."

Caleb stepped aside and held the door. Violeta read the disinterest on his face with having to deal with one of Sarah's friends. Or maybe he just didn't like uninvited guests.

She walked over the threshold, feeling every bit a vampire who needed an invitation into the home of the people she would consume. The screen door closed with a slap behind her.

"Since Sarah won't take my offer, I wondered if I could leave it behind with you two."

"No, that won't work," Caleb said. "Sarah won't take it from us on your behalf as much as she wouldn't from you."

"I thought you'd say that. You see, I, too, have a daughter."

Amelia entered the front foyer, a dishtowel in her hands.

"What is that you're cooking?" Violeta asked. "Smells wonderful."

"I'm making paella tonight," Amelia said. She had aged into a beautiful woman. The kind Violeta had seen in magazines offering life insurance plans for people about her age. "I have to get back to the stove, but I have a quick second. What's this all about?"

"Well, my husband left me four months ago," Violeta said, wiping at the corner of her eye as if she was about to cry. "He traveled to Europe to escape justice because of what he had been doing to my daughter."

"Oh, that's terrible," Amelia said, turning to look at her husband. They exchanged a glance, but Violeta couldn't tell if they were still buying what she was selling. At least Caleb wasn't.

"It was Sarah who stopped the abuse." Then she set her face to a look of dismay. "Oh, I'm so sorry. How rude of me. Are you aware of what your daughter can do?"

"Yes," Caleb said. He did not look impressed. If it weren't for Amelia, Caleb probably wouldn't have invited her inside, and this meeting would have already gone to the gun stage.

"Sarah came to me a year ago," she said, hoping her lies would at least allow them to get away from the front door before she had to pull the gun out. "She told me what was happening in my home. She even went so far as to predict the time and place that another *event*," she used air quotes for that word, "would happen." She sniffled.

"Caleb, can you get her a Kleenex?"

Caleb grunted and walked off.

"Why don't you come in, and I'll get you a glass of water?"

"What I really need is a hammer."

Amelia frowned. "A hammer?" she asked tentatively.

Violeta pulled out a locket. "Inside this pretty gold locket is a picture of my husband and me on our honeymoon. I thought it appropriate if I broke it in the home of Sarah's kin. She saved my daughter's life. I would be paying homage to Sarah the only way I know how."

Caleb returned with Kleenex and handed one to Violeta. She made a display of blowing her nose and then scrunched the Kleenex up and dropped it in the pocket with the gun.

"Okay, I have to get back to the stove," Amelia said. She turned to her husband. "This won't take a moment. Caleb, go get this nice lady." She stopped and turned to Violeta. "I'm sorry we didn't get your name."

"Violeta Payne."

"Haven't we heard that name around here?"

"You might have." She told them about her business and the distribution warehouse she owned. "My husband and I have operated out of Santa Rosa for some time now."

Amelia waved her index finger. "I thought I'd heard of you." She turned back to Caleb. "Honey, I'm going back to the kitchen. Go to the toolbox in the basement and get the hammer. We're going to break a locket at the kitchen table before dinner."

"But, Amelia, aren't we—"

"Shhh." She touched his lips with her finger. "Just do it. After that, we'll eat in ten minutes and watch *Sons of Anarchy*."

Caleb looked between the two women and then headed for the stairs.

Amelia ran for the kitchen. "I can't let the paella burn. Come on up and have a seat at the table."

Violeta followed Sarah's mother to the kitchen. From outside, Violeta had thought it was a bungalow, but the house was a back split. Halfway through the living room, stairs led to the kitchen, and more stairs went above that to the bedrooms. Caleb had descended a set of stairs to the left that led to the basement. There were many benefits to this design that Violeta picked up on right away, one of them being able to survey the entire living room area from the kitchen, separated by a small white railing.

For people on their income, they had extra nice furniture. The suede sofa set belonged in a more expensive home than this one, but not everyone could have Violeta's money.

Not everyone can be like me.

She shuffled across the floor, animatedly using her cane. At the stairs, she used the railing and took her time.

If Sarah only knew where I was right now.

Violeta grinned so wide her teeth showed.

"You look happy," Amelia said. She stood over a large wok, stirring the contents with a big wooden spoon.

"Very happy." Violeta leaned on the corner of the kitchen table. "This concludes a terrible era of my life."

Footsteps on the stairs behind her announced Caleb's return. He set the hammer on the table in front of Violeta.

"Okay, it's nice to meet you and all," Caleb said, catching his breath from the stairs. "But let's do this, and then we have a dinner to get to."

You bastard.

"I'm sorry to be keeping you from your dinner. The last thing I wanted was to inconvenience you." She bowed her head and stared at the locket. She could almost feel the look Amelia just gave Caleb. "I'll be gone in less than a minute."

Caleb stepped back and leaned against the counter beside his wife as she stirred their meal.

Their last meal.

The perfect family. The nice daughter. The small humble home and home-cooked meals. They had everything and nothing. It disgusted her to no end that people like this actually thought they were happy. How could they excel in life? Where would they go from here? Making dinner, watching a TV show, and pretending to be in love? Why was Caleb coming off so angry if they were really in love? The man obviously had issues, which probably came as a result of the woman he married.

He leaned back on the counter, his hands flat. She wondered what he was up to.

She sniffled. "I need to blow my nose again," Violeta said. She reached into the pocket with the Kleenex and the gun and wrapped her hand around the grip, slipping her finger inside the trigger guard.

As she did this, Caleb moved. Suddenly she realized what he was doing.

The knife block.

His right hand was touching the knife block's base. He didn't trust her with a hammer and was ready to attack with lethal force.

Well, fuck him!

All in one motion, she withdrew the gun, aimed it between their heads at the fan above the stove, and fired before either one could scream.

Chapter 37

Sarah pulled the ambulance over about half a mile from her parents' house. It was a little bit of a walk, but she didn't want the vehicle discovered near her parents' home.

Her headache had increased, and fatigue set in to the point where she wondered if she would fall asleep if she closed her eyes for a few seconds. As a set of headlights passed, she had to squint. Driving had become a chore, which made it dangerous. She was close enough to walk now, and the two men in the back eventually had to be let out.

She placed the two guns she took from the men in Parkman's apartment in the back of her pants, handles facing outwards toward her hips, and then got out of the ambulance.

The key slipped into the lock effortlessly, making no sound whatsoever. Leaving the key in the door would allow whoever showed up to open it and let the two men out easily.

See, I still care. I've got a heart.

The walk would take five minutes or so under her present condition. Going too fast, getting her heart rate up, would only cause her migraine to pulse more than she could bear at the moment. Even with a high pain threshold, getting shot in the head was off the charts.

As soon as she got to her parents' house, she would place an anonymous call about two men in the back of a modified ambulance on Piner Road, just outside of town.

She walked on, her feet heavier with each step.

Why aren't the Advils doing anything yet?

Off in the distance, a police siren turned on. Suddenly back to full alert, Sarah turned around, trying her best to ignore the flaring pain.

The siren was coming from somewhere behind her. She increased her pace, trying to distance herself from the ambulance. About a mile back, a police car turned a corner, the lights on the roof flashing, its headlights blinking on and off, the engine revving.

She had to turn away and close her eyes. After a deep breath, she dropped down the embankment and entered the vineyard that stretched across a rolling field. It sat directly behind her parents' house. She still had a full five-minute walk to get to the house, but this way, no one would see her in the dark, and she could enter through the back door.

Less than a minute later, the police car stopped, and the siren abated. She stopped along the edge of a row of grapes and turned back to see what they were doing.

The cop car had stopped at the ambulance. The side door was open, and the two men in the back were just getting out as she watched.

What the hell?

How could anyone know that fast? Unless they were tracking the vehicle and she just got out in time.

That meant they would know how close she was. If they were to do any fast research on her, they would also discover where she was headed.

Maybe she shouldn't go home right now. The last thing she wanted was to walk in the front door, say hello to dear old mom and dad, explain how she had been shot in the head, and then get arrested for some stupid assault charge.

A warm night under the stars in the vineyard would be better.

Perhaps her headache would be gone by the morning, and she could think better and figure things out.

She had never been this lethargic. Aggressiveness was more her nature. But what could she do with her head hurting this bad?

The ground was grassy under her feet. She found a spot relatively secluded from the road where she sat and rested her back against a stake with a vine tied to it.

Her eyes fluttered in the dark, then closed.

Maybe she would just rest for a few moments and then decide what to do.

Chapter 38

Amelia recoiled from the sound of the gunshot so violently that she hit the wall beside the stove and then crumpled to the floor, a look of utter shock on her face.

Caleb had jumped up and landed on the edge of the counter but then dropped fast to the kitchen floor and ducked his head low while staying on his feet.

As Violeta turned her aim toward him, he glanced at the knife block on the counter, but now it was too far away.

"Don't even think about it," Violeta said.

Amelia whimpered on the floor, her hands partially covering her surprised face.

Smoke billowed up from the wok on the stove as the paella began to burn.

"Caleb, stand up, and then come and sit down at the table." She jerked the tip of the gun, gesturing for him to move. "You too, Amelia. Come, sit down. We need to talk."

Violeta edged backward until she was at the entrance to the kitchen, wanting to keep at least five feet between her and Caleb. He was the hero of the family. He was the alpha male. She had to stay ready for his charge.

The sound of the sizzling paella increased, as did the smoke. She would have to make this quick or turn the stove off.

"Faster," she shouted.

Caleb sat in the chair as he was told and stared at his wife, who was struggling to get off the floor.

"Hands on the table," Violeta said. "Lock the fingers. Anything other than what I ask gets you killed."

The hammer was in Caleb's reach now, but that was what she wanted. At least Caleb hadn't tested her yet by reaching for it.

Violeta moved closer and gently placed the gun's tip against Caleb's head, pressing it behind his left ear.

"My daughter shot your daughter in the head earlier this week." She cleared her throat and adjusted her stance in case Caleb jumped up. "Move, and I'll do the same to you. Go ahead, be the hero. Act the tough guy. You'll look good in a suit and tie," she leaned closer to his ear, "in your *fucking* coffin. A cheap pine box. Then how will you provide for your family, huh?"

Amelia scrambled across the floor on her knees after having abandoned her efforts to stand and walk.

Firing the gun in their kitchen, shocking the shit out of them, had quelled any ideas of rebellion. Inwardly, she was so proud of herself for having thought of it.

Be aggressive, or go home.

In Caleb's eyes, she saw what amounted to acquiescence.

At least for now.

Amelia crawled up into the chair opposite Caleb and stared across the table at him.

"What do you want?" Caleb asked.

Smoke billowed along the ceiling of the kitchen. Maybe five more minutes before the house would be too smoky to stay. But she couldn't back away from Caleb yet.

"Amelia," Violeta said. "Pick up the hammer."

Amelia continued to stare at Caleb.

"Pick it up!" Violeta screamed. "Or watch your husband die on your kitchen table because that's what we're having for dinner. A brain roast."

Amelia took the handle of the hammer into her hand but kept it on the table.

"Caleb, put your right hand in the center of the table, fingers splayed. Do it now."

Caleb moved his hand without hesitation.

"I have no beef with you two. Neither one of you has harmed my family or me. But your daughter has. And that asshole, Parkman. Since I can't get my restitution with them, I choose you. Now, I really want to kill you both." She paused to let that sink in. Amelia shuddered, then coughed as the smoke began to bother her. "But I won't kill you if you do what I ask. And if you do, I will leave in five minutes, and you'll never see me again. Is that understood?"

Caleb's head moved up and down so subtly she wouldn't have noticed the movement if the gun hadn't been pressed against his scalp.

"Good. Now, Amelia, I want you to use the business end of that hammer to smash your husband's fingers. Are you willing to do that?"

Amelia swiveled her glazed, bloodshot eyes to meet Violeta's gaze.

Oh, how I'm loving this. Who knew I was cut out to make people learn shit the hard way.

Amelia shook her head. "I can't … I can't hurt my husband. Please don't ask me to do that—" She coughed again.

"What would happen if a mouse was loose in your house? What would you do?"

"What?" Amelia's voice cracked.

"A mouse! What would you do if you found a mouse in your house?"

"We would kill it or try to get it out," Caleb answered for her.

"Right. Now, what happens if a bear wandered into your house and got aggressive with you, and you had a rifle? What would you do?"

"Shoot it."

"Right again. So, Amelia, this situation is either the mouse or the bear. Is your husband a mouse or a bear? If he's a mouse, kill it with the hammer. But if you can't, that means your husband is a bear, and I'll be forced to shoot him. This is entirely up to you, but we're running out of time because that paella doesn't smell as good anymore. You've got ten seconds to kill the mouse or face the alternative. Go."

Amelia's hand twitched.

Caleb nodded at her. "Go ahead, honey. I don't mind. It'll be okay. Fingers heal. Heads, not so much."

"Five seconds," Violeta reminded her. "Listen to your husband."

Amelia lifted the hammer. It wavered in the air as

everything in her body was probably telling her not to do it.

"Make it count," Violeta said. "Something has to break. Do it now."

Amelia raised it higher, then brought the hammer down. It missed Caleb and dented a circular hole on the top of the wooden table.

"What are you doing?" Violeta shouted. "Do it again and make sure you get a finger, or it'll be your last chance."

Amelia cried a torrent now. Her lips moved like she was praying. Caleb was a pillar of stone. The only thing moving on him was sweat as it leaked down from his forehead. His face had paled as he waited for the hammer to fall.

"No countdown this time," Violeta said. "Just pick it up and do it."

Amelia lifted the hammer above her head. Caleb nodded and closed his eyes slowly, then opened them.

"I love you, Amelia."

"I love you, too, Caleb."

"Oh, how sweet," Violeta said softly in a gentle, motherly voice. Then she screamed, "Fucking do it!"

Disgusting human beings.

The smoke detector screeched at that exact moment, startling all three of them. Over the high-pitched agonizing wail of the unit, Violeta shouted for Amelia to hit the mouse or kill the bear.

Amelia brought the hammer down. This time the business end hit Caleb's middle finger dead on, snapping it at the knuckle and denting it below the rest of his fingers. He bit his lip and withdrew his broken hand to hold it close to his chest.

Violeta ripped the hammer out of Amelia's hands and

swung it above the stove at the offending smoke detector on the ceiling. It tore into the white plastic casing and broke it clean off. The unit shot into the wall and dropped at Violeta's feet. She stomped on it until the screech quieted.

Hammer in her left hand, gun still firmly in her right, Violeta stepped back to the table, lifted the hammer, and brought it down on Amelia's wrist. She didn't see it in time to react. The hammer snapped her wrist, bending her hand at an odd angle. It reminded Violeta of a YouTube video Tam had watched where a skateboarder had fallen and snapped his wrist back.

Amelia screamed and held up the offending wrist.

Violeta swung again, this time aiming for Amelia's other hand. Because she was using her left hand, she pivoted on her feet at the unexpected weight of the hammer missing its target.

The table moved, skirting fast at Amelia. Her chair tipped back, and then she was falling.

It happened too fast for Violeta to realize what was going on.

Now she was falling as something heavy banged into her. She landed on her left shoulder, and pain shot up her side and into her neck. The hammer flew from her grasp and tumbled a few feet away, but the gun stayed where it was, locked on her finger.

Caleb's weight was on her, and she understood quickly what had happened. The hero had shoved the table out of his way, knocking Amelia down, and then he dove on Violeta. Even with the pain of a broken finger, it hadn't dampened Caleb's will to fight the intruder in his house.

But Violeta had the advantage.

Amelia screamed on the floor beside her. The hammer was on the floor somewhere, meaning Amelia could grab it at any second.

Violeta had no choice but to use the gun. She had come here with violent intent and had wanted to leave murder as a last resort, but this was self-defense now. She was being attacked. Any jury of her peers would see that.

Caleb applied pressure to her throat with his unbroken hand. She had failed to get a good breath while under his weight and couldn't maneuver him off yet. Even as her breath was cut off and her face reddened from the pressure, she winked at him and attempted to smile as she brought the gun around and set the tip against his side.

His hand wrapped tighter as he pushed down toward the floor, cutting off all chance at air.

She pulled the trigger.

Amelia shouted in surprise at the loud report and shambled away from them. Caleb's body went rigid, his hand locked in place. For a brief moment, she wondered if he would go into spasms, his hand clenching, squeezing her throat until he crushed it in his death throes.

Something warm trickled over Violeta's stomach and waist.

Caleb was bleeding on her.

His body relaxed as he lost consciousness, allowing her to roll sideways. His weight eased off her as she breathed in deep, coughed, and breathed again. Her eyesight cleared, and the room came back into view.

Amelia's high-pitched scream reminded Violeta of the smoke alarm. Amelia scrambled to her husband on her one good hand, hugged him, and called his name over and over.

As Amelia clung to her bleeding husband, it riled Violeta to intense anger that boiled over. She raised the gun and fired at Amelia. The gun wavered in her weakened hand, and the bullet went wide.

Amelia, with a stunned expression on her face, leaned down and hugged her husband.

"Why aren't you running?" Violeta shouted.

Amelia kept her head down, her arms wrapped around Caleb.

Violeta got to her feet, using the counter for support. The paella smoke rolled just above her head. She kicked the hammer out of the way, picked up her cane, and aimed the gun at the top of Amelia's head.

"Goodbye, you stupid bitch."

The front door opened.

"Momma?" Tam called. "I'm here."

Chapter 39

Parkman sat beside Aaron in the cruiser's back seat as they pulled up on the ambulance.

"We need to continue on to the house," Parkman said.

"We will, but I want to know what I'm walking into," Gibbons said.

The tires squealed when he stopped. Even as the car settled on its shocks, he was already hopping out, leaving the car door open.

"Are you in charge here?" Gibbons asked the first guy he saw in a suit. The man nodded. His tie was loosened around the neck, and his shirt unbuttoned. He looked ragged, like he'd worked an extra shift. Parkman had been there and done that in his time.

Gibbons identified himself and then asked, "What happened?"

"We got a call from a cop named Carson Dodge down in

Florida.”

"Florida? What the hell has that got to do with this?” Gibbons asked.

"Hell if I know. All we heard was there was this big ambulance carrying an expensive package. Something extremely valuable. He had a reason to believe it was in our town. Then one of our guys spotted it.”

"What was in it?”

"A doctor and an off-duty cop.”

"They were the expensive package?”

The suit shook his head. "Apparently, that package walked away. We've got a couple of cruisers driving around, and K9 units are on their way.”

"You guys got the name of this valuable package that walked away?”

"Sarah Roberts. Mean anything to you?”

Gibbons looked back at Parkman. "Yeah. I think I know where she might be.” Gibbons pointed at Parkman. "Or at least he does.”

Chapter 40

Violeta lowered the weapon.

"Tam, what are you doing here?"

"You told me to meet you here, remember?"

Violeta didn't remember that. She recalled telling Martin to return in an hour, but not Tam. So much was happening she couldn't be expected to remember all of it.

She knew where Tam had been. Conspiring with Oliver. Meeting with cops. Calling the brigade on her. Violating her trust. Betraying her every which way.

You're just like the rest of them.

"Right, yes, I remember now," Violeta said, her voice soft, reassuring. "Come over here."

"What happened?" Tam asked as she started through the living room. "Where's all the smoke coming from?"

No one had touched the paella. It had become a blackened mess in the wok. Violeta was surprised she wasn't coughing more because of it.

"Did you do as I asked? Is Sarah dead?"

Amelia's head shot up at the mention of her daughter's name.

"Yes, Momma." Tam nodded as she came up the stairs. "When I got to Parkman's apartment, those guys you hired had hurt her real bad. I actually did a good thing. Putting her out of her misery like that was humane."

Violeta couldn't contain her anger toward Tam anymore. Suppressing it was like trying to contain the explosives inside a grenade after pulling the pin.

"I didn't ask you to do anything humane." She spit the last word out and brought the gun around to bear on Tam.

Tam stopped on the top stair just before entering the kitchen. Her eyes widened. "Momma, what are you doing?"

"I heard you talking to your dead father."

"But Momma, he's not dead."

"He will be when I'm through with him. I heard you conspiring against me."

Tam shook her head back and forth, the frightened look on her face giving Violeta pause. Something about causing terror in her daughter had always pleasured her.

"Now, here's how I see it," Violeta said as she moved slowly toward Tam. "I'm going to shoot you. Then I'm going to kill Sarah's mom."

"No, no—" Tam wailed. "You can't, Momma. No more hurting anyone."

"Shut up!" Violeta flicked hair out of her eyes with a jerk of her head. "Once this is done, I will leave here and go to your father and fix that mess. When the police show up here, they will see everything." She placed the gun against her daughter's forehead. "Don't move an inch, my darling." Violeta stood over her, looking down as Tam was still one stair below. "I will tell them how you went to Toronto and shot Sarah. Then followed her back here and killed her in Parkman's apartment. To rid the world of this wicked family, you came here and killed Sarah's parents. It was and always has been about killing Sarah. Everything is about killing Sarah. That's what I'll tell the authorities." She leaned in close and whispered as if they were the only two in on the wonderful joke. "You would wake at night from a nightmare yelling those words. Killing Sarah. When I would ask about it, you would—"

"Momma!" Tam yelled. "Look out!"

She had taken her eyes off the broken-down Amelia. Instantly she realized what a horrible mistake that was. She had thought Amelia didn't have a broken wrist but a broken spirit.

She ducked and tried to bring the gun around, but when she did, Amelia was still on the floor, clutching at her husband.

Hands grabbed at her arm and pushed. Violeta lost her balance and fell. The steps behind her led to a back door before turning and heading to the basement. She landed awkwardly on the top stair, her head dropping below it, arching her back until the strain was too much. Pain shot up her spine, and she cried out.

Tam landed on her, scratching at her face, screaming like a demented hyena, shredding the skin on her cheeks as if it was the skin of a kiwi.

She fought back, flailing uselessly with her arms, but Tam was younger and stronger.

The gun.

She looked for it, but the gun was gone.

Tam's hands jabbed, cut, and punched at her as the teenager bellowed insanely. Violeta feared for her eyes, her looks. Spinning her head back and forth to disengage Tam's fingers, she wondered for a brief second if this was the end. Would she die under the weight of the daughter she had labored over and given birth to? She had changed her diapers, helped her through homework, and was trying to teach her survival in a world that would eat you up if you weren't quick and smart.

Her mind floundered, her will weakening. Then her hand bumped the cane. She gripped it with the tenacity of a dying soul's last chance, flicked the knife's release clasp, and brought it around blindly.

It hit something hard, and the scratching stopped. The weight holding her down fell away. She tried to open her eyes but only blinked through the blood that seemed to be coming from all over her face.

She tried to get up, but sharp pains screamed through her lower back. A shout escaped her lips. A roll to her side allowed her to maneuver herself into a sitting position. Tam lay on the kitchen floor, holding her own face.

Violeta wiped at her eyes and blinked away the crimson to see. The knife had sliced from Tam's hairline across her left eye and finished on the bridge of her nose. Tam had both hands over her eye as blood seeped through her fingers.

Violeta grinned. She had won. The battle was over. Tam would have to respect that she had been bested even when Violeta was on the losing end. Her dominance would go a long way in teaching Tam what a woman could do.

"This is just the beginning," Violeta murmured through dampened lips. She spit blood out in order to speak better, "of the horrors I'm going to do to you, you little whore scum. You will be the doormat you have been destined to become since you were born."

She pushed up against the wall and got to her knees, breathing heavily to manage the pain in her back.

Amelia had gotten up and now stood over her husband.

Violeta's gun was in Amelia's unbroken hand.

Several cars pulled up out front. Amelia snuck a glance through the large living room window at the arriving vehicles. From the slightly elevated kitchen, Violeta had a good angle to see police cars, unmarked cruisers, and an ambulance.

The cavalry was here. But the Roberts family wasn't dead yet. Her word against theirs wouldn't work now.

She had to leave. Turn up somewhere later. Claim she wasn't here at all and never had been. She would pay Martin a million dollars to swear her an alibi.

How did the police get here so damn fast?

Amelia coughed. The smoke had subsided as there was nothing much left to burn in the wok. But Amelia was standing closest to the stove.

The front door opened.

Amelia looked toward it and coughed harder.

Violeta took her chance. She pushed her bum off the top of the stairs and dropped three feet to the bottom, where she almost fell headlong into the door from the pain in her back. She got the deadbolt unlocked and threw open the back door.

A bullet would enter her from behind at any second, but she had nothing else to lose. It was either getting out alive or dying in prison.

She ran into the night with no bullets chasing her.

One quick look over her shoulder, and she saw Tam coming out the back door after her, one hand still covering her wounded eye.

Tam had the hammer in her other hand.

Then the grapevines of the vineyard behind the Roberts's house swallowed Violeta, and she disappeared in the darkness.

Chapter 41

Parkman watched from the front of the house.

"I'm so scared of what they might find in there." He hopped from one foot to the other. "Was there something I missed? Could I have done something different to avoid all this? Because you know it's all my fault. I took this client on in the first place."

Aaron slapped his shoulder. "Don't talk so stupid. You did your job. You found her missing husband. How could you know she was a fucking lunatic? The important thing is to find Sarah. If she wandered off from that ambulance, she could be anywhere." He gestured at the house. "Unless they find her in there. Which I hope they don't."

"I know. She has a head wound. She needs rest, not violence. Shit, the stuff she's been through. It's got to be killing her right now."

"It has been. That's why she wanted to quit."

"Maybe that's the best thing for her."

Movement in the dark behind the house caught his eye.

"Hey, Aaron," he pointed. "Look. Is that someone running?"

They both leaned sideways, away from the light coming out of the big living room window. A short woman or a young girl ran into the vineyard and disappeared into the darkness.

Her arm had been raised with something in it.

Parkman took off in a sprint with Aaron close behind.

No one shouted after them. Parkman hit the vines first, then ducked down and clamped his eyes shut.

Aaron dropped beside him. "What are you doing?" he whispered. "Trying to hear better?"

"No," Parkman whispered. "Acclimating my eyes to the darkness faster."

After a few more seconds, Parkman opened his eyes and could now see the tops of the rows of vines from the dim light coming from the few houses that rimmed the vineyard.

Aaron tugged on his arm and leaned in close to his ear. "Do you think that was Sarah?"

Aaron's breath tickled Parkman's ear. "No. I think it was Violeta's daughter."

"What would she be doing in Caleb's house?"

"Let's find her and ask. I'll go that way."

They split up. Before Parkman got five feet, someone grunted and gasped about three rows over.

The rows were too long to run to the end and then run down the next, even if he knew which one to go down in the dark. There had to be a way to sneak under.

He got on his hands and knees and touched the base of

the stakes attached to the vines, but most of them were too close for him to fit through.

Another grunt close by.

"Stop it," a woman said. A voice he recognized. She was moving closer to him. "We have to leave together." Then in a lower voice. "I'm not the enemy. We, together, can fix this."

Violeta.

Parkman continued his search and found a spot he could fit his shoulders through. He got down and pushed.

Then stopped.

Someone was standing above him.

***

Violeta had made it down half the length of the first row she ran into, but her breath coming out in fits and starts slowed her pace. She could never outrun her teenage daughter.

Footsteps approached in the dark and slowed. The silhouette of Tam's head was easy to see with the lights of the Roberts's house behind her.

Violeta walked backward, trying to imagine what she could say to Tam to calm her down.

Why was she fighting me, anyway? I'm her mother.

What stories could Oliver have implanted in her head?

Tam tugged on Violeta's jacket. But it wasn't a tug. It was the hammer coming down, barely missing her skin.

Her bones chilled at the thought of being whacked with a hammer.

Tam swung again.

"Stop it," Violeta said. "We have to leave together." She

lowered her voice to a whisper. "I'm not the enemy. We, together, can fix this."

"Yes, you are an enemy." Tam swung again. "You're a horrible person. You're cruel and mean. All you do is hurt people unless they're useful to you. You're like Caligula. Some insane ruler who wants to be fed grapes while the people around you are murdered and raped, and violated. You take pleasure from other people's pain, and you have taken pleasure from my pain." Tam stepped closer. "Not anymore." She lunged.

Violeta saw the glint of light off the business end of the hammer. In the blink of an instant, she saw how close it was and knew she wouldn't be able to jump back in time.

But then, something was under her, and she was falling.

And thankfully, the hammer missed.

***

Parkman had managed to climb between the stakes but stayed low to not be detected. They were only steps away.

Something about nabbing Violeta himself felt right after all that had happened. She would serve a long prison sentence when everything was tied back to her.

But Tam was advancing on her mother. She had a weapon in her hand and was trying to hit her mother with it.

Parkman remained on his hands and knees and waited quietly, watching as the dark figures took one more step.

Tam cussed her mother out and lunged.

Parkman hopped to his right about a foot and bumped the back of Violeta's legs.

She fell over him and hit the grass on her back.

Tam had lunged so fast and so hard that she, too, ran into Parkman's side and fell over him, landing on her mother.

In the darkness on the ground, he lost sight of them. The scuffling and grunts were close, but he couldn't tell if he was at their feet or their heads.

He got up and advanced forward, using the toe of his shoe to guide him.

Something soft brushed against his foot.

In order to break up the fight, he held onto a vine and kicked.

One of them moaned loud, and the scuffling stopped.

Five feet away, a head popped up, silhouetted by the houses.

Violeta.

Somehow she had managed to crawl away.

She turned and ran.

Chapter 42

THE DREAMS WERE PAINFUL. They hurt like a bone had broken inside her head. Someone was screaming. There was a pounding on a metal door. Or maybe it was something made of aluminum. The pounding became excruciating.

Her sister's voice shouted at her.

(*Wake up, wake up, wake up, wake up*)

Sarah snapped awake, blinking rapidly in the darkness to see through the inky black, but it was nearly impossible.

She closed her eyes and rubbed her temples. The headache throbbed behind her eyes.

Someone shouted something unintelligible off to her left.

She jerked in reflex, the pain in her head flaring.

More noises. Someone is running approximately two rows over. The authorities were here. Looking for her. She had to leave. She had to get up and walk away. Come back another day. Sort everything out, then. She was in danger until she had time to heal and a chance to regain her memories.

Violeta Payne.

The name angered her. She had sent those men to Parkman's apartment, and when they found her, Violeta had told them to hurt her. Do whatever they wanted, Violeta had said.

Sarah had to get to Violeta first. Once that cockroach was crushed, she could sleep. Maybe she'd sleep for a week.

Or a month.

She got to her feet gingerly, moving her head slowly.

Whoever they were, they were close. More than one person.

A grunt, then a moan. Quiet murmuring.

What the hell are they doing? Fighting while searching for me?

Unless they weren't searching for her.

Sarah looked at the back of her parents' house. Flashing lights bounced off the walls of the nearby homes. Several police vehicles were parked out front.

It came together slowly in her sleepy mind. Whatever had happened in her parents' house had spilled into the vineyard.

She crouched down and started along her row.

Someone was running close by. Footsteps pounded down, but they sounded lazy, strained.

Nearing the end of her row, Sarah saw the top of a woman's head ten feet away, running toward her.

Someone yelled for Violeta to come back and stop running.

Sarah got ready.

***

Violeta ran, fumbling along in the dark, knowing she wouldn't run into anything as the tops of the rows were barely discernible in the dark.

Parkman was behind her, but he would be delayed. He was a righteous man. He would tend to Tam first, losing precious seconds, then come after her. That would be too late.

She would be free from this mess in minutes and would call for Martin to come and pick her up.

It was over. She had made it. Her word against theirs. She had money, lawyers, and a reputation. They had only their word. She had leverage, they had nothing.

The excitement, the fighting, and the running made her feel youthful again. Maybe when this was all over, and she was a richer woman for it, living by herself in her large home, she would take up yoga or some other pastime to feel youthful.

At the end of her row of grapevines, she turned and headed away from the carnage behind. Someone shouted her name back from the area of the house. Flashlights bobbed as men ran toward the vineyard.

I'm leaving just in time.

She made another turn toward the open street and ran right into something. Pinwheeling her arms to maintain her balance didn't work. Violeta fell backward and landed on her spine, knocking the wind out of her lungs. She gasped, trying to catch a breath, and looked up at what she had run into.

A woman stood over her, a not-so-distant streetlight glinting off an object extended in her hand. There was enough light to see half her face. The woman was young and beautiful with long, flowing blonde hair and an intense, even intelligent stare. A white bandage was pasted on her scalp above one ear.

The impossibility of it made Violeta gasp. The improbability of it caused her to laugh as her breathing began to normalize.

Standing over her, a gun in her hand, was none other than her mortal enemy. The woman she had recently vowed to destroy could now become an ally in their escape because she had a gun.

She grinned and got ready to persuade Sarah Roberts to hand over the gun or be hunted down and murdered in her sleep.

Either that, or she would offer to give her one million dollars. Everyone had a price. All she had to do was learn what Sarah's was.

***

Sarah ignored the pain in her head, leaned closer to the woman at her feet, and said, "Violeta Payne. You're like a root canal."

"A …" Violeta gasped and tried again. "A what?"

It was hard to tell if Violeta was smiling or about to laugh, but her words had that quality about them.

"A root canal. Always digging into things, mucking about, on the pretense that you're doing something right. With people like you, it's never going to be right. Even once that tooth is fixed, it'll break within months. You're like a fucking root canal, and I hate the dentist."

Before Sarah said another word, someone materialized from the darkness and dove from between a row of vines on Violeta's side, startling Sarah to the point where she almost fired her weapon.

The person landed on Violeta and slammed something down hard. A loud thump, followed by a whistle of air sound, and then the movement at Sarah's feet stopped.

Sarah kicked at the new person. It was still so dark she couldn't tell if it was a male or female.

The newcomer rolled over after the second kick and lay on the grass.

"It's truly over," a soft girl's voice said. "My mom is dead."

Someone else ran up. Thick shoulders, the ungainly gait of a man.

Sarah kept her gun in front of her.

"Oh shit," the man said, looking down at Violeta. "No way, Tam. You didn't."

Parkman. I would recognize that voice anywhere.

"How did you get away from me?" Parkman asked. "Shit, Tam, what have you done?"

"On your knees, Parkman," Sarah said through gritted teeth.

The image of him firing his weapon from close range in Toronto flooded back. The time for calm was over. Her head hurt, and her body was stiff from sitting against the vines for too long. Men were moving through the vineyard a few dozen yards over with flashlights. Time was short.

"Sarah?" he said, his voice sounding hopeful.

Maybe she wouldn't kill him in cold blood in front of Tam or whoever it was on the ground at Parkman's feet.

Maybe just wound him. Wound for wound. That would work. A fast shot to the head.

She raised the gun higher. "We meet again," she said. "This time, the shoe is on the other foot. Look who's holding the gun now, traitor. I won't tell you a second time." She breathed out through her teeth and took in another long breath. "Get. On. Your. Knees."

Parkman dropped.

"Sarah, listen—" he said, his voice soft, pleading.

"Shut up. I'm done listening. You were my friend. A dear friend. Shooting me was the ultimate betrayal."

"I love you, Sarah, and I would never do anything to hurt you."

"Bullshit. I saw you pull your weapon and fire. I got hit in the head. I can't believe I'm still alive. Why even call the ambulance if you aimed to kill me?"

"That wasn't my aim."

"More bullshit." She tightened her grip on the gun as her eyes glazed over. "I saw you," emotion choked her throat, "pull the gun."

"Sarah?"

A male voice from behind the vines. A voice she recognized. A voice that warmed her on the inside and made her feel loved.

"Aaron?"

"Baby, put the gun down. Don't do this."

The warm feeling disappeared, and rage filled the void.

"You're on his side? What is this?"

Tam leaned up from her prone position on the ground. "Shoot me, then," she said. "It was meant as a warning shot. I messed up and hit you by accident." The girl sobbed. "I thought I'd killed you, and now my mom is dead. I killed her because she was insane. Shoot me. I don't deserve to live."

Thoroughly confused, Sarah changed gun hands.

"Nothing makes sense." She faced Parkman, who remained on his knees.

"Sarah," he said. "If you truly believe I would hurt you, then go ahead, make your peace with it. After all we've been through, the people we have lost together, the trips to Europe, fighting in those crypts together …" He trailed off. "If you believe in your heart that I would betray you, there's nothing left. For you, Sarah, I would do anything. Even die if it came to it. But one thing I won't do is beg Sarah Roberts for my life. She wouldn't respect me, and her last memory has to be the right one."

Before she had more time to think about it, she took one step back so no one could get the jump on her in the dark. If what they were saying was true, then how come she saw it differently in her head?

"Sarah?" Aaron again. "Did the doctor talk to you about your head wound?"

"What has that got to do with anything?" she snapped.

"Where was Parkman when you got shot?" he asked.

"Standing in front of me. I saw the gun. Heard it fire. Felt the impact of the bullet." She wiped at her eyes and took a step closer to Parkman. The gun's barrel was only two inches from his forehead now.

"The bullet entered your skull from behind," Aaron said.

Something clicked in her consciousness. She blinked, looked to the side where Aaron's voice was, and waited for him to speak again.

But there was nothing left for him to say.

"I pulled the gun, Sarah," Parkman said. "To fire back at the person behind us. We now know it was her." His arm moved to point at the girl on the ground. "Tam Rood, Violeta Payne's daughter." Parkman looked back at Sarah. "That was probably why Vivian asked you if you would quit the vigilante business to not meet me but talk to Tam Rood. Meeting me kept you involved. Talking to Tam might have cooled the situation down. Is it all coming together for you?"

A palpable silence fell over them. The men with flashlights were almost there.

The image of Parkman crucified on the cross in that church in Italy came back to her. She suddenly realized why it bothered her so much. Parkman had been like a brother to her. They had fought side by side so many times, got out of jams, and survived together. When she saw him hurt the way he was on that cross in a little town called Montone, she had become enraged. She remembered how later, when she had come up from the crypt below the church, Parkman had been taken down. He wasn't in the church anymore. A woman named Rosalie told Sarah that Parkman had picked up a gun and was outside, hunting the people responsible.

Her legs trembled with weakness. Her emotions were like the deluge of a monsoon flooding the banks of a river on an arid land, threatening her lavishly built home on its shores, her safety, her existence, where she felt one with the world and understood herself and her motivations without question. Emotional, spent, and disgusted with what she had been about to do, Sarah lowered the gun, unsure if she could ever trust herself again around the people she loved.

The bullet had entered from behind. On that fateful night, Parkman was standing in front of her. It couldn't have been him. He had done nothing wrong.

But what had she done? How could she have come so close to hurting him? How could she have come so far? And it was all because she didn't correlate the entry wound to where Parkman was standing in her memory.

She pivoted toward Tam Rood. The girl who had actually shot her. The gun was up again.

"No, Sarah," Parkman whispered. "Don't. She's seventeen. It's not her fault."

The flashlights were closer still, the men running their way.

People have to pay for their wrongdoings. They have to be accountable.

The men's voices carried over the darkened vineyard.

Sarah felt Aaron's eyes on her. Parkman watched from his knees. Tam waited for the bullet, defiance on her face, her one good eye unwounded and unyielding.

Sarah lowered the gun and slipped it away. The only person who needed to be accountable for their actions was her.

"There's been enough violence for today," she said. "I need rest. Then I need to figure out a way I can," she turned to face Parkman, "make it right with you."

She reached her hand out. He took it and stood to meet her eye to eye.

"Ever since you were snatched from the hospital in Toronto," Parkman said, "we have come across the country looking for you, and now we found you. There is nothing you need to make right. We're good. Hell, we're all alive."

As the authorities arrived and the flashlights found them, Sarah pulled Parkman in and hugged him fiercely, crying on his chest.

"I'm so sorry, Parkman. I actually believed what I saw."

"We all believe what we see."

He held her until something tugged on her pants. A weight lifted off her back.

The guns!

She pushed Parkman away and spun around. The flashlight brilliance from the men who had arrived fell on Tam's face.

Tam placed the gun she had grabbed under her chin and pulled the trigger. Nothing happened. She pulled it again. Then again.

Sarah swatted the gun out of Tam's hand.

"No bullets. You think I would pull a loaded weapon on a friend? This one is loaded." She pulled the second gun out and placed it on the grass as the men behind her shouted and moved in.

Two men subdued Tam while Parkman grabbed Sarah and pulled her back. Aaron stepped up and put a hand on her shoulder. Their eyes met, and he smiled.

"I'm sorry, Sarah, but there's more bad news."

He gestured with a slight nod of his head at Sarah's parents' house.

"Oh shit," Sarah said as she took off running, Aaron clearing a path, pummeling the men who tried to stop her.

Chapter 43

VIOLETA PAYNE DIED THAT night on the edge of the vineyard behind Caleb Roberts's house from blunt-force trauma to the throat. Tam's downward thrust of the hammer's claw end cut through Violeta's neck, severing her carotid artery, and she bled out in under a minute.

Sarah marveled at how a woman could die in front of four people, and no one seemed to notice or care at the time.

Tam Rood lost the eye her mother had hit with the knife end of her cane. Forever she would wear a patch in remembrance of the night she mortally wounded her mother. The weight of what happened to Tam would be on her shoulders longer than Sarah could imagine. Tam had entered a state of shock hours after they took her to the hospital and only recently started talking to investigators.

If only I had listened to Vivian and talked to Tam initially. None of this would've happened.

She rolled over in her hospital bed and stared at her father as he slept. It had been three days since the incident at their house. He was to be released from the hospital today on the condition he took it easy. Parkman, Aaron, and a few of the nurses signed the cast on his broken hand. The bullet wound had been superficial. It entered at the tip of his hip bone and exited through the fleshy other side at the top of the buttocks, missing everything vital. He would have a scar to match several of his daughter's.

With a cast on her broken wrist, Sarah's mother had left earlier to prepare the house for Caleb's return home. Oliver Payne had arranged for a private room for Caleb during his stay, and a bed was brought in for Sarah to continue resting from her head trauma. She planned on heading home with her father today, where she would rest and talk to her sister, who had been mysteriously absent the past few days.

Sarah had woken to a small message from Vivian explaining that this was how Sarah had wanted it. She had wanted to quit. Once Sarah had deviated from Vivian's warning to not meet Parkman, Vivian had seen what was coming and knew Sarah to be on the right path, so she let her navigate her course without interruption. But if Sarah decided to continue working with her, Vivian had a full agenda.

Aaron opened the door and stepped quietly inside the room, startling Sarah from her thoughts. She sat up in bed and took his hand as he sat in the chair beside her.

"Tam Rood admitted everything," he said.

"What's everything?"

"I understand they just finalized her statement. Violeta had orchestrated the attack on you. Oliver, Tam's father, came in and added his version of events. Together, they told parallel stories of what Violeta had been up to.”

“The police took my statement as well,” Sarah said. “I was shot in Toronto and came to Parkman’s apartment for help. Violeta sent two men to rape and torture me—”

“And then sent her own daughter to kill you,” Aaron added.

“I did what I had to do to stay on this side of the grass.”

“They believe you because they found Derek alive. You could’ve killed him but didn’t.”

“Did they get that other guy, Violeta’s driver?”

“Martin?”

“Wasn’t there someone who was supposed to pick Violeta up after she visited my parents’ house?”

Aaron squeezed her hand. “Yes. They don’t have much on him, but they did pick him up.”

She met his gaze. “How’s Parkman handling everything?”

“You mean with you?”

She nodded and looked away. The horror of mistakenly hating someone who had been so loyal hadn’t left her. There would be a mark tattooed on her soul for a very long time for holding a gun on Parkman.

“He hasn’t mentioned anything. I think he considers it a non-event. Although,” Aaron offered a crooked smile, “I don’t think he wants to be in that position again.”

Sarah took her hand away and lay back on the bed.

“I didn’t remember a lot of things when I woke up. It really scared me, and I don’t frighten easily. But the image of Parkman and that gun was quite vivid.” She stared up at the ceiling. “Crazy how things work out, eh?”

"Crazy."

The door opened slowly. Detective Joffrey, who Sarah had met a couple of times since the night in the vineyard, entered, a cell phone in his hand. He gestured at her sleeping father and asked if it was okay.

Sarah nodded.

Joffrey walked up and handed her the cell phone.

"You have a call," he whispered.

"Who is it?"

"A Florida cop named Carson Dodge."

Sarah frowned. Florida? She had never heard of a man named Carson Dodge.

She put the phone to her ear. "Hello?"

"Can anyone else hear me?" the male voice asked.

She recognized the voice but couldn't put a name to it.

"No."

"Confident? We're alone?"

"Yes."

"Sarah, it's Darwin."

"One sec," she said. She put the phone on her chest and looked at Aaron and Joffrey. "Guys, I'm going to need a minute here."

Joffrey stepped away. "I'll be just outside the door."

Aaron nodded and got up from the chair. "I'll go wait for your mother. I understand she's coming back before Caleb is released."

Sarah waited until the door closed.

"Darwin," she whispered. "How did you find me?"

"I've known where you were since the moment you got shot in Toronto just off Keele Street."

"How?"

"Remember how I told you I monitor cell phones? I listen in for chatter to make sure my family's name doesn't come out of the wrong mouths?"

"Yes. You have an impressive setup in Italy."

"When you were here, I got Parkman's cell number and was able to hack into it. I thought nothing of it when he called to meet you at midnight. That was nine in the morning over here. I was wide awake in my office, already on my third coffee, when I heard him call for an ambulance, saying that you had been shot."

Everything fell into place.

"I asked you when you were here," he continued, "if we were ever in need of help, would you look out for my family, and you said you would. That goes both ways. Since I didn't know who your enemy was or who I could trust, I called my handler, Carson Dodge, down in Florida, a man who can be trusted, and had him arrange the modified ambulance and the pickup at the hospital. I told him to make sure he made it out of that hospital alive and to have proper care until they delivered you to your parents. If he wouldn't do it, I made sure he knew that I would fly back to North America and do it myself, which is the last thing he wants. No one needs another mafia war."

"Wow, I had no idea that was you."

"No one does. Carson's connected to this, but that's where it stops. I thought you should know that I was behind Carson's motivation."

"I'm glad you called."

"You might want to smooth things over for Parkman, Aaron, and whoever else waited for you at the hospital in Toronto the night you got shot."

"Why? What are you talking about?"

"In order to delay everyone that night and get you secured away in my ambulance, I had *my* doctor come out and tell them that you were in bad condition, and it looked like you weren't going to make it. My guy gave you a twenty percent chance to live or worse. The other reason I did that was I didn't know who your enemy was. He could've been waiting in the hospital to hear news of your condition."

"Parkman and Aaron are fine. I don't have to explain anything to them. They're just happy I made it out of the hospital safe. Now that I think about it, no one cleared up the ambulance connection."

"But, hey, Sarah?"

"Yeah?"

"Next time I help, can you go nicer on the men that show up? They were just doing their jobs. A simple thank you would've worked. Drugging them and locking them in the back of the ambulance wasn't cool."

She heard the smile in his voice.

"I know how you are," Darwin continued. "I understand that they were at risk, but when people are doing nice things for you, maybe it's okay to let them sometimes."

"That's a tough one, but I'll definitely consider it."

She felt lighter hearing Darwin's laugh.

The door opened, and her mother walked in.

"Listen, I have to go. Maybe we can talk again soon."

"Not unless you need me, or I need you. Remember, I'm The Ghost now. They never found his body, so I've taken on his moniker. Carson has even taken up calling me that."

"Okay, Ghost, we will be in touch."

"Count on it."

"And thanks."
The phone line clicked. Darwin was gone.

Chapter 44

SARAH SLID THE MOTORCYCLE helmet over her head, careful to limit the rubbing on her wound. They had taken the bandage off last week, leaving a slightly hidden scar behind new hair growth. Most of her memories had returned in the month she stayed in Santa Rosa with her parents.

Aaron had gone back to Toronto and shipped her motorcycle to her. He hadn't understood her decision to stay but didn't fight her over it. He recognized those moments when there would be no changing her mind.

The bodies had been removed from Parkman's apartment, and Oliver Payne had hired a team to scour it clean after the police had finished with it. Oliver also refurnished Parkman's apartment and gave him a lump sum of money for his pain and suffering. Sarah's parents received a payment, too.

Since Oliver had recently lost his wife, he was left with

the entire business, which he had begun to dissolve, selling off stores and reinvesting the money in mutual funds, bonds, and stocks.

Everyone was moving on, but Sarah would never be the same. A bullet to the head had changed something in her. She had wanted to hurt Parkman. The desire to kill him had consumed her. How she could forgive herself for that was a question she had no answer for.

Over the past few weeks, she had cooked for Parkman, brought him lunch to work, and considered how she could make it up to him.

"Sarah," he had said one day in his office about a week ago. "You have nothing to make amends for. You were acting on the information you had, which wasn't wrong in your mind at the time."

She had been staring out his office window at the pretty lights of Santa Rosa at night.

She turned to him. "You're wrong. The feelings I felt. The thoughts I had. They were terrible. Faint wisps of those feelings are still evident in the back of my mind. I feel like I betrayed your name, your memory. If I had been a hothead, maybe a couple of years younger, I wouldn't have taken the time to listen to you. I would've just shot you." She shook her head and walked to the office door. "Sometimes there are things that are unforgivable." She opened the door and waited. "Sometimes there are things that you pay for eternally."

"You're being too hard on yourself."

"Is there any other way to be?"

She had walked out and closed the door behind her.

She loved Parkman like a brother, a father. The debt

would be paid one day. She would save his life or take a bullet for him. It would make her feel better about what she had become in those moments of despair.

Until then, she needed to be away from Santa Rosa, from the vineyard behind her parents' house, and from Parkman.

Aaron didn't understand it when she said she wasn't coming back to Toronto for a while. She would eventually because the feelings she had for Aaron were intense and wonderful, but right now, she needed time on her own to figure out her direction in life.

Most of all, though, she didn't deserve to be held, to be loved, to be *in* love, not after what she had almost done to someone so close to her.

The pains of loneliness, sorrow, and misery were dangerous and could lead her back to a life of depression, a place she did not want to return to. But what had helped her out of that depression years ago was Vivian and the purpose Vivian gave her. It was Vivian who gave her a life in the first place.

That life had been violent and filled with turmoil, but she always made it out with Vivian by her side. Telling Vivian to leave her alone and disregarding her final message about meeting Parkman almost changed the course of her life forever.

She had almost murdered someone dear to her.

The life Vivian had offered Sarah not only had a purpose, but it gave her Aaron, it gave her love, and it gave her peace.

Yet Sarah had chosen to turn her back on that and quit. In doing so, her life broke down.

That meant only one thing. She could never quit working with Vivian. She could never stop what she was. Sarah

Roberts was a vigilante with a secret weapon: a dead sister.

No one else had that ability. Unequaled, unparalleled, Sarah could do wondrous things for people in need, and she had attempted to turn her back on that. She had grown selfish, wanting a life of her own, a borrowed life that offered her Aaron, domesticity, and comfort. A man she would have never met had she not been working with Vivian in the first place, doing what she was supposed to be doing.

She started her bike, merged into traffic on Olivet Road, and headed out of town. She was needed in a city called Kelowna in British Columbia, Canada.

Kelowna had the highest crime rate per capita of any city in Canada, so it was fitting she would be needed there.

Vivian's recent message talked about a huge bridge spanning the waters of Okanagan Lake where a woman would jump to her death during the first week of August. This woman wouldn't die as an RCMP officer would jump in and save her. Sarah needed to learn why this woman wanted to jump, and Vivian told her that the officer who saves the woman had to be antagonized. There was something about this man that needed to come out, and as *The Antagonist*, Sarah was the one who could do it.

On the open highway, she thought about her manuscripts. The books she had started writing about her life and the horrors she'd been through, from the day these dark visions had started to the warning Vivian had given her about the FLDS compound in the southern U.S. She recalled the crypts in Hungary and Italy that led her to the lunatic who kept women in cages in his basement in Toronto. The men from the Sophia Project had hunted her, the Rapturites, and her crazy time in Vegas. She had been the hostage, the victim, and the vigilante.

Recently, with all the mental and physical pain she had endured, it felt like everything was about killing Sarah.

They had succeeded, even just a little bit. A part of her had died. The part that was flowering, opening up, allowing possibilities of love and marriage. Maybe one day that would come back, but until then, she had a mission, a path. Until then, she would work with Vivian, deal with this woman from the bridge in Kelowna, and never deviate from her path again.

Sarah smiled. It was good to be grateful for who you are and work with the talents you were given.

It was time to get serious. It was time to get mean. It was time to antagonize people to get results.

Sarah's life was about to get darker, and she was ready. It didn't matter how dark. If anything, she deserved a little darkness after what she had done to Parkman.

Maybe one day, she would rekindle her ability to be trusted by honorable men like him. Maybe one day she could hold her head up high, look him in the eye and feel that she deserved his love.

But first, she had to prove it to herself, and Vivian said she would.

In time.

Sarah gunned the engine, feeling the vibration work through the seat between her legs as she pulled out to pass a slow-moving semi.

Her hands tightened on the handlebars.

It was time to do a lot of good things to make up for the one terrible thing she had almost done. Vivian had said that what she had just gone through was only a preparation stage for what was coming in Kelowna. Knowing that, Sarah looked forward to the challenge.

"Bring it on."

She hit the gas again, felt the wind push her back, and cried at the freedom coursing through her.

Someone once told her the most powerful thing in the world was the freedom to say no. She believed that and embraced it.

But what freedom meant for her was the ability to say yes, to walk into the fight and keep moving forward. That was what she intended to do.

She would never stop moving forward and never abandon Vivian again.

Until it killed her.

Afterword

Dear Reader,

During the winter of 2011, I lived in Greece in the village called Agios Adrianos, the same village where Oliver Payne escaped to at the beginning of the novel. The walk into Nafplio that Oliver took that fateful morning when Captain Elias Kostas picked him up under the relentless sun of southern Greece was the very same walk I would do for groceries. On these walks, I made up impromptu stories of tension and drama. Oliver running from Violeta and her hunting him, even the missing passport in his villa, was one of those stories. I discovered the best stories were the ones that made me shiver, the personal ones. So I wondered what would happen if I went back to my villa and discovered my passport was missing and the police were looking for me after my ex-wife made up more false claims (which was something she always did).

Well, you get the picture.

That story never left me.

Lina and the Sugar Spell Spa are both real. She is the owner of the elegant spa mentioned in the novel and a family friend. I recommend her spa if you, dear reader, ever find yourself in Nafplio, Greece. Say hello from Jonas when you go. You will make Lina smile.

Here's the link to her webpage: http://www.sugarspellspa.gr/en/

In *Killing Sarah*, I wanted to explore the feeling of killing her off. Not *actually* killing her off from the series, but taking her out of the picture for a while.

I felt it important before the series went on for another couple of dozen novels, that you, the reader, got to see how Aaron felt about her, how Parkman would die for her if need be, and how Darwin was watching, listening, and had resources to snatch her away while still maintaining anonymity.

The people around Sarah, her friends, and her family don't always get their due.

In addition to that, I wanted you to see a side of Sarah that people don't always see, which is the side that I see. With her fast-paced, tension-filled life, that side doesn't come out all that often. I wanted you to see a softer Sarah, a nurturing Sarah who is human on every level, who cries, has weaknesses, and cares about the people around her and not just those she strives to save from fate.

As one of us, Sarah also has flaws. She isn't always right. Mistakes can happen, and she made a huge mistake with Parkman. How she feels about that, as you probably detected at the end of the novel, is horrible. She feels she can't face him, redeem herself, or make up for it. Having nearly killed the man who has spent years being there for her, backing her up, just because she missed the entry wound detail has mortified her. All she had to do was realize the bullet had entered from behind. All she had to do was think. How many people make mistakes without thinking? How many people lose someone in their life through self-sabotage? How many people struggle with relationships in their lives?

Sarah, in my opinion, is one of us. The only difference is tenacity. I've got an attitude. Sarah's got an attitude. We all have an attitude. Whether it's kind to others or rough, we all have an opinion.

With Sarah, she just wants everyone to love one another, be nice, and stop the hatred. The only way to do that is through education, and Sarah is a teacher. Unorthodox, but she is one. Sarah teaches through accountability and consequence. Do a harmful thing to someone else, pay for that. Become someone who is harmful, and die for that.

In Sarah's world, there are no in-betweens, no half-measures. That's why in her mind, Parkman had to pay for what he did. When she found out he wasn't guilty, she now has to account for her actions.

Sarah understands there are two elements involved in committing an act of violence or a crime. In Latin, it's called *mens rea* and *actus reus*, which simply means the *intent* to commit the act, and then the *performance* of the act itself.

She already had the intent with Parkman and was very close to doing the act. The intent isn't just halfway there for Sarah; it's a box already checked off.

But now Sarah is on her way to Kelowna, and things are

back to the way they were in *The Enigma* and *The Vigilante*. Sarah and Vivian have their work cut out for them, and things will get serious from here on in.

Hold on to yourselves because we're going for a ride. Sarah and I are happy you're coming along …

Be well, and get caught reading.

Love as always,

Jonas Saul

About Jonas Saul

Jonas Saul is the bestselling author of the Sarah Roberts Series—more than two million sold!—and has written and published over sixty thrillers. After acquiring an agent, he signed several deals in Los Angeles, with MadRiver Pictures optioning his Sarah Roberts Series— over forty books!—(currently in development).

Jonas has often outranked Stephen King and Dean

Koontz on Amazon over the past decade. He's regularly invited to be a guest speaker, teacher, or workshop presenter at international writing conferences and film festivals worldwide. He hosts an annual writer's retreat in Greece, where he currently lives. He focuses his teaching on how to get tension and emotion in every scene, on every page, how he made it as a creator/writer, the path to success in this business, and the pitfalls to avoid. He also hosts a reading retreat in Greece with guest authors, yoga retreats, and hiking retreats. Visit the Imagine Greece Retreats website at www.imaginegreeceretreats.com, or email him directly to discuss an opportunity to join one of the retreats at jonas@imaginegreeceretreats.com.

Jonas is also a professional freelance editor. He works for several publishers and does private editing for clients, with many testimonials on his website at www.imaginepress.org, which details each author's response to Jonas's editing skills. Email Jonas directly for an editing quote at editor@imaginepress.org.

To book Jonas for a speaking engagement at a writer's conference/festival, to have him on your jury at a film festival, or even to say hello, email Jonas directly at jonassaul@icloud.com.

For updates on releases, hit the "Follow" button on Amazon or Bookbub, and join Jonas on Facebook, where he's most active.

Contact Jonas Saul

Linktree: Find me here

Email: jonassaul@icloud.com